'To think,' Ringlets murmured bitterly; 'to think I loved him once.'

Ah, so Ringlets and the poet! Things were beginning to make se...... ...... want to know the squ......

'Are you a....... .... like something to drink in ....'

Then, as she .... stared at me, I almost swooned myself. Her eyes were terrible! Black, imploring. It was as if something else was staring out ......, something foul and ancient and unbearably s........ ...ked. It was impossible to hold the gaze of those eyes without feeling faint.

D1148532

www.kidsatrandomhouse.co.uk

Other titles by Susan Davis and available from Corgi Books:

The Henry Game
Delilah and the Dark Stuff

MAD, BAD AND TOTALLY DANGEROUS

MAD, BAD AND TOTALLY DANGEROUS
A CORGI BOOK: 0 552 55191 0

Published in Great Britain by Corgi Books,
an imprint of Random House Children's Books

This edition published 2004

1 3 5 7 9 10 8 6 4 2

Copyright © Susan Davis, 2004

The right of Susan Davis to be identified as the author of this
work has been asserted in accordance with the Copyright, Designs
and Patents Act 1988

All rights reserved. No part of this publication may be
reproduced, stored in a retrieval system, or transmitted
in any form or by any means, electronic, mechanical,
photocopying, recording or otherwise, without the
prior permission of the publishers.

Papers used by Random House Children's Books are natural,
recyclable products made from wood grown in sustainable
forests. The manufacturing processes conform to the
environmental regulations of the country of origin.

Set in 12/14½ pt Bembo

Corgi Books are published by Random House Children's Books,
61–63 Uxbridge Road, London W5 5SA,
a division of The Random House Group Ltd,
in Australia by Random House Australia (Pty) Ltd,
20 Alfred Street, Milsons Point, Sydney, NSW 2061, Australia,
in New Zealand by Random House New Zealand Ltd,
18 Poland Road, Glenfield, Auckland 10, New Zealand
and in South Africa by Random House (Pty) Ltd,
Endulini, 5a Jubilee Road, Parktown 2193, South Africa

THE RANDOM HOUSE GROUP Limited Reg. No. 954009

A CIP catalogue record for this book is available from the British Library.

Printed and bound in Great Britain by
Cox & Wyman Ltd, Reading, Berkshire

RE-VALUED CITY LIBRARY
ACC. No. 000531
CLASS No. J
INVOICE
PRICE

Mad, Bad
and Totally
Dangerous

SUSAN DAVIS

CORGI BOOKS

CAVAN COUNTY LIBRARY

ACC No. C/183501
CLASS NO. J /12-14
INVOICE NO. 6349 IES
PRICE €6 66

Thanks to Desi and Jenny for doing the reccy.

Also, thanks to Terry for taking me there.

CAVAN COUNTY LIBRARY

Prologue

All present life is but an interjection,
An 'oh!' or 'ah!' of joy or misery
Or a 'ha, ha!' or 'bah!' a yawn or 'pooh!'
Of which perhaps the latter is most true.

I really can't believe what's happening to me this summer. Things have got so bad that I, Abigail Carter, seriously suspect I might be *cursed*. You know, like, *cursed* cursed? Doomed to an eternity of abject misery type cursed? It wouldn't surprise me at all if I had an enemy somewhere. Maybe Tamsin French at our school, for instance. Maybe she never forgave me for giving her that duff palm reading back in the third year, when I told her she'd have six kids and live a life of total poverty. Maybe she is at this very moment melting down her leg wax into an Abbie doll and stabbing a large hatpin in my most vitally *vital* organs. Why not? Listen – believe me, stranger things have happened. And they've happened to me!

All right, maybe it's some kind of judgement then. Yeah, could be. I'm being punished for not giving up my occult practices, for studying the ancient art of phrenology and stuff. (That's telling your personality from the bumps on your head, in case you don't know.)

1

Or could it be that the gods have just got it in for me? Like they're saying: 'Hey, that Abigail Carter – she's been having it too good lately, let's give her a bit of a shake-up and see what happens!' Call me paranoid if you like, but I reckon they're all up there now, leering down from the toxic yellowish clouds that lurk above Northgate and tittering their heads off.

Well, I've got nothing to laugh about. There I was one minute, having an 'all right' life, thank you very much, the next . . . Well, let me give you the precise sequence of events as noted in my diary.

THURSDAY 3RD AUGUST: After seven months, three and a half days and two hours of delectable dating, my boyfriend Joel, the bloke I intended to share a duvet and a shopping trolley with for the entire rest of my life, takes off for a year in Australia and breaks my heart.

SATURDAY 5TH AUGUST: Attempt to distract myself from broken heart at the Next summer sale. Whilst rattling through a rail of micro minis, some lowlife nicks my purse clean out of my bag, and makes off in the scrum with my life savings.

SUNDAY 6TH AUGUST: I wake up screaming from this nightmare that makes *Blair Witch* look like *The Teletubbies*. It begins OK. Here I am sashaying down the street, feeling like hot stuff in my new micro skirt, when a car pulls up behind me. I turn, hoping to see Justin Timberlake behind the wheel of his open-top Jag. Sadly, it isn't Justin. It's not even a car. Parked in a disabled parking bay is an old-fashioned carriage drawn by six black horses.

This is where the dream changes. There is something horrible about this carriage, the way it glitters like the shiny casing of a black beetle. Even the horses are sinister. Their flanks gleam with sweat, their eyes roll, their hooves stamp and the black-feathered plumes on their heads remind me of death.

One thing I know – I'm not getting inside that thing, no way. When the window rolls silently down, I try to run. Trouble is, my legs seem to have sprung roots and I'm stuck to the spot. I look inside. I can't help myself. But instead of the monster I'm expecting to see, the carriage is empty, the scarlet padded interior yawning like a great mouth.

Then I realize. The carriage has come for me. *I* am the passenger. Well, that's when I wake up screaming and then my mother sticks her nose round the door and says I'm overwrought, and puts me on a cocoa and night-nurse routine for a week. Or tries to.

MONDAY 7TH AUGUST: Lauren comes round, and she's in one of her bossy, Lauren-knows-best moods. I tell her about my nightmare and she says I've seen too many costume dramas recently. And there's nothing 'weird' going on, for heaven's sake, because we've grown out of . . . you know . . . *that stuff*.

By *that stuff*, she means those visits from the Other Side that we're a little prone to. I should explain. Lauren and I have this, like, fatal attraction for the undead. The first time, it was Henry VIII who took a fancy to us. There we were, messing about with our home-made Ouija board and thinking we'd be dead lucky if someone's granny turned up, and who should we get but the randy royal, determined to see off our boyfriends and add us to his collection of doomed wives. Then there was the seventeenth-century Witchfinder, Matthew Hopkins, who even locked us up and accused us of cavorting with the devil, if you please. That was all thanks to our friend Delilah, who really is a witch. Delilah is Joel's sister, and it was her spells that attracted the witchfinder's ghost in the first place. Not that we blame her. In fact, I wish she was here right now so I could tell her about my dream and that. But she and her mum have gone off to visit some long-lost aunty in Transylvania.

So you can hardly blame me from panicking when I get this weird feeling in my scalp. I know this feeling. It means Lauren may have 'grown out of that stuff', but I haven't. It means that some *seriously supernormal type thing* is about to happen any day now. And don't ask me why; I just know that the festival Lauren is rabbiting on about has got something to do with it.

The poetry festival is coming to Northgate next week, and Lauren's idea was that we both apply for some holiday work there.

'Poetry festival? Eugh!' I scrunched up my features into an expression of utter disgust when she first

4

mentioned it. 'I mean, if it was a rock festival or something, then I might consider it.'

'What's wrong with poetry?' Lauren arranged her skirts carefully before sitting on my bed. Ever since being cured of her eczema by Delilah's moon-dew, she's been planning on becoming a healer – once she's finished her A levels, that is. She's taken to wearing these white cotton garments that look like a bunch of tea towels strategically arranged. There was one on her head too, knotted jauntily over her plaits.

'Think about it, Lauren. The last thing a person with a broken heart needs is to listen to a lot of drivel about lovers skipping hand in hand through the bluebells and stuff.'

'Really' – Lauren sighed – 'poetry's got nothing to do with bluebells these days. And anyway, all you have to do is serve coffee and give out leaflets and show people where the loos are and that kind of thing. You need the money, don't you?'

She had me there. I was hoping the police might show up one day with purse and life savings intact. There was a hundred and fifty pounds inside, which I'd dug out of my post office account when Joel left.

'I suppose,' I murmured grudgingly. The money I got for cleaning my mother's chiropody surgery, Feet First, would barely keep me in styling mousse.

'So . . .' Lauren smoothed her saintly white petticoats over her knees. 'So what about the festival? Oh come on, Abbie, think of all those gorgeous poetic types wandering about. We might be serving coffee to some famous literary genius. It's not every day people like that come to Northgate.'

'No ... but ...' I couldn't explain what was really putting me off. I wasn't even sure myself. Just some gut feeling I had. A hunch. It was as if some clever, more evolved part of myself knew the future already and was trying to warn me. The poetry festival had something to do with that nightmare I'd had about the empty carriage with its stifling crimson interior, waiting to suck me in. I was sure of it. Yet how to explain this to Lauren?

Still, if it hadn't been for my stolen purse and the fact that there was virtually nothing left in my post office account, I don't suppose I would ever have agreed so feebly.

'Oh all right then. But it's under protest, mind. Because I don't have a good feeling about this.'

Lauren inspected her pale face in the mirror. 'Face it, Abbie,' she said, 'you never have a good feeling about anything.'

Chapter One

She walks in beauty, like the night
Of cloudless climes and starry skies;
And all that's best of dark and bright
Meet in her aspect and her eyes:

Actually, Lauren was usually the one having bad feelings about things. The difference was, while she gave herself premature frown lines fretting about UV rays and irradiated tomatoes, my worries were mostly of the unearthly kind.

Next day, as we crossed Bromfield Park on our way to our interview at the festival office, my scalp was prickling so much, you'd think a giant head louse was moving in. 'Get a hold of yourself, Abigail Carter,' I told myself.

After all, there was nothing spooky about the park, which was down the road from our school, where I'd had my very first snog with Mark Cristofolus in the second year. I'd also planted a gladiolus bulb in the Millennium Gardens there – part of a magic ritual which had made Joel fall hopelessly in love with me. That is, until some hooligan with a football snapped its blossomy head off about a month ago. The exact same week that Joel had told me about Australia.

The festival office was actually a paper-strewn room in

the park keeper's lodge. Goodness knows where old George the park keeper was. He'd been replaced by a middle-aged bloke with a pony-tail and a shirt exactly like my neighbour Mrs Croop's flowery wallpaper.

At the sight of Lauren and me, the man clutched a hand theatrically to his chest and uttered: 'I wandered in a forest thoughtlessly, And on the sudden, fainting with surprise, saw two fair creatures, couched side by side . . .'

As we stood there, trying not to look too mortified, he explained, 'John Keats, *Ode to Psyche*. Sorry, couldn't resist – Lauren, isn't it? And Abigail? I'm Giles, by the way.' He held out his hand. 'Oh damn, excuse me a moment!' The phone was ringing, and a long conversation ensued – something about train times and herrings.

Finally slamming the receiver down, he apologized again. 'Accommodation arrangements for our poets – you wouldn't believe how difficult it is to get the right kind of hosts. I don't suppose either of your parents have a spare room going, do they?'

'No, sorry,' I said at once. 'Not an inch to spare, I'm afraid.' Our flat in Smedhurst Road was so cramped there was barely space for me. And anyway, the idea of some versifying old beardie being fussed over by my mother was too excruciating.

'Sorry, we're decorating,' Lauren said, alarmed. This was understandable. Lauren's mum's hobby is belly dancing, and she's well known for her impromptu practice sessions. Enough said.

'Ah, well, never mind.' Giles glanced at his watch. 'Actually I was expecting another young lady to turn up at this interview, but she's late. We'll just have to start without her. So . . . ladies, tell me, what is your favourite poem?'

'Er . . . favourite?' we both stammered.

'You must have one, everyone does. Come on. Don't be shy. Anything you like.'

Was this some kind of test? Lauren must have thought it was, because she launched straight into the first verse of 'Tyger, tyger burning bright'. Not that it was her favourite poem or anything. We'd done Blake for our GCSEs, and it was, like, imprinted for ever on our brains. Thankfully she'd only got as far as 'In the Forests of the Night' when the door was suddenly flung open. Whoever pushed it used so much force, the rush of air scattered papers from Giles's desk onto the floor.

A girl about the same age as Lauren and me stood there panting, hand clasped to her chest as if she were about to draw her very last breath. 'Oh, you've started. Look, I'm reelly reelly sorry . . . but my mum was held up, and I had to look after my baby sister, and then the bus was late . . . But anyway, I'm here now! I'm Ruby. Ruby Blagg.' She held out her hand. 'Nice to meet you, Mr . . .'

'Giles.' Giles held onto Ruby's hand longer than is usual with your average handshake, I noticed. This was hardly surprising. Bleary eyed from nightmare-ridden nights I might be, but even I could see that Ruby was definitely a babe. As well as a stunning figure, she had these wide blue eyes (which means friendly and carefree, according to my face/head reading chart), topped with silkworm-type eyebrows (which is, like, dead lucky). Her nose was the kind I'd pick for myself if I could ever afford

9

a nose job – cute with gently rounded nostrils; a sure sign of success, according to my chart.

OK, her get-up was a bit unfortunate. Black mesh top and pink frilly mini with white wedge-heel sandals is a cringe-making combo in anyone's book. As if that wasn't enough, her shoulder bag was pink and heart shaped, with a sequinned butterfly. A fake carnation bobbed about in her long red hair.

Lauren, miffed at not getting to recite 'Tyger, tyger', raised her willow-leaf eyebrows at me, a gesture I translated as 'Tacky or what!'

'So, Ruby . . .' Giles was warbling. 'Tell me, what do you think that you, personally, can bring to this job? I want people who have a "gut feeling" for poetry . . .'

'Oh, I've got the *feeling*, Giles! I *so so* love poetry – always have since I was a tot. I make up little rhymes myself all the time. Like, I'll just be lying in the bath . . .' Ruby waggled her fingers, as if to emphasize her point. She had those funky talons you'd spend a fortune on in a nail bar. Dancing in the air like exotic insects, they seemed to hypnotize Giles, as she continued, 'I'll just be lying there, like, miles away, and this rhyme'll come right into my head, like *ping* . . . an' then I got to scribble it down right away—'

'Well, look,' Giles interrupted, looking flushed. 'Frankly, I've had enough of interviewing all week. I'll take you girls on, but I warn you, it won't all be cavorting about with famous poets, you know. You might have to take tickets, or serve coffee in the refreshments marquee, or do a bit of promotion. Talking of which, I hope you three are free tomorrow.' He gathered a wad of flyers from his desk and waved them at us. 'I want you out on the High Street first thing: I want every single person in Northgate to have one of these brochures by tea time.'

As we turned to go, he caught hold of Lauren's arm and coughed discreetly. 'And can I just mention the outfits, girls . . . ?'

'Outfits?' Lauren looked puzzled. She was dressed as usual in her saintly white cottons, while I'd stuck to my crop top and combats look.

He looked embarrassed. There were no uniforms or anything, he mumbled, but if we could take a leaf out of Ruby's book, and dress a little more . . . 'A little more . . . you know . . .' His hands fluttered at thigh level. 'A little more, or a little less, I should say . . . ha ha . . .'

'Totally gross!' Lauren decided as soon as we were outside in the park again. 'Did you get that, Abbie? He wants us to wear miniskirts. Correct me if I'm wrong, but this is meant to be a poetry festival, not an amusement park.'

'Well, it was your brilliant idea to work here,' I grumbled. My head was aching. No wonder, with this horrible sunlight dazzling my eyes. I wished it would rain. I longed for a dirty great cloud to blot out the sun, so I could be miserable in comfort.

Ruby piped up that we should think ourselves lucky about the short skirts. 'When Pizza Pronto first opened – that's the place I work at during the day time, right – I had to dress up like a giant pizza, with this great big pineapple thing on my head. You should have seen me!'

11

I'd expected this Ruby would just melt away, with the interview over, and leave us to go our own way. But, to my horror, she had wedged herself between Lauren and me, catching hold of our arms as if we were great mates from way back.

'Hey, anyway, we got it! We all got the job. Isn't that fantastic!'

'Wonderful,' I grunted, 'if your great ambition in life is to serve cappuccinos all day.'

'Still, it's a bit of extra cash, isn't it?' Ruby said. 'I mean, just 'cos I work at the pizza place all day doesn't mean I haven't got ambition myself.' As she steered us along the avenue of sweet-scented chestnuts, she added that she was probably going to be famous. *Very famous.* In fact, she fully expected to be 'a household name' by the time she was twenty.

'Oh yeah?'

I was just wondering how to break free of Ruby's clutches, when Lauren said, 'Excuse Abbie, she's not herself just now. She's had a bit of a rough time lately.'

Ruby peered anxiously into my face. 'Oh, I'm sorry. Did someone die?'

'Die?'

'In your family . . . ?'

'No, of course not.' I jerked my arm free of hers. 'It's not *that* bad.'

'To look at her, you would certainly think someone had died,' Lauren said.

'*Love* has died, as you very well know, Lauren Alexander.' I sniffed. 'At least, it hasn't died, but it's in Australia, which is a bloody long way away.'

'Well, you know what I think,' Ruby burbled happily. 'I think we're all going to love working at the festival. It's so exciting. And just think, Abb, you might meet a famous poet!'

'Oh yes, I hadn't thought of that. I feel so much better now. My name's Abigail by the way.' (I can't stand people who shorten your name when they've only known you, like, five minutes.)

'Never say never, Abb, that's my motto!' Ruby chirruped, unperturbed.

I ground my teeth together. 'Is it really? How fascinating.'

Sadly, the subtleties of my famed sarcastic wit missed their mark completely. It was like Ruby was wearing invisible sarcasm-proof armour. My poison-tipped arrows just pinged right off her.

'You've got to have faith, Abb. Hasn't she, Lor? It's like my dream of being famous. The girls at my school used to sneer, but it didn't bother me or nothing, 'cos I know I will be one day.'

'Famous for what though?' Lauren was using her kind-to-lesser-beings voice, which was beginning to give me the hump.

'I'm not sure exactly,' Ruby admitted happily. 'I'd really love to be an actress, but I can't afford to go to drama school. But a lot of singers go on to acting, don't they, and I love singing. I'm always singing, dancing and that. I used to do lessons, right from when I was little. Then, when my mum had Rosie, there just wasn't any . . .'

What there wasn't any of when Ruby's mum had Rosie, I didn't hear, because I'd just dodged across

Bromfield Road, narrowly missing being run over by a screeching fire engine. Even that would be preferable to Ruby's life story, come to think of it. Who wanted to know? Imagine having to put up with her for a whole shift! It didn't bear thinking about. Where did she live anyway? I hoped to God she wasn't going my way.

She was. I could hardly believe my bad luck when she joined me at my bus stop.

'Oh, are we on the same route, Abb? That's so great! We can travel into work together of an evening.'

I glared at Lauren as she turned towards the stop that would whiz her safely to leafy Highgate. 'See you two tomorrow then,' she called. 'I'll, er . . . I'll ring you later, Abbie.'

'Yeah, right.'

It was stifling on the bus. The plastic seats almost boiled my bum. Ruby plonked herself next to me, her perfume whooshing up in my face, sickly and somehow waxy, like a scented candle. As we lurched along, Ruby chattering beside me about her family and Pizza Pronto and getting famous, I stared miserably out of the window.

Why did Ruby have to be on my route? I was just cursing my luck and wishing myself a thousand miles away, when suddenly, horribly, I *was*.

At first I thought I'd got something in my eyes. I rubbed them cautiously, trying not to smudge my eyeliner. I blinked. Several times. But rather than going away, the blurring took on a strange rosy hue. This was mad. Now red bloody splashes were floating before my eyes like daubs of paint.

At this point I had a few stern words with myself. *OK, it's cool, everything's fine.* My fingers grasped hold of the seat rail in front. *Whatever you do, don't panic.* I stared and stared at the metal rail, and the blob of dirty grey chewing gum that adorned it, willing my sight to return to normal. Then I had a terrible thought. Perhaps I was going blind?

So much for keeping cool! Now my palms were sweating so much, my fingers slipped from the metal rail. Or had the rail slipped from them? Funny thing – the rail didn't seem to be there any more. Something weird had happened to the bus seats. Where was the graffiti-covered plastic? Where was the chewing gum? The seats had turned into crimson plush, that kind of rich, fuzzy stuff you get in old-fashioned cinemas.

Taking a deep breath to calm myself, I realized that Ruby's waxy scent had disappeared too. In its place, the spicy tang of old leather and rotting velvets.

Why me? I heard myself whimper into a vacuum of red-plush silence. *Leave me alone. I want to be normal, understand? I can't take this any more.*

My dream had come back to get me. How could this happen in broad daylight? How could I be sitting here, in the beetle-black carriage I'd seen in my dream? My dream. An image flashed before me of black-plumed horses, the kind you see in historical movies, in funeral processions. Suddenly I knew that's what this was. A funeral. The plush seats felt rough as my fingers dug into them. Somehow or other I was mixed up in somebody's funeral. But whose?

The carriage rocked so hard it seemed it would tilt on its side. Grabbing the leather hand strap to steady myself,

15

I turned to the window. The High Street had disappeared. There was only the slick of darkness, my own petrified face reflected in it like the moon.

Then, 'Hey, Abb, are you OK?' Ruby's voice seemed to come from miles away. Ruby? Oh, thank God for Ruby!

She was giving my shoulders a little shake and peering into my face. 'You sound like you've got a pain or something. There's a funny bug going round – our Roxie was in bed with it all last week.'

'No.' I smoothed my sweaty palms on my knees. 'I mean, yeah, I'm OK, thanks.' I'd never imagined I'd be so glad to see Ruby.

I got off at the next stop. As I turned up Smedhurst Road towards home, my mobile rang.

'Hey, Abbie.' Lauren's voice at the other end was oddly hesitant. 'You know I was going to recite "Tyger, Tyger" . . .'

'Mmmm . . .'

'Well, it's totally bizarre in my opinion. All the way home on the bus, I had this poem going round and round my head, like it came out of nowhere. I wrote it down soon as I got home just now. Want to hear it?'

'Not really, but I've just heard Ruby's life story, so your poem won't make much difference.'

Lauren ignored me and began to recite in a doom-laden kind of voice:

'Start not – nor deem my spirit fled;
In me behold the only skull,
From which, unlike a living head,
Whatever flows is never dull.'

'So,' she said, 'what do you think? Do you recognize it from anywhere?'

'No, but it sounds like something you'd write on someone's tombstone. Have you been hanging around graveyards recently?'

Lauren said she wouldn't even dignify such a cretinous remark with a reply. 'Maybe I'll show it to some cultured, intelligent person like Giles.'

'Yeah, good idea, you do that, Lauren.'

Well, I was hardly in the mood for poems about 'spirits' and 'skulls'. Lauren couldn't see me shudder as she read out her creepy little verse that she said came from 'nowhere'. And I wasn't going to tell her about my traumatic experience on the bus just now. Not yet. Not until I understood what it was all about myself.

From the sound of Lauren's verse, I somehow didn't think that would be too long.

Chapter Two

I lived, I loved, I quaff'd, like thee:
I died: let earth my bones resign;

Next day was scorching. The steel and glass shop fronts in Northgate's pedestrian zone were glinting like knives in the sun. A scent of coffee wafted onto the street, as Lauren and I patrolled in front of the café awnings. We were wearing our regulation minis, and armed with enough flyers to inform half of Europe of Northgate's looming literary event.

'Want some?' Since Ruby had wandered further down the street, I waved my slab of chocolate enticingly beneath Lauren's nose. 'Hurry up, it's melting all over my bag.'

Lauren asked if I had entirely forgotten about her chocolate allergy? 'Not that I want to worry you or anything, but I think you may have one yourself actually, Abbie.'

'What – a chocolate allergy? No way. I'd rather be dead.'

'No, I seriously think you might. You've got the telltale signs, if you want my opinion.'

'Oh yes, and what are they?'

Lauren ducked to avoid the drips from a hanging

18

basket. 'Shadows under the eyes, pasty look, classic symptoms of cocoa-bean intolerance, I'm afraid.'

'Thanks for the warning.' I broke off four squares and stuffed them in my mouth. Lauren would look a bit rough herself if she'd had my experience on the bus yesterday. I very nearly said, *Oh yeah, and does cocoa-bean intolerance give you hallucinations as well?* Luckily the mouthful of chocolate stopped me from saying anything. And anyway, I had other things to worry about. Like . . .

'Nathan Daly, from *The Buzz*.'

The newspaper guy jumped from a car which had lurched to a halt right in front of us. 'Nice to meet you, girls!' He held out his hand.

I almost lurched myself. OK, I might still be pining for Joel, but I still knew a hunk when I saw one. He had that kind of lean, tough, go-anywhere look that heroes in movies have when they're leaping across rooftops to rescue some girl. This and the cheeky grin were a winning combination. I mean, it might have been, if I weren't still in love with someone else, of course.

Oh dear. Just as I was extending my hand to meet his, I noticed the chocolate smeared all over it. Except it didn't look like chocolate. It looked like something much more disgusting.

'Sorry . . . I, er . . .' I waggled my fingers in embarrassment. 'It's um . . . melted a bit.'

Lauren groaned. She hissed at me, 'It's all around your mouth.'

To my horror, just as I was wiping it off, Nathan Daly angled his camera at us both. 'Take no notice of me. I'll just hang around for a bit and catch you girls in action, handing out leaflets and that. All right?'

'No' – I glared at him – 'it's not all right actually. Look, I just don't want my face in your paper, OK?'

He gave me a quizzical look. 'Why's that then? Wanted by Scotland Yard, are you?'

'Ha ha.'

'The FBI, then?'

I rolled my eyes. 'It's just that I'm not smiling for *anyone*. And anyway, I can't understand why you want pictures of us in the first place.'

Nathan said Giles had called up his editor demanding a centre-page spread. 'Don't know if you two have read *The Buzz*? The entertainment guide no girl should be without? No?' He clicked his tongue in mock disgust. 'Well, anyway, my editor wants the works. It's not every day we get a poetry festival in Northgate.'

'But we're only handing leaflets out,' Lauren objected. 'Surely you want pictures of the poets themselves, not us?'

The photographer scratched his head thoughtfully. 'Don't know about that. Poets aren't exactly photogenic – know what I mean? All those beards and hairy sweaters can be a bit of a turn-off. Thought we'd catch you girls first, for a bit of glamour. Help pull in the crowds.'

Glamour! Was he being sarcastic or what? Ever since Joel left, I'd been feeling about as attractive as a facially challenged warthog. Plus my thighs were way too chubby for last year's suede mini. I glared so hard at Nathan Daly it's a wonder his camera didn't break. Something about him really wigged me off. With his creased, hanging-out shirt and stubbled chin, he'd got this cheeky, rumpled look, like he'd just spent a hot night with some Northgate babe.

Lauren, who was wearing opaque black tights beneath her mini and a funky cap set askew on her plaits, said that glamour had very little to do with poetry, in her opinion. 'If it's glamour you're after, why don't you just take Ruby?' She nodded over to where Ruby was throwing herself at the passers-by.

'That's Ruby, is it?' The photographer's eyes lit up.

Not surprisingly. Resplendent in a bum-skimming micro dress, Ruby was giving it all she'd got. Every now and then she'd break into a little impromptu dance routine right there in the street.

'Ruby!' I called out to her, signalling wildly. 'Over here! There's a photograpgher to see you.'

At the word 'photographer', Ruby's head swivelled instantly in our direction. She tottered up the street towards us in her baby-pink stilettos, waving her remaining flyers in triumph. 'Guess what, I've shifted half of these already. You wouldn't think so many people would be keen on poetry, would you? Who's this then?'

'Nathan.' Nathan held out his hand. 'From *The Buzz.*'

'*The Buzz?* Reelly? Hey, terrific!' Ruby was impressed. She whipped out a mirror to check on her lippy. Anyone would think this photographer was from *Hello!* magazine, not just some local entertainment guide that hardly anyone read.

But, annoyingly, Nathan was insisting on pictures of all three of us. 'Come on, girls. It won't hurt. Just give us a smile, eh? Job done and everyone's happy.'

'Everyone is *not* happy,' I reminded him. 'Excuse me,

21

madam, would you like to take a leaflet about the poetry festival?' The old woman I accosted shrank from me like I was trying to pass on some infectious disease. It was all right for Ruby, with her winning smile that stopped people in their tracks, but I'd be hours getting rid of the things at this rate.

'Tell you what,' Ruby suggested to the photographer. 'Why don't you take me handing a leaflet to some, like, really *interesting*-looking person?'

I laughed bitterly. 'Interesting? There *are* no interesting people in Northgate.'

'Oh, I don't know. What about him?' Ruby nodded down the street a bit. 'He looks dead artistic, if you ask me.'

Dead artistic, she said. As we followed Ruby's gaze, something made me catch my breath. The man gazing into the window of Hot to Trot wasn't your usual Northgate type. No self-respecting Northgate bloke would be seen dead in a green velvet jacket, with a silk scarf fluttering at his neck, for a start. At first I thought he was checking out the trainers, but then I realized he was studying his reflection. When he tossed back his chestnut locks, it was like he'd been practising that gesture in mirrors his entire life. You couldn't blame him. I mean, if you were that totally gorgeous it'd be hard not to fall in love with yourself.

'Come, Smut,' he called carelessly over his shoulder to an overweight bulldog, which was trying to chew its stump of a tail.

'Bet you that's one of the poets,' I murmured to Lauren. 'Wonder who. D'you reckon he's someone famous?'

The man was walking uphill towards us. Or rather, he was *limping* towards us. I couldn't help wondering what had caused the limp. Some kind of sporting injury maybe, or a fall from a horse. He looked that kind of dashing type who rides with the hounds by day, and parties with blue-blooded It girls by night. Whatever had caused it, the limp gave him a lopsided gait, which didn't go with the superior expression and tossing curls. Obviously this bloke fancied himself Big Time! The sneer took in the passers-by, the shops and the whole of Northgate High Street; as if it was the saddest place he'd ever seen in his life. But if I hadn't been 'totally off men', I would have said it was the sexiest sneer I'd ever seen. Would the sneer stay in place when he kissed? I wondered.

Ruby didn't waste any time. 'Excuse me, sir, would you like to take a leaflet about the poetry festival which is opening on Saturday?' She paused. 'Oh, what a cute dog! Is it safe for me to stroke him? He won't bite me?'

The man halted. He stared at Ruby as if she was some kind of mythical treasure he'd crossed oceans to find, and now he couldn't believe his luck.

'Stroke away, dear girl,' he drawled at her, pushing the tumble of curls from his forehead as if to see her better. 'My Smut has a soft spot for the ladies.'

'Perfect,' Nathan murmured, camera whirring as Ruby crouched down by the dog.

'Smut? That's an unusual name for a dog,' she was saying. 'Who's a luverly boy then. Who's a luverly doggie-poos?' She was tickling the rolls of fat round the dog's neck with her sparkly talons.

23

'This is embarrassing,' Lauren declared. I had to agree with her. We both cringed in the doorway of Vita's Vestments, a frumpy dress shop favoured by my mother, and pretended to be interested in the polyester blouses on special offer.

Next time we looked, Ruby had left off assaulting the dog and was concentrating on its owner. 'If you don't mind my saying so, sir, you look like a gentleman who enjoys a good poem.'

'A good poem?' The man lifted a corner of the silk scarf to his mouth, as if to check the sneer was still in place. It was. 'Actually, I dabble a bit myself, you know.'

'Oh go on!' Ruby shrieked, clasping a hand to her chest. 'You mean you write poems yourself? You're one of them poets who's reading at the festival? Well, fancy me stopping you. That's just the most amazing coincidence!'

The poet cast a weary eye about the High Street, now thronged with Friday lunchtime shoppers. 'Quite so. Although often I think scribbling is a disease I hope myself cured of.'

'Oh you mustn't say that. I'm sure we'd love to hear your work. You must be on the brochure somewhere – what's your name again?' Ruby shook out the leaflet and scanned the photographs. There were about twenty poets in all, and a quick glance told me that none of them looked anything like this one.

'No, I can't see you here,' Ruby said. 'You must be one of the special guests that Giles told us about.'

The poet examined the cuffs of his jacket, beneath which a frill of white shirt peeped out. He sighed. 'Well, now you find me out. I am indeed a special guest. A surprise item, you might call me. And you, dear girl, what is your role exactly in this establishment?'

'Me? Oh, I'm just one of the helpers. You know, taking the tickets, helping out at the stalls, that kind of thing. Keeping everybody happy, I suppose you could say.' Ruby beamed.

'A quest in which you will surely succeed. And your name is . . . ?'

The way he was staring at Ruby made me feel faint with jealousy. His eyes just gobbled her up, bit by bit, like she was edible; like he was trying to decide which were the juiciest parts to start with.

'Ruby. Ruby Blagg, sir.'

'Ruby. Delighted to make your acquaintance, Ruby.'

As the poet bent his face to Ruby's hand, Nathan Daly snorted quietly behind his camera. 'Knows how to play his cards all right.'

I ignored him. Personally, the very thought of those sexily sneering lips brushing Ruby's skin made my knees feel weak. Even Ruby seemed lost for words, for once. She looked pretty foolish, still standing there, her hand held out as if she'd been turned to stone.

'Now, Ruby,' the poet said in a more businesslike tone, 'can you tell me where I may find a decent gentleman's outfitters? The footwear in this place is of a strange fashion.'

Glancing disdainfully over his shoulder at Hot to Trot, he added, 'I am afraid I am most particular on this matter, Ruby. One must be well shod, do you not agree?'

'Oh yes, I do. I'm a bit of a shoe-freak, me,' Ruby

giggled, displaying her neat ankle in the pink stiletto. 'I've got stacks of them at home. But I'm not sure about a gentleman's outfitters. I don't think there's anything like that round here.'

The poet clicked his tongue impatiently. 'This place is the devil!'

Ruby sighed. 'Northgate? Yeah, it is a bit of a dump. Mind you, it's a posh sort of dump. Better than where I live . . .' She stood, head cocked on one side, waiting to be asked her address probably.

I murmured to Lauren, 'Sneaky or what? She's picking him up.'

'Warren Road,' Ruby continued boldly. 'That's one of them streets that runs along the back of Wood Green tube – you know, near the Shopping City? No? Well, you haven't missed anything. It's a right dump there. Not even safe to go out after dark – know what I mean?'

Lauren groaned. 'She'll be giving him her address next. He could be a pervert, for all she knows.'

But sadly for Ruby, he failed to take the bait. He just muttered something about nothing being safe after dark. Gazing up into the steamy skies above Northgate, he declared mysteriously, 'Give me a *sun*, I care not how hot, and sherbet, I care not how cool, and *my* heaven is as easily made as your Persian's.'

As Ruby stood speechless, trying to make sense of this, he called to his dog again, 'Come, Smut,' and went limping on past us up the hill.

Nathan Daly whistled silently. 'Is that guy for real?'

Ruby seemed to think so. 'Can you believe it?' She came prancing over to us. 'Fancy me hitting on a real live poet! Did you see the way he looked at me? Did you see him kiss my hand? No one's ever kissed my hand before. Oh no!' She clapped her hand to her mouth. 'He never told me his name. And I can't see him on the brochure.'

'Probably because he's not a poet at all,' Lauren said doubtfully. 'If you want my opinion, Ruby, you're far too trusting.' Casting a withering look over the passers-by, she added, 'There are some very strange people around.'

'Yeah,' I said slowly. 'What did he mean by "nothing is safe after dark"?'

'Oh, you two kill me!' Ruby shrilled. 'You fuss over me like two old mother hens. Did you get some good pictures then, Nate?'

'Perfect.' Nathan was packing his camera away. 'You're a natural, Ruby. And that guy! What planet is *he* living on? I mean, what kind of prat ponces about in clobber like that?'

I stood uneasily, hoping he hadn't taken any sneak shots of me. Although the way my luck was going, he probably had, and I'd wake up tomorrow morning and find my hideous warthoggy self emblazoned over the centrefold of *The Buzz*.

Maybe he guessed what I was thinking, because he winked at me in a reassuring, friendly sort of way, and said he'd see us all tomorrow then.

'Will you?' Lauren said stiffly.

'Course I will. Grand opening, isn't it? Got to get Northgate's first event for a decade on camera.'

Funny, but as Nathan Daly drove off, I was secretly pleased at the thought of him being there tomorrow. A wink is not the same thing as a kiss on the hand, but it made me feel kind of warm inside, considering that my heart was still in a zillion pieces and I was totally off men.

By now it was almost two, and the High Street had emptied as people went back to their offices. Ruby had got rid of all her brochures, and was heading home. Deciding that Giles wouldn't be any the wiser, Lauren and I dumped our remaining flyers in a bin, Lauren agonizing a bit over such a waste of the earth's resources.

'Know what I'm gonna do soon as I get home?' Ruby said.

We shook our heads.

'I'm going to write a poem of course!' Ruby announced triumphantly. 'I'm going to write a poem and show it to that really cool poet guy with the dog. And if it's any good, well, he might be able to help me. He might be able to help me get famous!'

'Sad,' I said to Lauren, as ten minutes later we were sipping our cappuccinos in Costa Coffee. 'That girl is seriously sad.'

I couldn't have faced going home on the bus with Ruby again, so Lauren and I had pretended we were visiting a friend. Even Ruby couldn't invite herself along to the house of a complete stranger, I reasoned. But in any case, so anxious was she to write her poem, she seemed quite happy to say goodbye to us.

'Do you reckon that guy was a nutter?'

'There was something really . . . odd about him. And I don't just mean his sense of style. Although the romantic look is hot this summer, the velvet jacket

28

was taking it a bit far, don't you think? Lauren, I said—'

'Hmmm . . .' Lauren sucked on the end of her plait. She had an odd, dreamy look on her face suddenly. 'Abbie, you know that verse I told you over the phone yesterday?'

'Something about a skull?'

'Yes. Well, I've just got another verse. I mean, it's just come right into my head.'

'Oh, don't you start,' I groaned. 'You sound like Ruby in the bath.'

'I can't help it. It's true. Wait a minute!' Lauren held up her hand for silence, although I wasn't even speaking. 'Wait . . . yes' – her head was cocked, as if she could hear a voice speaking just to her from the heavenly spheres – 'just let me get this down.'

Grabbing a napkin, she began to scribble on it in green felt tip. I watched uneasily as the pen whirred back and forth, her plaits trailing in a puddle of spilt sugar. It seemed a bit unfair. Here were Ruby and Lauren hotwired to some poet in the sky, while all I got was that hideous empty carriage and some snorting old nags.

Lauren had finished. Gazing at what she'd just written, she shook her head. 'This is majorly weird. I mean, I've no idea where it came from. Do you want to hear it?'

I shrugged. 'Spit it out then.'

Lauren cleared her throat and read aloud:

> *'I lived, I loved, I quaff'd like thee;*
> *I died: let earth my bones resign;*
> *Fill up – thou canst not injure me;*
> *The worm hath fouler lips than thine.*

'So. What d'you think?'

'I think it's stupid. For a start, worms don't have lips, do they? Anyway, can't we just forget about bloody poetry? We'll have enough of the stuff tomorrow, won't we – poetry coming out of our ears.'

'That's just it,' Lauren said. 'It's coming *into* my ears. From nowhere. I mean, I don't understand it either. The same thing happened yesterday. I'll just be thinking of something, and suddenly there's this verse in my head and I have to get it out.'

'Amazing,' I said sarcastically, dusting muffin crumbs from my fingers.

'It's like a gift, like someone is just giving it to me. You know, like Mozart, when he wrote his music, he never knew where it came from, he was just like a . . . genius.'

'So all of a sudden you're a poetic genius?'

'I didn't say that.' Lauren stirred her coffee slowly. 'I'd rather it didn't come into my head at all. But there it is.'

We were silent a moment. I was thinking about my hallucination on the bus again. The empty carriage, the six black horses. That older, wiser part of Abigail Carter seemed to know it all. She knew that the carriage, and Lauren's poem, and Ruby's sexily sneering 'poet' were somehow connected. The other part just said, *Listen, Abigail Carter, you don't want to go there.*

When you worry about things you give them a shape. It was Delilah who told me that once. I took another whacking great bite out of my muffin.

'OK, Lauren, get a move on and "quaff" your coffee,

will you, before the earth your bones resigns, whatever that means.'

'Before I die, of course.' Lauren looked straight at me. 'Surely you realized? That poem, Abbie, it's about death.'

Chapter Three

Poetry is a passion, or at least it was so ere it grew a fashion.

So Lauren was writing poems about death, and I was dreaming of funerals. Maybe someone was trying to tell us something?

You could hardly blame me for being edgy, stuck in Northgate for August and feeling like the victim of an ancient Egyptian curse. I was doomed. Deserted. I was also broke. The gods were definitely out to get Abigail Carter.

Why should I believe this? Well, let me just update you on the latest sequence of events:

1. Boyfriend buggers off to Australia;
2. Life savings stolen along with beaded purse;
3. Have to take job at tedious poetry festival to make ends meet;
4. Plagued by recurring nightmare, despite cheese on toast curfew;
5. Nightmare turns into daymare when I hallucinate on bus;
6. Dentist tells me I need to wear my brace for another six months at least;
7. I'm stuck working with Ruby Blagg for an entire three-hour shift.

The way things were going, it had been no surprise to me, when, on Saturday night, and the grand opening of the festival, Giles informed Ruby and me that we'd be serving drinks together in the café.

Giles seemed nervous. He kept flexing his arms as if he was worried that the sleeves of his jacket might be too short. It was one of those crumpled beige linen affairs that doesn't really go with a pony-tail.

'Prepare yourselves for a bit of a rush, ladies,' he told us. 'We're expecting an enormous turn-out for our first performance.' Gazing heavenwards, he added, 'Stella Paddock, a rising star in the poetry firmament . . .'

I tried not to look too devastated as he went on waxing lyrical about Stella whatshername. Actually I was inwardly cursing myself. If only I'd worn my brace! No way would Giles have given me such an upfront job with a mouthful of metal.

'Isn't that great?' Ruby was burbling. 'Us two working together, Abb! Such a shame about poor Lor, though.'

'Yeah, poor Lor,' I said with a sarcastic look at Lauren as she scuttled off happily to sit at the ticket desk. All Lauren had to do was take the tickets, hand out questionnaires to the audience and ask if they had enjoyed themselves. Whereas I was about to be rushed off my tootsies, wiping down tables and having to be pleasant to people.

'I'm not cut out to be a waitress,' I grumbled to Ruby, as we tied on the frilly aprons over our minis. 'I can't even make my parents a cup of tea without slopping it all over them. Supposing I spill coffee down someone? Supposing I give one of the customers third-degree burns?'

33

'You know your problem, Abb?' Ruby adjusted her carnation hair slide. 'You put yourself down too much. Course you won't spill anything. Know what, I'll bet you're a born waitress. Anyway, I'm glad we're in the café, 'cos if *he* comes in for a coffee, I'll get my chance, won't I?'

I stared dumbly at her. 'If *who* comes in? What chance?'

'That poet bloke, of course, the one with the cute dog. The one who kissed my hand. You remember!' She nudged me so hard, I nearly fell over. 'Oooh, I hope he does come. I was going to show him this.' Fumbling in her bag, she drew out a scrap of paper and stuck it in front of my face. 'It's my poem. Told you I'd write one, didn't I? It was a piece of cake. Just came to me in a flash. Will you do me a favour, Abb, and give it a quick read – per-lease? Tell me what you think.'

I didn't have much choice. Ruby had thrust the page right under my nose.

I scowled at it. 'Ruby, I know nothing about poetry. I don't even like poetry.' The poetry we did at school, I meant. Old Wordsworth flitting among his daffodils, that kind of stuff.

'Please. Please, it won't take a sec,' Ruby urged.

Wearily I read aloud:

> *'I saw him walking up the street*
> *And thought uh-huh, he looks neat.*
> *He's got this little dog called Smut –*
> *He really is the cutest mutt.'*

It went on like this for several verses. 'Er . . .

Ruby, you're going to show this to that man with the dog?'

'Yes, I told you.' Ruby snatched it back, and folding her masterpiece into a neat square tucked it in her bra. 'Then I can get an expert opinion.'

We went back to the café, where a couple had wandered in for a drink before the performance. Normally the park café did a roaring trade in crisps and Victoria sponge cake and tea. The building, which overlooked the duck pond, had once been a museum – the old-fashioned kind with a stuffed fox in a glass case and drawers of dead butterflies. When vandals had managed to burn half of it down, it had been refurbished as a gallery, a cool white space dotted with the odd sculptural plant and arrangement of pebbles. Sometimes the Northgate Amateur Dramatics used it for their dodgy pantos, or there were photography exhibitions of historic Northgate. Now it was to be centre stage for the poets.

Behind the café bar, a tall, self-absorbed woman called Amelia stood polishing glasses.

'Not exactly rushed off her feet, is she?' Ruby whispered. 'Let's have a peep at this Stella woman.'

'OK.'

We snuck in by one of the side doors, into the churchy hush and new-paint, composty smell of the gallery. Stella Paddock, a tiny woman with wind-chime earrings and cropped magenta hair, was standing up on the shallow platform, which served as a stage. She was reading from a loose sheaf of papers, in a squeaky voice that hardly carried beyond the front row. Unfortunately it was just loud enough for me to get the general gist. I shuddered.

Call me squeamish, but blood-soaked placentas and breast milk are not exactly my thing.

'Oh look, it's that photographer bloke who fancies you.' Ruby nudged me suddenly, nodding towards the back of the room.

'Fancies me? I don't think so,' I mumbled. All the same, my heart quickened as I noticed Nathan Daly, his camera trained on Stella. To my embarrassment he noticed me looking and grinned.

'See?' Ruby muttered with satisfaction. 'What did I tell you?'

I glared at her. 'He's just doing his job – he doesn't fancy me, for goodness' sake. And anyway, I'm not interested.'

'Oooh, tell me another one!' Ruby hissed, adding that she didn't think much of Stella's poem. 'Doesn't even rhyme. If you ask me, a poem should always rhyme. I could do better than that myself.'

'Mmmm.' I didn't argue with her. I was too busy avoiding Nathan Daly's glance. He didn't really fancy me, like Ruby said, did he? Well, tough luck if he did, because I didn't fancy him. At least I didn't think I did.

Even so, I was just the tiniest bit sorry when the doors opened a crack, and Giles beckoned us into the passage. 'I've been looking for you two.'

He dangled a bunch of keys in front of Ruby. 'Ruby, would you mind going to the storeroom? There should be a box of candles on the right-hand shelf. Be careful, though – you might need a stepladder.'

'Candles?' Ruby looked puzzled. 'Oh, for the tables, you mean? Romantic, eh, Giles? I like that.'

36

Giles looked disconcerted a moment. He frowned up at the ceiling where the spotlights were flickering slightly. 'Romance wasn't my first thought, Ruby. These lights are worrying me actually. There were storm warnings earlier, so best to be on the safe side.'

Storm warnings? I hadn't heard any storm warnings. Yet even as he spoke, we heard the faint rumble of thunder in the distance.

'Oh, and, er . . . Abigail' – Giles turned to me – 'there's a fellow sitting in the café waiting to be served. He's got a dog. Could you tell him politely about the rules?'

'Rules?'

'No animals. Health and safety and all that. It's not hygienic.'

Back in the café, I couldn't even see this solitary customer at first.

'Over there,' Amelia mouthed at me, nodding over to the corner table. I stared. The table was partly obscured by a giant fake banana tree and a coat stand. Through the jungly silk leaves, I could just make out a glimpse of green velvet.

The poet! My heart sank. How was I to tell Mr Drop-Dead Delicious that he and his 'Smut' weren't welcome here?

'Er, hem' – I coughed – 'excuse me, er, sir.'

He didn't even look up as I approached. He was too absorbed rolling dice across the metallic top of the table. I watched, bewildered, as two sixes landed by the sugar bowl.

At last he spoke in a disgusted voice. 'Stella Paddock! I care not for a scribbling woman, myself.' Reaching for the bottle of red wine at his side, he topped up his glass. Smut was curled beneath the table, wrinkly snout resting on his paws.

'Excuse me, sir,' I began. 'I'm very sorry, but dogs aren't allowed in this place. It's the rules.'

My heart shrank as I was treated to the full lip-curling sneer. '*Rules?*'

'Um . . . erm . . . yes . . . er . . . you know, like . . . hygiene rules and that . . .' Up close to those disdainfully drooping lashes, those sensuous lips, it seemed like I'd lost the power of speech.

'Hah!' He laughed shortly as if this was the most ludicrous thing he'd ever heard. 'Rules are made to be broken, are they not?'

I tried not to look at his hand, carelessly stroking the side of the bottle, his long, elegant fingers weighted with rings.

'Sorry, but it's the organizer's rules.'

Gently, the poet nudged his dog with the toe of a boot. 'Hear that, Smut? We're not welcome in this establishment.' Still he made no move to leave. He just leaned back, one arm flung across the back of the chair, like he was staying the night.

'Personally, I care nothing for rules.' He looked me up and down, studying me as if I was a fairly interesting specimen he'd found under a microscope. 'It was the rule at my college at Cambridge. No animals. I kept my tame bear there in my rooms, and they liked him so much, he became the house mascot. What think you of that?'

'A bear?' I said. 'At university? Isn't that, like, *cruel* – to the bear, I mean?'

The poet made a spluttering noise of contempt. 'Pah! My bear was better treated than many humans I have known. Rules! Poppycock. Send your manager over to my table and allow me a word with the fellow.'

I glanced over my shoulder. Giles had disappeared and I had no idea where he was. I rubbed my palms against my apron. They were sweating, which was odd, because I noticed for the first time that I was actually quite cold. But since the temperature outside had barely dipped below the eighties, I figured it must be the air-conditioning that was on too high.

'Unless, that is' – his eyes challenged me – 'you would care to escort me from the premises yourself?'

Just as I was wondering how to answer this, there was another roll of thunder, and the room suddenly fell dark.

'Oooh, just in time,' Ruby panted, returning with the candles. 'Better light these quick, Abb – looks like there's going to be a right storm.' She paused and gazed out of the window. 'Hope it's not too bad. Our Rosie – that's the baby – she's terrified of storms; screams the place down, she does.'

Really. I was about to scream the place down myself when Giles appeared and instructed me to please go and light some candles in the gallery at once. 'Before poor Stella Paddock trips over on the stage. We don't want any accidents on our opening night.'

Silently I cursed Giles. It was kind of exciting, that shivery feeling you got when the poet looked at you. And now I had to hand him over to Ruby, just when we were beginning to strike up an . . . um . . . acquaintance. Damn these power cuts! And anyway, who cared if Stella

Paddock tripped over her long floaty scarf and fell flat on her backside?

The candles Ruby had given me were the huge sort that look like Greek columns. It was a bit awkward, creeping about the gallery and trying to find the sconces to stick them into. The power cut had done nothing to put Stella Paddock off. She had now progressed from breast milk to nappies; although how anyone could wax lyrical about baby poo beat me.

Somehow or other I fumbled my way around the back of the audience and found a twisted black metal sconce. I struck a match, and as I did so, Nathan Daly caught hold of my forearm.

'Hey, Abbie, got a minute? I want a word.'

'What about?'

From his tone, it sounded serious. Urgent even. I couldn't think what Nathan Daly wanted with me, unless it was to try and con me into grinning idiotically for more photos. In which case he was totally out of luck.

As I lit the last sconce and the gallery filled with a yellow flickering light, Nathan motioned me towards the door. 'Out here.'

The passage, which linked the café area to the gallery, was still in darkness. But at least it was warmer here. Stifling even. The more the thunder rolled, the hotter it seemed to get.

'I should get back to the café,' I said. 'Soon as that woman stops gassing about nappies and stuff, they'll all be straight into the bar, and Giles—'

'Giles can wait a minute,' Nathan said. 'That customer,

the guy with the dog – the one who fancies himself as a poet . . .'

'What about him?'

'I came in a minute ago to grab a drink, and saw you talking to him.'

'So?'

Nathan scratched his head awkwardly. 'When you were talking, did you, er . . . notice anything – anything . . . strange?'

'Strange?' I laughed. 'Did I notice anything *normal* about him, you mean?'

Nathan smiled. 'Yeah, yeah. Look I'm not talking about the dodgy clobber, or the antique chat-up lines or anything.' He paused, as if he was struggling for the right words. 'I mean, just *strange*.'

I hesitated. What was all this? I hardly knew Nathan Daly. If I told him what I really felt about this awkward customer, he'd think *me* strange. In fact he'd think me a total nutter. For instance, I'd noticed that when the lights went out, the darkness had seemed to gather more thickly around the poet's table, as if it was there for a purpose, shielding him. Then there was the temperature. Just crossing from the bar to his table had been like leaving the jungle for the freezer aisle at Sainsbury's.

I decided not to mention this, though. That kind of 'strange' can't be explained, at least not to a boy.

'He's just a bit eccentric, I suppose,' I said finally. 'I mean, he was going on about some tame bear he'd kept at college. And he was rolling dice on the table, you know, like he was playing a game all by himself. Which is pretty weird.'

41

Nathan grunted. 'Yeah. Pretty weird. I tell you what's even weirder . . .'

As he leaned down towards me, I breathed in the tangy scent of his leather jacket, mingled with warm skin. It was hard not to compare Nathan's smell with the poet's musty charity-shop scent.

'Those pictures I took of you lot yesterday,' he murmured; 'there's something funny turned up in the development.'

It didn't surprise me. 'Something funny' was probably my face.

'Is it me?' I said faintly.

'You?' He laughed. 'Nah. I mean the ones I took of your mate Ruby, when she was chatting up his lordship out there.'

'She's not my *mate*,' I snapped, backing away slightly. 'She's just someone I work with.'

'Whatever. Anyway, there I was using up about half a roll of film. Thought my editor would love that – you know, local eccentric chats up pretty young festival warden.'

'And did he?'

'Didn't get a chance. Because he didn't show up on the prints, did he?'

'What d'you mean?'

'I mean,' said Nathan, 'that the pictures I've got are all just of Ruby. Just Ruby. Like she's talking away to thin air. There's nothing else there. Not a sign of our friend. And I've eliminated all the technical reasons. It's not over-exposure, nothing like that. I've been taking pictures for a while, you know, and I've never come across anything like this before.'

42

Nathan and I were standing really close together by now. So close, I could hear the cottony rustle of his shirt as he breathed. This was all a bit disconcerting, when I was totally off men. It was true that part of me liked this Nathan a lot. Part of me found him interesting. Part of me was tempted to blurt out all the strange things I'd noticed about the poet, and all the strange things that had happened to Lauren and me. Perhaps if Lauren hadn't materialized at my elbow that minute, I would have done.

'In case you'd forgotten,' Lauren said, 'I have been sitting out there in reception without any lights for the past twenty minutes. Then Giles turns up and tells me you've got the candles. Do you think you could let me have one? That's if it's not too much trouble.'

Nathan held up both hands and said it was all his fault, and anyway he really ought to get some more pictures of Stella by candlelight. 'See you later, yeah?'

It was late by the time Lauren, Ruby and I were grabbing our bags from the cloakroom. The café had been hectic, and it wasn't until the lights had flashed back on about half an hour before we closed that I noticed the poet had gone. I imagined Ruby must have got rid of him after all.

Out in the park, the night air was thick and moist. The thunder had rolled away, leaving a faint electrical pulse behind it. The chestnut trees shivered softly as we hurried toward the park gates and the steady rumble of traffic.

Being a waitress was harder work than I'd imagined. Lauren complained she had a sore throat coming on, and my legs ached from running round the tables. Only

Ruby seemed unaffected as she boogied along the tarmac cycle path. 'Guess what, you two? I've just shown him – I've shown Ron my poem.'

'Ron?' Lauren and I queried together.

Ruby nodded. 'Ron Lord, that's his name – he just told me.'

When we looked blank, she sighed and said, 'Ron Lord, the poet? With the cute dog? You naughty girl, Abb' – she pointed accusingly at me – 'you tried to throw the poor bloke out, he told me. Anyway, about my poem – know what? Ron absolutely loves it. And know what else? He reckons that I show great promise. In fact, Ron reckons I could be famous. He reckons I could be just about anything I want. What d'you think about that then?'

'You showed, er, Ron, your poem?'

'Course I did. We had quite a chat while you were fussing about with those candles. Ron is so, like, cultured and interesting. *Ruby*, he says to me at one point, *Ruby, I won't talk, I won't flatter, I don't listen, except to a pretty or a foolish woman*. Then when he ran his finger up my arm, and said how fine my skin was, ooooh . . .' She demonstrated how it felt with a little shudder.

'Pretty or foolish?' Lauren said in a jealous voice. 'I hope he didn't mean you're foolish, Ruby – which, of course, you aren't.'

'Lauren, I'm sure he meant she was pretty,' I said, although actually I was jealous too. The poet had made no attempt to stroke my arm, after all. What did Ruby's arm have that mine didn't?

Then I remembered the photograph, and wondered if

I should tell her about Ron's mysterious non-appearance. Perhaps not, or we'd be here all night. And anyway, maybe it really was a technical fault and Nathan had made a mistake?

Nathan. Hadn't he said something about seeing me later? I glanced over my shoulder, hoping to catch sight of him among the crowd. But he must have slipped out early. There were only the trees, and a few stray festivalgoers making their way slowly home.

'That's really sweet of you to say I'm pretty.' Ruby took my arm. 'Hey, are you OK, Abb? Not going to have any more funny turns on the bus, I hope?'

I hoped so too. But judging from the bad feeling deep in the pit of my stomach, I had more than a few funny turns in store for me yet.

Chapter Four

In short, he was a very pretty fellow,
Although his woes had turn'd him rather yellow.

The tarot cards spread out upon the table had a menacing look. And that was even *before* I'd turned them over! My heart raced as I rattled the curtains across the living-room window and lit the candles. It was early Tuesday evening and Giles had told us he wouldn't be needing us until eight. Dad was at some union meeting at the ambulance station, and my mother was giving a talk on 'Foot Care for the Over Fifties' to the Townswomen's Guild. For once I had the flat to myself, yet I felt so guilty, you'd think I'd invited all the hunks in Northgate over for a private salsa session.

I had good reason to feel guilty. Hadn't I promised all sorts of people – my parents, our headmaster Mr Bullet, the vicar, God, the Angels of Light, my dead ancestors and Lauren Alexander – that I would never ever again dabble in the unknown? Hadn't we had enough close encounters of the undead kind to make me shun the occult for ever?

My finger traced a pattern on the back of the first card. Supposing it turned out to be the Hanged Man? Just my luck if I got the Skeleton.

It was my waitress job which had brought on this panic about the future. It had made me think about Life After School. I had to face facts: the chances of finding a vacancy in *Prediction Monthly* for a qualified phrenologist were remote. I had no 'calling' like Lauren to counsel the suffering, no dreams of becoming a superstar like Ruby had. And my hopes that Joel would whiz back from Oz and carry me off to a white fisherman's cottage on the shores of Loch Lomond were fading by the day.

'Ah well, here goes nothing.'

Taking a deep breath, I turned over the first card, and hah! Just as I feared, a rotten one! The Moon stared up at me. This was no romantic 'by the light of the silvery moon' type of moon, but a sinister, smirking kind of moon, flanked by a howling dog and a wolf. Beneath it, the Crayfish crawled from a slimy pool. Oh well, perhaps the next one would be better, but *slam*! Just as well my mother came pounding along the hall at that minute, or who knew what horrors my future might reveal?

'What on earth are you doing sitting in candlelight, dear?'

'Just doing my homework. What else is there in life but study, Mother?' There was just time to shuffle the cards into their box. Not that Mum would have had the faintest idea what they were.

'Well, you'll ruin your eyes like that.' She snapped on the glary central light.

'Anyway, what happened to Foot Care for the Over Fifties?'

My mother eased her own feet into a pair of furry

slippers. She sighed. 'Such a shame. One of the townswomen went and fainted. Went down with such a thump I thought she'd dropped dead. When she came to, she was muttering on about ghosts.'

'Ghosts?'

Mum shook her head ruefully. 'Said there was a man hobbling about the hall, trying on some of my demonstration corn pads, if you can believe it. Poor woman. Apparently she's not been quite right in the head since her husband passed on. Still, it quite put a damper on things. I thought it best to cancel till another night.'

'A ghost? Interfering with your corn pads? Ha ha—' My laughter was cut short as I remembered something. 'Did you, er . . . say . . . hobbling?'

'*I* didn't say "hobbling", *she* did. There was no one in that hall tonight except us seven women and Mr Tarrant the caretaker. A fine upstanding man, he is, with no trace of a hobble. And I should know because I service his corns regularly—'

'Oh, all right, Mother, please spare me the details!' I clapped my hands to my ears. The very thought of other people's feet makes me sick. I don't even like my *own* very much.

But the fact that my mother should even mention the word 'ghost' was worrying. A ghost with a hobble? A ghost with a limp? Put that together with a limping poet who was there one minute and gone the next, and a man whose image had somehow evaded the camera lens, and what had you got?

Flicking through to the back index of my tarot book, I read for the Moon: *Deception, Confusion, Despair.*

A chill ran through me. Maybe I should tell Lauren. Maybe I should persuade her to look for another pocket-money job somewhere else. Before things got out of control.

But there was no chance to tell Lauren anything. I arrived at the festival later that night to find the place heaving. It looked like half of Northgate had turned up for what Giles called 'the People's Poetry Blast'. Not real poets this time, like Stella Paddock, but Northgate's very own Poetry Circle, thick manuscripts tucked beneath their arms. Skulking just inside the doors of the gallery, Ruby and I watched the audience take their seats. There were a lot of old-looking blokes wearing patched green corduroy, and women in cobwebby shawls.

'I hope they're not going to read their Complete Works,' I muttered to Ruby.

Nathan Daly wasn't here tonight, I noticed. Obviously *The Buzz* hadn't thought the Northgate poets worth photographing. It was odd, but I kind of missed that grin of his.

'Are they any good?' Lauren, having done her stint with the tickets, came and joined us after about ten minutes.

'Pretty rubbish, if you ask me,' I whispered.

The wannabe poets droned on and on: a lot of stuff about first love, and somebody's granddad dying. In fact I was almost asleep on my feet when Ruby nudged me.

'Omigod, look, it's him! It's Ron!'

We stared. A second ago the stage had been taken by an old lady rhapsodizing about her cat – 'Ode to Blackie' or something. I hadn't actually noticed the poet get up on stage. It was like he'd just materialized there somehow; as if he'd sprung from a trap door.

'D'you think he's one of them?' Lauren murmured. 'The Northgate poets, I mean?'

I shook my head. 'Not a chance.'

How could she think such a thing? The Northgate poets all had chunky sandals and beards a vulture could nest in (at least, the men did). Style-wise, Ruby's poet knocked them all for six. I gazed at the shirt frothing creamily at the neck, the matador jacket straining across the shoulders as he pushed the curls from his eyes. One scornfully sweeping glance was enough to silence the entire room.

A weird feeling came over me. I even forgot that I had certain suspicions about this bloke – like, just how much of a real man he actually was. For, as I leaned against the door, order pad in hand, I began to long for him to notice me, me, Abigail Carter! If only that scornful gaze would come to rest on me, just for a second!

Ruby hissed in my ear, 'Did you see that? Did you see him smile at me?'

'Shhh! He's started.'

I must admit I was curious to hear what kind of stuff he wrote. Yet, so entranced was I by that honeyed drawl, I hardly noticed the actual words. It was only about three lines in that bells began to ring. Hadn't I heard those lines somewhere before?

'I lived, I loved, I quaff'd like thee;
I died: let earth my bones resign;

50

The poet raised his glass of ruby wine to the audience, took a slow sip, savoured it, then continued:

Fill up they canst not injure me;
The worm has fouler lips than thine.

That worm again! Slowly I turned towards Lauren. She looked pale, although that was normal.

'That's mine,' she whispered. 'That's *my* verse. The one I showed you. How did he . . . ?'

'Maybe you just read it somewhere and you'd forgotten,' I suggested. 'You know, it's, like, subliminal.'

'Subliminal?'

OK, it was a pathetic explanation, but I might have gone on with it, had it not been for the disturbance at the back of the hall.

A woman in the back row of seats just stood abruptly, like she needed the loo or something. But instead of making for the exit, she stayed put, staring at the stage and muttering.

Ruby nudged me. 'Uh-oh, we've got ourselves a loony. What's she up to? Looks like she's wearing her gran's nightie.'

The long, flimsy white dress was very low cut, and gathered beneath the bust. It did look a bit like a nightie, but not many grannies I knew would flash their cleavage like that! And the only time I'd seen elbow gloves before were in old photos of the Queen at a night at the opera. As for her hair, the style mags would have it that curls were coming back, but *ringlets* were going too far, surely? They were the kind you see in the ballroom scenes of costume dramas, dangling in black sausagey corkscrews.

I stood rubbing my forearms. Goose pimples. The air conditioning was too high again. Either that or—

'Such fine words! Hah . . .' echoed from the ringleted one.

If the poet heard his heckler, he gave no sign. Finishing the 'worm' poem, he started on another – something creepy about 'a shade on earth'.

'Such pretty words, hah! Hah!' Ringlets cried again. 'Be not seduced by such fine words; be not seduced as I have been.'

Maybe it was the acoustics in this place, but the voice had a strange echo, as if it was carried from a long way off.

There was a moment of confusion as all heads turned towards the back.

Looming up behind us suddenly, Giles murmured in my ear, 'Abbie, see if you can get that woman in the white dress out of here, there's a good girl. Offer her a drink on the house or something. We don't want any trouble.'

I scowled. Why me? Why did I get all the rubbish jobs?

I was a bit wary as I edged around the back row seats. But luckily, Ringlets just vanished out of the side door at my approach. Since Giles was still watching me, I followed her into the passage to show willing.

I was hoping she'd just leave. Instead, I found her leaning against the front entrance doors, in a kind of swoon of despair.

'To think,' Ringlets murmured bitterly; 'to think I loved him once.'

Ah, so Ringlets and the poet! Things were beginning to make sense. Embarrassing sense. Frankly I didn't want to know the squalid details.

'Are you all right?' I asked her. 'Would you like something to drink in the café?'

Then, as she raised her head and stared at me, I almost swooned myself. Her eyes were terrible! Black. Imploring. It was as if something else was staring out of them, something foul and ancient and unbearably sad. I blinked. It was impossible to hold the gaze of those eyes without feeling faint.

'Do you know what he called me?' her voice rasped huskily. ' "That odd-headed girl".' Ringlets gestured at herself and laughed. 'Odd-headed. Me! *He* called *me* odd-headed, if you please.'

Personally I wasn't surprised. 'Are you, um . . . one of the Northgate poets?' I asked her.

She looked down at her hands almost coyly. 'I thought I might be once, but alas, I had not the talent. Yet' – pausing to allow a dramatic sigh – 'I had the heart of two fine poets in my time. What think you of "Comet beautiful and fierce, Who drew the heart of this frail Universe"?'

'Sounds good,' I agreed.

She didn't seem to hear me. 'Such fine curls,' she moaned. 'So handsome. Yet he used me so ill.'

As the dark eyes bored into mine, slimy tentacles of misery reached out to grab me. I could actually *feel* her despair. The weight of it was like a great cat squatting on my shoulders. My whole body seemed to slump. I managed to take a step backwards.

53

'So that's . . . nothing to drink then?'

'What has he done with her?' When her hand shot out and gripped my wrist, it was all I could do not to scream.

'Sorry. I don't understand. Done with who?'

'What has he done with my Allegra?'

'Allegra?'

'You may know her by another name. Alba, we first named her. Such a pretty child. Why, everyone said so.'

'Sorry, look, there aren't any Albas or Allegras here. There's only Amelia behind the bar. But I'll, um, ask around, OK?'

Not OK. For without any warning, Ringlets suddenly threw herself at the gallery doors. Bursting through them, she flung out an accusing gloved arm at the poet. 'What have you done with her? Where have you taken my Allegra?'

Fortunately this outburst was drowned out by the sound of clapping, as the audience gave a standing ovation. I heard voices buzzing about me – What talent! Had anyone caught his name? And was he likely to become one of their members? Such a pity he'd just gone off without a word.

The platform was now empty, except for Giles, asking if everyone would like to make their way to the café for refreshments.

'I wish he hadn't rushed off like that,' Ruby said, grabbing her order pad. 'I was going to read him my new poem. I never got a chance. I reckon that stupid woman scared him away.'

'That stupid woman', as Ruby called her, seemed to

have scared herself away. At least, there was no sign of her in the café; I even checked the toilets just to be on the safe side.

Lauren had been asked to stay behind in the hall to stack chairs, and I went to find her. After all that, I really needed to talk; to tell someone about Ringlets. But Lauren hardly noticed me come in. She was just standing there, surrounded by half-stacked chairs, holding a bunch of questionnaires in her hands.

'Lauren, I've got to tell you—' I broke off. Wait a minute. They weren't the questionnaires at all. These papers were stiff and yellowing, edges crumbly like stale cheese. The words were dashed off in spiky green lettering. Silently Lauren handed one of them to me.

'Oh no' – seeing her face I knew even before I read – 'not again.'

> *Better to hold the sparkling grape,*
> *Than nurse the earth-worm's slimy brood;*
> *And circle in the goblet's shape*
> *The drink of gods, than reptile's food.*

by Ron Lord

Another verse of the 'worm' poem. Only this time, not in Lauren's hand but in the poet's own. He'd even signed his name at the end.

'Ron Lord,' I said slowly. 'Never heard of him. Lauren, listen to me. Remember Nathan, that photographer from *The Buzz*?'

'Don't tell me he's asked you out?'

55

'No, stupid.' I told her what Nathan had told me last night, about the pictures he'd taken of Ruby and the poet.

'This Ron Lord, he just never showed up in the prints. *We* saw him, and Nathan saw him in the camera lens, but the camera didn't record him. Don't you think that's a little strange?' When she didn't answer, I persisted, 'Lauren, you know what this means. You know what I'm trying to say.'

What was the matter with Lauren? She was stacking up chairs so fast, the metal frames clanked together.

I went on, 'Then there was my dream about the black carriages – I never even told you about that.'

'Oh, your dreams!' Lauren rolled her eyes.

I sighed. 'That crazy woman tonight, you should have seen her eyes. Lauren, it's *happening* again. You can't just turn your back and ignore it.'

'Can't I?' Lauren said. 'Just try me, because that's exactly what I'm going to do. I'm going to ignore it all, OK?'

'But what about your poem? Ron Lord's poem, I mean.'

Lauren turned on me, a pinched, obstinate look on her face. 'Maybe it's like you just said, subliminal. I picked the verse up from somewhere – the radio, a book – and it got filed away in my subconscious.'

'Well, I—' But as soon as I opened my mouth, she jumped down my throat.

'I told you, Abbie, I don't want to know. And if you keep on about it, then sorry, but I just don't want to be friends any more. Understand?'

56

With that, Lauren grabbed the piece of paper with Ron Lord's poem from my hand, and began slowly and deliberately to tear it up.

Chapter Five

In play there are two pleasures for your choosing:
The one is winning and the other losing.

Sprawled on my bed, I flipped the pages of *J-17*, trying to concentrate on the latest must-have lippy shades for autumn. There were two hours to kill before my stint at the festival, and I wasn't looking forward to it. Something about my encounter with Ringlets and the poet yesterday had given me the creeps. Were they somehow connected? In the poet's presence, I'd felt all shivery and weird. OK, getting up close to a seriously sexy bloke would give any girl the shivers, but I couldn't help feeling there was more to it than that. I'd felt a real chill coming off him. It was like the feeling you'd get if you opened the door of a cellar where daylight hadn't penetrated in years.

When the telephone rang, I had a sudden, mad conviction it was him.

'Abbie, dear, it's for you!' my mother called from the living room. 'A young man,' she said, eagerly passing me the receiver.

But the 'young man' turned out to be an 'old man'. It was only Giles asking could I do him a favour please? Apparently Ruby had taken the storeroom keys home with her by mistake, and now the electricians needed access to the meter or something. The problem was, Giles couldn't get through to Ruby's phone.

'I just keep getting this message – number unavailable. So, Abbie, if you could just pop round to her house and tell her to bring those keys straight away, that would be great.'

'But, um, I don't even know where Ruby lives.' Well, only that it was somewhere near the tube station. Why was it everyone seemed to think Ruby and I were mates?

'Oh?' Giles sounded surprised at first. 'Well, the address is twenty-seven, Warren Road. I'm sure you'll find it easily enough. And I'll put a bit extra in your pay packet for your trouble, OK?'

NO, I wanted to say. No, it is not OK. But Giles had already put down the phone.

Half an hour later I was getting off the bus outside Wood Green tube station. My dad, who as an ambulance-driver knew all these streets like the back of his hand, had given me directions for Warren Road. I was just about to cross the main road by the Esso garage, when a car drew up alongside me.

'Hey, Abbie, thought that was you. Not working at the festival tonight?'

I turned to see Nathan Daly grinning at me through the open window. There was a girl sitting next to him. A girl with sleek brown hair and a sulky mouth. The pang of jealousy I felt took me by surprise. After all, I didn't fancy Nathan, so why should I care if he had a girlfriend?

'Oh, um . . . no,' I stammered. 'I mean, yes, I am, later.

I'm on my way to Ruby's. She's got some important key or something, and I've got to get it off her.'

'Oh yeah?' Nathan scratched his head. 'I looked for you the other night after the lights went out, but you must've left before me.'

'Oh, yeah, probably.'

'Meant to call in last night and say hello,' Nathan went on, ignoring the sulky girlfriend. 'I was wondering, did our poet friend with the dog turn up again?'

'Yeah, he did. Actually, he gave a performance, and everyone went wild. Except for this one crazy woman—' I broke off. It was a bit awkward, stooping to talk through the open window of the car, with all the rush-hour people pushing past me on the pavement. Not to mention Nathan's girlfriend giving me the evil eye beneath her fringe.

'Crazy woman?'

'She was heckling him from the back – it was really embarrassing. I had to, like, escort her outside, and she was slagging him off and everything. She told me he'd called her an "odd-headed girl".'

Nathan threw back his head and laughed out loud. He was the kind of bloke who sees everything as a joke. The odd thing was, I felt I could tell him anything. I mean, all my worries about the poems, and the nightmares, and the madwoman's burning eyes. Somehow I just sensed that Nathan had an open mind about such things.

'Damn!' He slapped his forehead with the palm of his hand. 'Looks like I missed all the action last night then.'

'He left one of his poems lying around,' I said. 'Bit

morbid. Something about a skull and worms and that. His name's Ron Lord.'

'Ron Lord?' Nathan laughed again. 'Never heard of him.' He turned to the girlfriend. 'You heard of a Ron Lord, Tracey?'

Tracey shook her head, like she wasn't the slightest bit interested.

'Don't think anyone has,' I said; then, catching the girl-friend's eye again, I straightened. 'Well, better go and find Ruby.'

Nathan leaned his elbow further out of the window and looked up at me. 'That reminds me – tell your mates those pictures will be in *The Buzz* on Saturday. I'll call into the bar then, and we can talk, OK?'

With that the car sped off, leaving me standing there, wondering what he meant by 'talk'. I also wondered where he was going with that snotty-looking Tracey, and why I seemed to be the only girl on the planet – apart from Lauren, of course – without a boyfriend.

Crossing the High Street, I could see Ruby's road right ahead. There was a Spar on the corner, and a gang of lads lurking outside.

'Hey, dahlin', fancy a quick one?' one yelled out, like this was an offer no girl could resist.

As I hurried on past, I heard exaggerated retching noises behind me. 'Phaw! See that? What a dog!'

Normally, being called a 'dog' by a bunch of yobs with more bling than brains wouldn't have bothered me. Tonight though, the insult really hit the mark. For a start it was one of my warthog days; one of those days when you feel that only a lifetime of extensive facial surgery would make you human. Secondly, I couldn't help thinking about Nathan and Tracey. Together. An item.

With the Spar gang now making 'woof woof' noises behind me, I hurried past houses covered in pimply grey rendering. Warren Road was just as Ruby described, a right dump. Tiny front yards sprouted knackered old sofas and bicycle parts. Twice I had to step over puddles of curdled sick. Still, here it was at last, number 27, no better or worse than the others. No need to open the gate; broken off its hinges it lolled sideways against the hedge. Walking up the front path, I had to sidestep a nude plastic doll with no legs and an old TV aerial.

'Damn you for taking those stupid keys, Ruby Blagg,' I hissed under my breath. It was all a waste of time anyway. If no one was answering the phone, then it followed there was no one at home. One knock, that was all, I decided, and if there was no answer, Giles would just have to manage without them. Tough!

However, just as I was lifting the knocker, something soft and warm plopped onto my head. I squealed out loud. 'What the hell was . . . !' Furiously shaking my head, I heard a snort from above, giggles, whispers, then another soft, slug-like thing caught the back of my neck. I plucked it off. A chip!

'Hey! Stop that!' I looked up to see two demonically grinning faces at an upstairs window. Kids! They seemed to be chucking their chips out of the window for a bit of a lark. At the same moment Ruby opened the door.

'Oh! Abbie. It's you.' She seemed shocked to find me standing there plucking chips out of my hair. Not half as surprised as I was though. I hadn't expected to find Ruby at home. And certainly not with a baby astride her hip, apparently trying to wrench her nose off.

'Yeah,' I said, 'it's me. I've just been pelted with someone's dinner actually.' I lifted another chip from behind my ear. 'Are those little horrors up there anything to do with you?'

Ruby looked stricken. 'Oh, Abbie, I'm sorry, really. Look, you'd better come in.' She stood aside to let me pass.

Still I hung back. Set foot in that hell house? She must be joking! 'Er, no,' I said. 'Better not. Got to get to work. Giles just sent me to ask if you had those keys.'

'Keys?' Ruby jerked her red hair free of the baby's fist.

'To the storeroom. He reckons you took them home by mistake, and he needs them urgently. He's been trying to ring you but he couldn't get an answer. That's why he sent me.'

'Oh no.' Ruby clapped a hand to her mouth. 'I probably did, though God knows where I've put them. Look, Abbie, can't you come in – just a minute? I feel so bad about the mess. Let me get you a cloth at least. You've got grease on your top.'

She seemed so concerned, I felt mean for having such snotty thoughts about her house. It wasn't Ruby's fault after all.

'OK then.' I stepped inside. Then wished I hadn't. The smell was the worst thing: a toxic mix of hair spray, poo and mashed swede. I tried not to breathe. A girl of about four or five was hobbling down the stairs, tights around her knees, whining, 'Rube, I just done a big poo and I can't pull the handle.'

'Shh, Roxanne,' Ruby snapped. 'Can't you see we've got a visitor?'

'But it's a big poo' – the child glared at me, as if it was my fault – 'an' it won't go down.'

There was a sound of charging footsteps from upstairs, and the two chip-hurlers appeared to give us a chorus of: 'Roxie's done a floater . . . Roxie's done a floater . . .'

'Shut up, you two, and where's my mobile?' Ruby shrieked. 'I know you've hidden it somewhere – and what've you done to my friend?'

Friend? Ruby thought I was her friend? I began backing towards the front door. If this was Ruby's family, I was sorry for her. But my one thought now was to escape. I would have escaped, if Ruby hadn't suddenly shoved the baby into my arms.

'Please, Abb, can you hold Rosie for a sec while I look for my mobile, and those flaming keys? The phone's been cut off since last week – that's why Giles couldn't reach me.'

'Hey, um . . .' I was about to say I didn't, like, *do* babies, but Ruby had already rushed off to locate keys and mobile. Roxanne gazed up at me. I held Rosie well out of reach of my nose and hair. She was much heavier than I'd imagined. Her face was framed with sticky curls, the bright orange of tinned spaghetti. She gave me a suspicious look, as if she was trying to decide whether it was worth screaming her lungs out or not.

Roxanne demanded suddenly, 'Wass your name?'

'I'm Abbie. What's yours?'

'Roxanne!' She shrieked with hysterical mirth, as if I was stupid not to know. 'I'm Roxie, an' that's our baby, Rosie.'

'Is it? Look, can you go and get your big sister? Only I have to get back to work, see.' My knowledge of infants was zero, but I knew you couldn't just dump them and leave them to their own devices.

'Rosie cried all night 'cos she's getting teef like wot I got.' Roxanne grinned to show me.

'Really? Ouch!' I jerked a strand of my hair from the baby's grasp. So much for the careful streaks of Definitions colour gel I'd used earlier. Since then it had been coated in chip grease, and was now being wrenched out by the roots.

'You got shiny bits on your teef,' Roxanne pointed out.

'Have I? Oh yes I have.' In my rush, I'd forgotten to take out my brace before coming out. The realization that I'd been close to Nathan Daly, flashing crustaceous bits of metal at him, made my face grow hot with shame.

I glared at Roxanne for reminding me. How much longer was I going to have to stand here, loaded with a baby and discussing orthodontics with a four-year-old, for heaven's sake? It seemed like for ever before Ruby reappeared, a hand clamped on the neck of either brother. 'Say you're sorry, you little toads. Apologize to my friend.'

'Sorry!' the two boys yelled. They gave me a look that suggested they'd throw far worse things than chips next time.

Ruby had managed to get her mobile back, I noticed, and was tucking it up in its furry lilac holder. She jangled a bunch of keys at me. 'You'll never guess where I found these. Down the side of Rosie's cot. Right little magpie, aren't you, Rosie?' Ruby glanced at her watch and frowned suddenly. 'If you just hang on a minute longer, Abb, we could go together.'

This was my cue to leave. I was about to pass the baby back to her, when the door burst open behind us. A girl who looked like a skinny bad-tempered version of Ruby pushed right past us into the living room. She flung herself on the sofa, demanding to know if someone was going to make her a cup of tea.

'I'm all done in, I don't mind telling you.'

Still holding the baby, I hardly knew where to look. How many siblings did Ruby have, for God's sake?

'Phaw, it's stinking hot out there!' The girl kicked off her shoes with relief. She made impatient beckoning motions at me suddenly. 'Give her over. She bin changed yet?'

I shrugged. Who did Ruby's sister think I was? The nanny?

'I told you seven,' Ruby grumbled mildly. 'You know I got to leave for work by seven.' As she slipped on a pair of yellow sling-backs and tried to fix her hair, I sensed an edginess. Was Ruby scared of her sister?

'Sorry. Forgot.' The girl jiggled the baby with one arm, while extracting a long paperchain of tickets from her purse. 'Bumped into someone getting my lottery tickets and we went for a quick drink. Couldn't be antisocial, could I?'

I couldn't help staring. The lottery tickets were draped over the arm of the sofa – at least twenty of them. Not only that but the room was littered with old scratch cards. There must have been hundreds of them. I could just imagine the frantic scrape of fingernails, then the disgust as yet another losing ticket was tossed aside.

'Well, I'm off now, before I get the sack,' Ruby said. Giving the baby a quick kiss on the cheek, she prodded me towards the door.

'Don't worry,' the sister retorted, 'if I win the jackpot I'll leave you a note.'

As soon as we were out of the house, we began to run.

'I'm sorry about that, Abb,' Ruby panted. 'I suppose you'll tell Lauren and Giles and everybody.'

'Tell them what?'

'It's too bad of my mum being late,' Ruby said in her chirpy voice.

'Yeah. Good thing your sister came home when she did.'

'Sister?' Ruby glanced sideways at me as we paused to cross the High Street. 'Sister? That was my mum, you gawk!'

'That was . . . your *mum*?'

She didn't laugh at my mistake, as we ran the rest of the way to the bus stop, and neither did I. So I supposed I wasn't the first person to make it.

Chapter Six

There is a tide in the affairs of women
Which, taken at the flood, leads – God knows where:

It was all a hive of activity at Lauren's house. Her mother Izzie, dressed in paint-daubed dungarees and baseball boots, was perched on top of a ladder. She was slapping crimson paint on the living-room walls in bold, bloody splashes, and singing along with Van Morrison in her husky, out-of-tune voice.

Outside in the garden, her partner Harvey (referred to by Lauren as Harv-wit) was madly sawing up sheets of MDF to make Moorish arches.

'It's bye-bye to boring old suburbia, sweeties,' Izzie told us, 'and hello to the exotic East. This house will look like a Moorish palace by the time we've finished.'

'Looks more like *The Texas Chainsaw Massacre*,' Lauren said. She apologized to Ruby. 'Excuse my mother. Ever since she took up belly dancing, she's been slowly turning a perfectly nice house into a harem.'

'Oh.' For once Ruby seemed speechless. She had a dazzled look in her eye as she gazed about the room. 'I think it's wicked,' she managed finally. 'Is this all your house?'

'Of course it's all our house. I mean, we haven't got lodgers or anything,' Lauren said, puzzled.

'And are these all your books?' At least two of the walls were lined with books. 'Did you read all of them?'

'Are you kidding?' I joked. 'Lauren only reads medical dictionaries, don't you, Lauren?'

'What?'

'Never mind.'

We trooped up to Lauren's white-walled, coir-matted sanctuary at the top of the house, since the pong of paint fumes, Lauren claimed, was making her feel sick.

So how come Ruby was here with us on this Saturday afternoon, when we weren't due at the festival until our seven o'clock evening stint? Well, naturally I'd told Lauren everything about my visit to Ruby's house. The last thing I'd expected was that Lauren would take Ruby up as a charitable cause.

'It explains everything.' Lauren shook her head sadly when I told her. 'Ruby's obsession with fame, I mean. It's all a fantasy. An escape from the reality of her life.'

'It doesn't explain why she has to be so bloody cheerful all the time though,' I protested.

Sorry for Ruby though I was, I wasn't too sure about the wisdom of getting too thick with her. It wasn't just her family that worried me. That night I'd gone to tell her about the keys, Ron Lord had turned up at the festival again, and given his usual hypnotic performance. The odd thing was, while he had the audience mesmerized, later, no one could remember a word he'd said. I also noticed that whenever he showed up, Ringlets wasn't far away. I'd catch a glimpse of her at the end of a

69

row, or passing the ticket desk, or flitting across the empty stage. Then I'd look again, and she'd be gone.

After Ron's last performance Ruby had fluttered about his table, flirting so shamelessly, she'd practically climbed into his lap at one point. She probably would have done, if Giles hadn't reminded her that there were other customers waiting to be served.

'I tell you, this poet guy is seriously weird. I've got this feeling he only turns up because of Ruby. I think she may be one of *them*,' I told Lauren. 'You know, like a magnet for the undead.'

Lauren said this was rubbish. 'Ruby is a simple soul, Abbie. She's far too down to earth to be a psychic. Ruby is in need of our support and guidance. Surely you can see that?'

'I so-o-o love your room, Lor!' Ruby's heels clattered across the bare polished boards. 'You've got so much space. Oooh, what's this?'

The pentagram, she meant. Lauren had painted the pentagram across her floor during our frantic time with the ghost of Henry VIII.

'Oh, that,' Lauren said, embarrassed. 'I've been trying to scrub it off for ages. We—' she shot me a warning look – 'I mean, I used to think it might protect me from, er . . . evil spirits. Hah. You know, when I was younger, of course.'

Ruby looked mystified. 'You don't believe in spirits, do you? You're as bad as our Roxie. She sees this woman sometimes, she says, leaning over Rosie's cot. Got a vivid imagination, that one.'

'What's it like coming from a big family?' Lauren

quickly seized the opportunity to change the subject. 'Abbie and I are both only children, so we have no idea.'

Lauren had one of those basket chairs in her room that looks like an upturned lampshade and gives you bum-ache to sit in. Now Ruby curled up in it as naturally as a cat. Grabbing the cushion, she cuddled it on her lap, like it was Rosie. As if her arms felt empty without a baby to cuddle.

'The kids are a bit of handful,' she conceded. 'Don't get me wrong – I love them to bits. It's just, well . . . sometimes it gets a bit much . . .'

'Do you have to look after them much?' I said. 'Like the other night?'

'Oh, I don't mind really. My mum can't cope sometimes, see. She gets in a state.'

'Why on earth did she have so many then?' Lauren said. 'There's no excuse with modern birth control. I don't personally plan to have children until I'm at least thirty-five, when my healing work is completed.'

I glanced sideways at her. This was a new one on me.

Ruby plucked awkwardly at the cushion. 'I know, but my mum loves being pregnant, see. She meets a new bloke, and before you know it there's another baby on the way.'

'She loves being pregnant?' I said, surprised, for I couldn't imagine anything worse.

'Yeah. She loves babies and stuff, like, when they're really tiny and newborn. It's when they start toddling they drive her up the wall. She always says that if she ever wins the lottery the first thing she'll do is get a live-in nanny.'

I remembered the lottery tickets I'd seen the other night, but didn't mention them. Personally I couldn't see there was much for Ruby to laugh about.

She went on, 'She can't help herself really. She's got this like . . . *addiction* to the lottery. She thinks it's the only way out of Warren Road. She buys so many scratch cards, sometimes there's nothing left over for food. That's when I have to help out a bit.' Seeing our shocked faces, she added, 'Well, I get good tips at Pizza Pronto, so what can I do? I won't see the kids go hungry.'

'No,' Lauren said slowly, 'but they're not your responsibility, are they, Ruby.'

'Maybe not . . .' Ruby pretended to study the cushion in detail. 'Anyway, I won't be living at home for ever. When I've saved up enough money, I'll get my own place. I might even put myself through drama school, although that costs a bomb, unless you get a special award. But I'm not worried.' Her face lit up. 'Not now I have Ron to help me.'

'Ron? You don't mean the poet, Ron?'

'Course I do. He's being so kind to me, really. So helpful.'

'I'll bet he is,' I murmured, at the same time feeling a peculiar twinge of jealousy. Which was ridiculous. If Ron was not exactly the man I thought he wasn't, then how could I be jealous?

Ruby leaned forward in her chair. 'No, it's not like that. Ron is a real gentleman. If I tell you two a secret, promise not to tell? I don't want it getting around. I don't want Giles to know . . .'

'Of course we promise.' Lauren sounded offended.

Ruby smiled, the slightly smug smile of someone who is privy to secret information. 'Well, it turns out that Ron Lord is absolutely *loaded*. And I mean loaded. He's got this estate up north somewhere. Some big old house that's been in the family for centuries, with massive grounds. And there's all these animals roaming about, and lakes with swans on, and statues, and peacocks . . . and . . .' Now Ruby was warming to the theme there was no stopping her. We heard more than we ever needed to know about this fabled estate up north.

'If this place is so marvellous,' I interrupted at last, 'what's he doing in London?'

Ruby leaned forward eagerly, arms resting on the cushion. 'He needs a base, doesn't he? When you're mega-rich and like a famous literary genius, you got to have a place in the town and one in the country. And guess what, I found out where his London house is!'

'It's not in Northgate, is it?' Lauren said.

'No, silly.' Ruby giggled. 'Where do all the famous poets and artists live? Hampstead, of course!'

'Hampstead?' I could hardly believe this. 'You mean he actually invited you round to his place?'

Ruby's eager expression faltered a moment. 'Well, he hasn't exactly *invited* me. Not yet. I just went to look – from the outside, you know?'

'But how did you know where he lives then?' Lauren said.

Ruby fiddled with her carnation hair slide and giggled softly. 'To tell the truth, I'm a bit embarrassed to admit this, but I followed him home one night, from the

73

festival. I saw him getting on this bus, and I just hopped on too – sort of spur-of-the-moment thing . . .'

I gaped at her. It was hard enough to imagine Ron Lord on a bus. He was surely the type to take taxis everywhere. Or – I shivered at the memory of my dream – a coach and horses maybe.

'He didn't see me,' Ruby added hastily, as if this was all that mattered.

Lauren was staring at the faded lines of the pentagram as if she couldn't believe what she was hearing. Neither could I. I knew Ruby was a bit on the pushy side, but following someone you fancied home on a bus was going a bit far. That was the kind of thing a stalker would do.

'I didn't realize he'd be going so far, of course,' Ruby continued, 'but once I was on the bus, I thought I might as well go the whole way. He lives right on the heath practically. I followed him from the stop, and then I stopped across the road from his house. I waited ages, hoping he might come out again.'

'And did he?' I said.

'No. But I saw this woman scurry out – a tiny little woman, foreign looking. Must've been a maid. Anyway, I'm not bothered, 'cos Ron says I can visit him up at his estate when he next goes up there.' She laughed. 'You know how he talks . . .' Imitating Ron's cultured tones, she drawled, ' "You would be most welcome, dear girl." He's so funny. He told me that when he took over the place from his uncle, he sacked most of the servants because they were ugly.'

Lauren was disgusted. 'That's unfair dismissal. You can't

sack people because they're a little facially challenged.'

Ignoring this, Ruby rushed on. 'That's not all. Ron has all these contacts in the theatre and stuff. Sometimes he puts on shows, concerts and that on his estate. And he's going to put in a good word for me, y'know, with his mates, and . . .'

Ruby wasn't boasting exactly. She was just bubbling over with excitement, and wanting to share it with us. For the first time, I began to feel seriously worried for her.

'Ruby,' I interrupted her, 'I don't want to be a damper or anything, but maybe you should . . .' I hesitated. What could I say? *Watch out for Ron the poet, because I think he's some kind of ghoul?* 'I mean,' I tried again, ignoring Lauren's stern warning look, 'don't take everything he says at face value. He might not be . . . all he *seems* exactly.'

'Don't look so worried, Abb. I can look after myself, you know.' Ruby jumped up and patted my shoulder as if I were her poor old granny, cautioning her on the Wicked Ways of the World. 'I know what! Why don't I show you both where Ron lives? Hampstead's not far from here. We could make a detour on the way to work tonight.'

Hampstead was a pretty big detour, as it happened. Lauren and I both opened our mouths to protest, then closed them again. Maybe we were just a little curious ourselves. And anyway, Ruby had made up her mind.

The weather changed dramatically as we left Lauren's house. The sky had been growing hazy all afternoon. Now it darkened to a purplish colour, like wet silk. By the time we got to the street where the poet lived, rain was falling so fast, we were obliged to huddle under Lauren's umbrella.

'This is it!' Halting beneath a Victorian carriage lamp, Ruby pointed across the street.

We stared. This was a world away from Warren Road. Here the heath was practically an extension of the gardens; steep gabled rooftops peeped out from jungle-like creepers. Cars purred softly over the pedestrian humps. Even the rain hissed respectfully down on the cobbles. The clack of Ruby's stilettos scraping over the kerb sounded loud and intrusive.

As for the poet's house, you couldn't see much of it behind a thick wall of evergreens. There was a pillared gateway with a blue plaque on the wall. I didn't pay much attention to this. Almost every house had a blue plaque to say that someone famous had once lived, died or visited there.

'Yeah,' I said. 'Very nice. Can we go now? I'm getting wet.'

'Yes, let's.' Lauren sniffed. 'This place disgusts me. You could house an entire African village in one of these houses.'

'Yeah,' breathed Ruby. 'Fabulous, isn't it? I'm going to live somewhere like this one day. You can laugh if you want, but I just know I will.'

We didn't laugh. It was just too pathetic. To indulge her, I said, 'Well, you never know. Tell you what, Ruby, I'll read your bumps one day – the ones on your head, I mean,' I added quickly in case she thought me some kind of pervert. But Ruby declined my offer.

'Thanks, Abbie, but I don't believe in fate, or the stars, or any of that stuff. I just believe in myself. You've got to if you want to get on in life.'

This was too much for Lauren. She adjusted her umbrella more firmly over her own head, as the rain began to swish down even harder. 'We should go. The Northgate bus comes in fifteen minutes; if we miss it, we'll be late for work.'

'OK, but just wait a mo' – Ruby caught hold of her arm – 'I'm going to ring the bell to see if he's coming tonight.'

'What? Oh Ruby, you can't . . . wait . . . !'

Ruby ignored me. She was already clattering over the cobbles towards the pillared gates.

'What *is* she like?' I gasped, as Ruby disappeared from sight. 'Talk about throwing yourself at someone.'

'She'll get herself arrested if she's not careful,' Lauren said. 'And personally speaking, I for one don't want to get involved. Let's move on up the street a bit. We'll give her five minutes, and if she doesn't come out, we'll just have to catch the bus without her.'

It seemed a bit mean, just to go off without Ruby. But I needn't have worried. No sooner had Lauren and I turned away than we heard the clatter of heels behind us.

'The maid answered the door,' Ruby said breathlessly. 'She couldn't understand English so I just gave her my note.'

'Note?'

'Just one of my poems. I was going to put it through the letterbox, then I thought, why not knock, since we're here?'

I couldn't help feeling relieved as I glanced across at the shadowy house. Supposing Ron Lord had been at home? Supposing he'd invited us all inside? Supposing . . . ? I stopped supposing and blinked. Towering in front of the poet's boundary hedge was an enormous lime tree. Behind the patchy grey bark, out of the corner of my eye I caught a movement. Something stirred. Shimmered. My heart jumped. Someone was watching us.

'Shh!' I gestured to Ruby. 'Who's that?'

The minute I said, 'Who's that?' she showed herself. It was like she'd just been waiting for us to sense her presence. Now we had, she stepped right out from behind the tree. Despite the summer rain, it wasn't exactly cold; yet as the figure in white floated towards us, I shivered as if my blood had turned to ice.

That woman. Ringlets. The one who had shrieked abuse from the back row, and demanded to know where 'Allegra' was.

'What's she doing here?' Lauren whispered unsteadily.

The scariest thing was the way she just seemed to hover there, gauzy and pale as a moth. She was still wearing the nightdress thing. Rain glanced off her white skin as if she was made from glass.

'Is my lord not at home?' Her dark eyes settled on Ruby. The imploring look I'd seen in them the other night had hardened to a mischievous glitter.

'Lord?' Ruby faltered. 'Ron Lord, you mean? The poet? Do you know him?'

'*Know* him? Oh yes, I *know* him!' The shriek of laughter was not really laughter at all. It had so many other emotions in it: sorrow, rage, a hatred so pitiless that Ruby actually lost her balance. The heel of her pink stiletto turned sideways. She winced, staggering into a nearby parking meter.

'Haven't I watched out here all those days?' The dark eyes seized upon her, as if to catch her, to pin her down. 'Have I not waited as you do now for an audience? Have I not sent my lord letters, stories, poems? Have I not given my entire self to him, body and soul?'

'I don't know,' Ruby stammered. 'Have you?'

There was a pause, as Ringlets – who was really just a girl, I saw now – gathered herself for a final onslaught. I held my breath.

'What has he done?' she hissed. 'What has he done with my Allegra?'

Lauren tapped my shoulder. 'Ignore her – come on. Let's go.'

I wanted to go. Oh, how I wanted to. But somehow my legs were stuck, the way they were in my dream, when the dark empty carriages rolled past. Beside me, Ruby was clutching hold of the parking meter, as if for support.

'Sorry,' Ruby was saying, 'I don't know any Allegra.'

I can't say I actually *heard* Ringlets scream. I *felt* it, though, in my head, like an electric drill boring its way through my temples. Somewhere in the region of my non-existent Bump of Wisdom a sharp pain stabbed.

Ruby made a whimpering noise of disbelief. 'What's going on? What does she want?'

In a lighter voice we heard, 'I want my Allegra. I want my child,' as if this should be obvious. Ringlets flounced, turned round and drifted back towards the tall scrolled gates of the poet's house. 'Is he at home? Is he hiding? Oh, this is most disagreeable. I know him. Yes, I know *Le Diable Boiteux*. The Lame Devil, some call him. The Lame Devil . . .'

This was enough. The minute Ringlets took her burning eyes from ours, her grip upon us weakened. My legs unlocked. Not wanting to hear any more about the Lame Devil, the three of us ran, stumbling over the slimy cobbles while the great gardens dripped and whispered around us.

Was she following? I hardly dared look over my shoulder. If only this had been Smedhurst Road, I thought. Someone might come to their gate, call from a window. There were always neighbours about, parking their cars, cleaning windscreens, putting out rubbish. But here, the occupants knew only their lighted islands, their leather sofas and silk cushions. What happened out on the street, in the dark, was no concern of theirs.

'Tell him, tell the Lame Devil, I *will* have my child!'

The voice wailed after us like a curse. I turned. Thank God she wasn't following after all. I couldn't even see her now – just a faint white blur blending into the lime tree outside the front gate.

'What a nutter! She ought to be locked up!' Ruby declared as we reached the corner of the avenue, the comforting blare of the main road just up ahead.

'Paranoia,' Lauren announced firmly, although she didn't sound too sure of her diagnosis. 'Probably it's a split-personality thing.'

'She's split all right,' I murmured. 'Split between this world and the next.'

I happened to glance down as I spoke. I hadn't noticed the street name before. Now it caught my eye, the stark black letters glossed by rain: BYRON DRIVE.

Suddenly everything clicked. Added up. Made sense. The terrible picture began to emerge, like something dragging itself out of the shadows.

Chapter Seven

My mother dream'd not in my natal hour,
That I should fall into a monster's power

Ruby's 'detour' had made us late. Jumping off the bus outside Bromfield Park, we had to run all the way from the gates beneath the dripping chestnut trees to the gallery.

There was only five minutes to spare before the first performance. Please don't let it be 'Ron Lord', I prayed silently. Those letters on the street sign, BYRON DRIVE, still blazed in my mind. Also the encounter with Ringlets had made me shaky. Supposing she turned up here again? As I busied myself about the tables, doling out menus, I hardly dared look towards the café entrance. If Ringlets was what I suspected she was, she could materialize here, right under my nose. Spirits do not have to catch the bus to Northgate, after all. They waft mysteriously through the layers of the world. They descend through ceilings and walk through walls. They travel faster than the speed of light. They— Oh my God . . . the doors were pushing open right now! I gripped the edge of the table, steeling myself for the drift of white dress, the gauzy, moth-like blur of misery which was Ringlets.

Then, 'Hey, it's Nathan!' Ruby cried out. 'Hiya, Nate.'

At the sight of Nathan Daly, I beamed with relief. Then quickly corrected myself. What was I thinking of? He might get the impression I fancied him. Looking away, I pretended to concentrate on the menus, propping them up just so against the sugar bowls.

Nathan made straight for the bar. 'How's it going then, Rube?'

'Oh, you wouldn't believe what happened to me and Abb and Lor just now,' Ruby said at once. 'We got, like, accosted by that crazy woman who comes here some nights. That one who looks like she's wearing her gran's old wedding dress. She just came at us from behind a tree. Gave us a right mouthful. Calling Ron all sorts – Lame Devil, you name it. Got more than a few screws missing, that one,' she declared, then broke off to give a little squeal of pleasure.

'Ooh, you got our pictures! Let me see them, Nate, please please please!'

There was no need, I thought, to loop her arms around Nathan's neck like that, practically knocking him off the bar stool. It was just as well there were no customers in yet – only Amelia, counting change out ready for the till. And me, of course.

I wondered what had happened to Tracey. Perhaps she was in the loo, making her sulky lips even sulkier, right this minute?

'Abb, what are you doing?' Ruby beckoned to me. 'Come and see the paper. Look, we're famous, we are!'

I had no choice. A copy of *The Buzz* was spread out on the counter, open at the centre page. Nathan smiled at me as I peered over Ruby's shoulder.

The pictures were mostly of Ruby flashing her teeth, eyelashes and practically everything she'd got at the camera. There was only one of Lauren and me. Not good. Lauren looked like one of those spindly meerkats you see on wildlife programmes, and my nose looked like the false kind that comes with a plastic moustache.

Nathan seemed to be watching my face for my reaction. His eyes had that crinkly, amused look, as if there was some joke I didn't know about. 'Looks like Ruby's taken over the show a bit,' he admitted wryly. 'The others didn't come out too well.'

Ruby looked puzzled. 'What happened to Ron, though? I thought you took me and him – you were snapping away all the time I was talking to him.'

'Yeah, well . . .' Nathan scratched the back of his head. 'Technical problems' – he looked me straight in the eye – 'over-exposure probably.'

Ruby seemed quite happy to accept this explanation. 'Is that what it is? Hey, look at me, I look a bit over-exposed myself, don't I? Oooh, I'm never wearing that top again – makes my boobs look funny, don't you think, Abb?'

'Oh come on, Ruby,' I muttered. 'You look fantastic, and you know it.'

'Yeah, yeah, well, don't let stardom go to your heads.' Nathan grinned. 'Where's your friend, by the way?'

'Lauren? Oh, she's in reception doing the tickets. Where's yours?'

Nathan lifted an eyebrow. 'Mine?'

'Your girlfriend,' I said as lightly as I could. 'Tracey.'

'Tracey?' He looked puzzled a moment, then

laughed. 'Oh, *that* Tracey. Tracey's my colleague. She's the new cub reporter on *The Buzz*. When I saw you, we were on our way to report on a gig down in Holloway Road.'

'Oh.'

Silly how pleased I felt. At the same time I realized that colleagues could very easily become girlfriends, especially when they have sulky lips and masses of silky brown hair.

'Abbie?' I turned to see Lauren standing behind us, holding a bunch of questionnaires. Her face had that pinched look that meant she was worried and trying not to show it. 'Look what I found, mixed up among the questionnaires.'

I knew at once what it was. The same yellowing paper, the same inky scrawl.

My throat went dry as I said, 'Looks like your friend's been here already, Ruby. He's left this behind.'

'What? Let me see.' Ungluing her eyes from her own image, Ruby almost snatched the verse from my hand and read in her shrill voice,

'Death, so called, is a thing which makes men weep,
And yet a third of life is passed in sleep – by Ron Lord.'

She sighed. 'That's so true, that is. Think of all the time we waste just sleeping! Funny he should just leave it, though. He might have popped in to say hello. Hey, Lor, have you seen these pictures yet? They're really good of you – you look all kind of sweet with your plaits and cap and everything.'

Lauren bent over the paper like she was really interested. She didn't fool me though.

I cleared my throat. 'Lauren, didn't you notice the name of the street we were in – in Hampstead?'

'Hmmm . . . ?' Lauren held the paper closer to her face. 'Can't say I did.'

'It was Byron Drive. And look at this – "by Ron Lord". That poet – d'you think he's trying to tell us something? For God's sake, Lauren, do I have to spell it out letter by letter? It's Lord Byron. Our mysterious limping poet is only *Lord bloody Byron!*'

Lauren held up her hand to stop me. 'Leave it, Abbie. Let's not go there, OK?'

'What's going on with you two?' The name Byron obviously meant nothing to Ruby. She was patting my shoulder in that infuriating way of hers. 'You're all on edge, Abb. Why don't you have a coffee, settle your nerves, eh?' Turning to Nathan she explained, 'Abb's still a bit upset about that awful woman tonight. I don't blame her. In fact, I'm gonna look for Giles right now, and tell him to have her banned from this place. Oh, and I'll take the paper and show him our pics while I'm at it.'

Grabbing Nathan's copy of *The Buzz*, Ruby whisked out through the doors. Lauren followed, muttering something about tickets and getting back to reception. Coward!

'What's all this stuff about Byron then?' Nathan looked closely at me.

'Oh nothing,' I said.

'Sounded like something to me.'

'Maybe, but you wouldn't understand.'

'Try me.' Draining his glass, Nathan swivelled round on his stool to face me. Something about his direct honest look made me feel I could trust him. Yet knowing how most males react to the idea of spooks, spirits and things that go bump, I hesitated.

In the end it was Nathan who came straight out with it. 'So you reckon our camera-shy poet is the ghost of Lord Byron?'

I glanced sideways at him. Amazing. He wasn't laughing at me. There wasn't the faintest trace of sarcasm in his tone.

'You probably think I'm mad,' I murmured.

Nathan shook his head. 'You think he's a ghost. Well, got to confess, it crossed my mind too, especially when I saw those pictures.'

'Really! I mean, I . . .' My mouth gaped open. A bloke who believed in the Other Side? That would have to be a first!

But Nathan was telling me about his gran, and how she had second sight. 'Reckons she saw Dick Turpin one Saturday afternoon in Highgate – broad daylight, and there was Dick galloping past the Spaniards Inn. She's seen more ghosts than you've served cappuccinos. Honest. Swear to God.'

I couldn't help laughing at the way he spoke. 'So you do, like, *believe* in them?'

'Why not? In my business I like to keep an open mind. Life is strange. I mean, half the people I photograph look like ghosts most of the time, and sometimes the ghosts look like real people. My gran has this phrase that used to give me the creeps when I was a kid: she says

"They walk among us." Just like that. "They walk among us." '

'Ergh, that's really creepy . . .' I took a deep breath. It was so so tempting to tell Nathan everything just then – I mean, all our ghostly experiences, the whole shebang. But then Ruby suddenly hurtled back through the door, shaking the paper at us like someone had just declared war.

'Hey, Abb, did you see this? Look what I just found on the back page!'

'What?' The way she was jumping up and down, I guessed it was another picture of her beautiful self she'd come across.

But the page she thrust inches from my nose was all advertisements: upcoming shows, films, personal column, lonely hearts, that kind of stuff.

'Yeah? So?'

'There, *there*!' Ruby stabbed the line she wanted me to read with a glitzy fingernail.

My eyes trailed down the personal column until the word 'AUDITION' caught my eye. The notice was short and to the point:

AUDITION TO BE HELD AT THE *FREE SPIRIT THEATRE,*
HAMPSTEAD
FRIDAY 25 AUGUST, 5 P.M.
CAN YOU SING AND DANCE?
WANTED: ATTRACTIVE, TALENTED GIRLS BETWEEN
AGES OF 16 AND 21 FOR VARIETY PERFORMANCE
P.O. BOX 6190 FOR DETAILS

'So? It's an audition.' I looked from the paper to Ruby.

She was sparking so much, it was a wonder it didn't just catch alight.

'Oh, Abb, this is my big chance, don't you see? It's my big chance to be famous. And it's like it was meant to be, 'cos I never get *The Buzz* usually. I'd never have seen it if not for our pictures!'

'Let me see that,' Nathan said, taking the paper from me. He frowned. 'Funny – never saw this when it went to print. Come to that, I've never heard of the Free Spirit Theatre.'

'Well, it's just opened probably,' Ruby said. 'You can't know every theatre in, like, the whole of London, Nate, come on.'

'That's just it, I do,' he murmured. 'It's my job to know.'

I couldn't say anything at that moment, because Ruby had flung her arms around my neck, as if she'd just won *Pop Idol* or something. Over her shoulder, though, I saw Nathan gazing towards the door with a strange expression on his face. And I shivered as I thought of that phrase of his gran's – 'They walk among us.'

A few days later Lauren and I were sitting in Ruby's bedroom, watching her preen and sing in front of an age-spotted mirror.

'*That boy makes me weak with des . . . iahh!*' Ruby trilled. '*Sometimes I think we can't get no high . . . ahh!*' It was a little number she'd written herself, and it wasn't half bad.

Song finished, Ruby paused as if for applause. She turned to Lauren and me. 'Well, what do you think? Shall I do that one on Friday night? For the audition?'

Five-year-old Roxie, who was shuffling around in a pair of Ruby's best stilettos, gave it a thumbs-down immediately. 'I don't like that one. I like "Wheels on the Bus", I do.'

Ruby sighed. 'Can't you go downstairs and play with Rosie, please? I'll be down in a minute.'

Lauren and I sat together on Ruby's bed, surrounded by a menagerie of fluffy lilac kittens and pink poodles, while cutesy Kylie beamed down at us from the walls. Roxie's bed was separated from Ruby's by a narrow bedside table heaped with cosmetics. There were only three bedrooms at Warren Road, so they had to share, Ruby had explained earlier.

Neither Lauren nor I were exactly thrilled to be stuck here in Ruby's House of Horrors, but what could we do? It was Wednesday, and since there were no events on at the festival that day, Ruby had begged us to come and take a look at her act.

'It can't be that bad,' Lauren had said when I tried to warn her on our way to the house. 'You always exaggerate, Abbie, that's your trouble.'

However, Rory and Rob always reserved a special welcome for new visitors, it seemed. Having pelted me with chips a few days ago, they nearly knocked Lauren flat, skateboarding down the stairs.

'*Wheels on the bus go round and round,*' Roxanne chirruped, spinning dangerously in the six-inch heels. She tapped Lauren on the knee. 'D'you know that one?'

'Shall I sing it again for you?' Ruby offered. 'It's so hard to know what the judges like. It's got to be something that grabs their attention. It's got to be, like – out of this world.'

'It's fine, Ruby,' I said. 'You've got a fantastic voice – hasn't she, Lauren?'

Lauren said that in her opinion auditions were totally competitive and unfair. 'You mustn't feel like a failure, Ruby, if you don't get chosen. It's not winning that counts.'

'Not winning? But I must – I *must* get chosen!' Ruby burst out, alarmed. 'They've got to choose me. I'm giving it everything. Everything I've got.' There was a desperate look in her eye as she grappled her shoes back from Roxanne and persuaded the kid into a pair of old flip-flops.

'Anyway, guess what?' Ruby's eyes glinted with mischief. 'I went to Ron's house again last night.'

'You didn't!' Lauren and I both said together.

Ruby seemed surprised at our reaction. 'Why shouldn't I? I told you, he's got friends in the theatre and that. I thought he might hear me sing.'

'And did he?' Lauren asked dubiously.

Ruby shook her head. 'That maid turned me away again. But I left a note with her, with my address and mobile number, and one of my own poems. So he's sure to get in touch soon.'

We hadn't planned on sticking around Ruby's house for long. The idea had been to watch her act, have a quick natter and split on some urgent business. But at Ruby's things were never that simple.

Somehow or other we'd been roped into various baby-related tasks and hours later we both felt like a pair of deflated balloons. It was almost as if I'd lost the will to live, never mind run.

Ruby poured us each a Coke, and slapped slices of the giant four seasons pizza she'd saved on the coffee table. 'Tuck in. You deserve it. Thanks for helping me out. Rosie's cutting her back teeth, poor little thing, so she's a bit whingey at the moment.'

I took a slice of pizza. 'Where's your mum tonight?'

'Oh, she goes to the bingo on a Wednesday night with her mate, Sian.'

'Oh.'

'Have you told her about the audition?' Lauren asked, picking vegetables out of the cheesy bits of pizza, because of her dairy allergy.

'Nah. I told her I have to work Friday night.' Ruby made a thing of brushing crumbs from her T-shirt, like she didn't want to meet our eye.

'But why? Why not tell her?' Lauren persisted.

'Didn't seem any point.' Ruby heaped a blob of Branston pickle onto her plate. Eventually she added, 'It's not like it's a big deal for her. I mean, she doesn't understand about auditions. She thinks they're a waste of time, and that people like us don't get famous. Not ever. She's always saying stuff like, "Oh, we're at the bottom of the pile, Rube," and "There's only two ways out of Warren Road, and one of them's in a coffin." '

'Charming,' I said, the word 'coffin' making me shudder suddenly. 'What's the other way?'

'Winning the lottery, of course.'

We all laughed. Actually it wasn't so bad at Ruby's with the kids in bed and her scary mother safely at bingo.

You might almost say it was cosy, what with the gas fire hissing and the giant screen TV flickering in the corner, sound turned down. The debris of toys had been swept into a box, bottles of milk, dummies and felt-tip pens were retrieved from the sides of armchairs. With the curtains drawn, their whirligig pattern of brown and orange dazzling the eyes, you might almost forget that Warren Road lay outside.

Ruby stretched out on the sofa, flicking through her latest *Crush* magazine. It was running a Britney Spears look-alike contest, and Ruby reckoned if she blonded her hair up a bit she might stand a chance.

'If you win, you get your picture in *Crush*, free tickets to a Britney concert and a week's try-out at the Avril James Stage School. Which is, like, only the top place where all the celebs— Oh no!' At the sound of Rosie crying, she broke off. 'Oh no . . . not now, Rosie . . . please.' Ruby glanced despairingly to the ceiling, the magazine slipping from her knees.

Lauren and I looked at each other, raising our eyebrows in sympathy. It was an odd cry for a baby. Sort of sudden and questioning, like a startled bird. There was a pause, followed by an outraged howl. The kind of howling that can't be ignored.

Ruby sighed. 'Not tonight. Please not tonight. She's only been asleep half an hour.'

Poor Ruby! How grateful I was at that moment for my own parents. At one time I'd longed for brothers and sisters; now I was thankful that I was the only miserable specimen they'd managed to produce. As Rosie's wailing worked itself up into a crescendo, the creaking quiet of the flat in Smedhurst Road, where we crept around in our slippers out of consideration for Mrs Croop downstairs, seemed like heaven.

Lauren took the opportunity to yawn loudly. 'Abbie, we should, er . . .' She nodded her head towards the door.

'Oh yeah, just remembered I promised to help my mum with her, er . . .' I paused, unable to think what I could possibly help her with.

'Choosing the new décor for the surgery?' Lauren suggested.

'Oh yeah . . . that's it. Anyway, I expect your mum'll be home soon, Ruby.'

I jumped up to grab my jacket from the back of a chair. Lauren was busily ramming on her cap and making faces at me. The faces indicated that baby Rosie wasn't our problem.

'We'll be off then,' Lauren said.

Ruby nodded. She was just getting wearily up from the sofa, when Rosie stopped crying. The silence was so abrupt it seemed unnatural. A baby wouldn't stop crying just like that, would it? Not unless someone picked it up, or . . .

Fear prickled my skin suddenly. It was as if my body knew what was coming before I did. As if it was already steeling itself for that voice, crooning horribly into the silence, 'Hush now, child. Go to sleep.'

A woman's voice. So clear and close, you could hear the breath between the words, like a slow, moist breeze. You could hear the stickiness of a tongue curving around the words 'sleep, sleep, go to sleep, my child . . .'

94

'Is that, er . . . your mother?' Lauren glanced nervously towards the hallway.

Ruby shook her head. She stood frozen, listening.

'Hush, my sweet one. Sleep now, for Mama.' This time the voice seemed to be right in the room with us.

Ruby clenched her fists. Her voice trembled as she said, 'That's the baby intercom. In Rosie's room.'

Next minute, Ruby had shot from the room and was taking the stairs three at a time. Lauren and I followed, Lauren tripping over a Lego tractor on the way up. We paused at the landing. The door to Rosie's room had been left slightly ajar at bedtime. Now it was open wide.

Ruby gulped. 'Who the hell . . . ?'

We followed her into the milk-scented gloom, almost afraid to look. Supposing the intruder was there, leaning over the cot?

But Ruby was standing there, hand clasped to her chest, laughing silently at her own foolishness. 'There's no one here.'

No one here *now*, she meant. At this moment. Or was there? The baby was lying on her back, rigid and flushed looking, and the cot was actually *rocking*? Rocking all by itself; rocking so hard, you almost felt seasick just looking at it. Cot hinges creaking and creaking like some strange sad lullaby.

Hush now, child. Hush now. Go to sleep for Mama.

Chapter Eight

And her voice was the warble of a bird,
So soft, so sweet, so delicately clear,
That finer, simpler music ne'er was heard;
The sort of sound we echo with a tear . . .

Absolutely no way would I have slept at the house in
Warren Road that night, not for a million pounds. But
Ruby was made of sterner stuff. She just shrugged it all
off – the ghostly voice, the cot creaking, everything. She
actually laughed at Lauren and me, shrinking in the
doorway of Rosie's room.

'What's the matter with you two? The way our Rosie
thrashes about, it's a wonder she doesn't shake this poor
old cot off its hinges.' Even so, I noticed she tweaked the
curtains open and had a peek down into the street. Then
she checked inside a wardrobe. Satisfied that no one was
there, she turned to us, explaining cheerfully, 'Walls in
this place are like cardboard. Probably that voice was next
door's telly. You can't fart round here without everyone
knows about it.'

'Neighbour's telly, my arse!' I said to Lauren as we
hurried back down towards the main road. 'It was that
woman. I know it was her. I recognized her voice.'

'What woman?'

'Oh come on, Lauren! *That* woman. Ringlets. The one who accosted us in Byron Drive. Isn't she always whimpering on about her lost Allegra? Supposing she's confused her own kid with Rosie? Supposing she's taken a fancy to her? No wonder the poor little thing howled like that. Imagine, opening her eyes, and there's Ringlets goggling over the bars at her . . .'

'All right, all right, I get the picture, thank you!' Lauren adjusted her cap firmly over her plaits and strode on ahead of me.

I had to break into a half-run to catch her up. 'Lauren, it's happening again. It's in the air. It's all around us. You can almost smell it. Can't you feel it, Lauren?'

Lauren spun round, flashing at me. 'NO! Look, I don't want to feel it, OK? I mean, what are you trying to tell me?' She waved her arms helplessly at the night sky. 'That we have some kind of fatal attraction for spooks? That wherever we go, for the rest of our lives, we'll be fighting the wretched things off? Because if that's what you're suggesting, Abbie, then I don't want to know. I'm quite happy to accept Ruby's explanation about what happened back there. Now do me a favour please, and let's change the subject.'

Lauren was In Denial. I could understand that. As for Ruby, she hadn't the faintest idea what was going on. Yet I couldn't help feeling that she, and maybe Rosie too, was in danger. *Grave* danger.

Over the next couple of days, though, Ruby had other things on her mind. Like the audition. The audition was to be held at five in the afternoon, and Ruby had wangled time off from Pizza Pronto to attend. She had somehow persuaded Lauren and me to go with her for moral support.

'Oh please please come, you two! We're good mates, aren't we? Most of the other girls will have their mums and that with them.'

That's how we came to be waiting outside Ruby's pizza joint that Friday; a day smelling like damp laundry, and the sky that kind of gun-metal grey that means rain.

'How do I look?' were Ruby's first words of greeting as she burst through the doors. 'I had to change out of my uniform in the toilets. If I'd gone home first, I'd have ended up with spaghetti or felt-tip pen all over my togs.' She gave us a little twirl. 'This thing cost me two weeks' wages. What d'you think? My make-up isn't too much, is it?'

What could we say? The gold-dusted cheekbones and neon lips wouldn't have been out of place in a circus. A glitzy hair slide secured a sweep of red hair, while earrings as big as minor planets dangled from her ears. Spangly hot pants and gold killer heels completed the picture.

'I haven't gone over the top, have I?' Ruby looked anxious suddenly.

Since Lauren appeared to be having trouble with her vocals, it was left to me to reassure her. 'Well,' I said, 'you'll certainly be noticed, Ruby. You'll probably knock the judges dead in fact.'

Ruby beamed with relief. 'You reckon? Really, truly?'

'Yeah, I do. Really, truly.'

Lauren suggested Ruby slip her shiny red raincoat over this flimsy ensemble. 'Have you seen those clouds overhead? You don't want to get your outfit wet.'

Ruby did as she was advised. This was a relief to us both as we hurried through the maze of narrow back streets to the theatre, which Nathan swore didn't even exist.

'He's talking rubbish,' Ruby said when I mentioned this. 'I looked it up in my *A-Z*. It's only ten minutes' walk from here, which is really, like, a coincidence, don't you think? You know, like it was meant to be.'

This strange borderland between Finchley and Hampstead was unknown territory to Lauren and me. The latticed passageways were cluttered with enticing shops. We passed bakeries wafting delicious smells, beamed antique shops and old-fashioned jewellers'. As we burrowed deeper into this labyrinth, a squally wind blew up, chasing litter along the streets, rattling street signs; hanging baskets swayed in shop doorways. Ten minutes' walk, Ruby had said. It seemed much longer than that before she finally halted.

'Well. This is it.' As if we still needed convincing, she read the gold lettering, which blazed across the awning – 'See what it says? THE FREE SPIRIT THEATRE. This is the place.'

We stared. The building, which dominated the mews of huddled shops, was a monstrous four-storeyed edifice of rusty red brick. From above the second-storey windows, rows of old-fashioned gas jets snaked out from spidery metal brackets. The entrance seemed to be shut up. In fact, the entire place was in darkness.

'Ruby,' I said slowly, 'are you sure you've got the right place?'

This couldn't be it, surely? I'd expected one of those swanky places with smoked glass and revolving doors and music spilling out onto the street.

'It looks like one of those old music halls,' Lauren said. 'How strange. Maybe you've got the wrong day, Ruby.'

'No, no, it says here in the paper – "The Free Spirit Theatre – Friday 25th August, 5 p.m." This must be right. Anyway, I'm not standing out here all evening – come on!'

Anyone with half a brain could see the place was closed. But Ruby didn't give up easily. She stood there, rattling the brass handles on the great oak doors and pummelling with her fists. 'Hey! Hey, anyone in there? Hell-oo-oo?'

'Ruby, it's no good, it's—' I was turning to go, when the doors suddenly gave under Ruby's weight.

She beckoned to us, beaming triumphantly. 'Told you it was open.'

'Call me suspicious,' I murmured to Lauren as we followed her inside, 'but I'm not happy about this. I mean, how come Nathan had never heard of it, for a start?'

Lauren rolled her eyes. 'Just because he works for an entertainment guide, he doesn't know everything, does he? I have to admit though' – she looked about uncertainly – 'it is kind of dead looking.'

This was an understatement. The foyer was completely empty. Dusty carpets lapped against oak-panelled walls. There was no receptionist in the confessional-like kiosk.

Nor was there any organizer, or stage manager, or assistant to welcome us; to take Ruby's name and number. There was only a cloistered mustiness as the doors swung closed behind us.

My eyes swept over the giant posters advertising future productions. The corners were curling, the colours faded, as if they had been up there a long long time. One of them caught my eye. *FRANKENSTEIN* – FROM THE NEW NOVEL BY MARY SHELLEY. New novel by Mary Shelley? My blood ran cold suddenly.

'Mary Shelley' – I pointed it out to Lauren – 'she was the author of *Frankenstein*. You know what else? She was a friend of Byron's. I remember reading something about it at school last term. How they stayed in this villa in Italy, and everyone was telling each other ghost stories. Byron suggested they write them all up, and that's how Mary Shelley wrote *Frankenstein*. And that was almost two hundred years ago.'

'Dust,' was all Lauren could say, running her finger along an oak picture rail. 'Dust.' She held up her finger, which was covered with powdery grey stuff. 'Inches thick. No one has cleaned this place for . . . for . . .'

'Centuries?' I finished the sentence for her. Turning towards the front doors, I called to Ruby, 'Ruby, Ruby . . . let's go. Look, there's no one here . . . Ruby?'

'Shh a minute. Listen!' There was a passage to the right of the main foyer. Ruby stood in the entrance, scooping her hair impatiently behind an ear, the better to hear. What did it take to convince her, for heaven's sake? Then I heard it too, faint and far off. From somewhere deep within this building, someone was singing. The tremulous notes floated down the passage towards us. They reverberated oddly, like the sound you get when you tap your finger against the rim of a glass.

'Hear that?' Ruby cried. 'I'm probably just a bit late, that's all.'

This time she didn't wait for us. She was off, shimmering in the dim passage like some gaudy butterfly. Lauren and I followed, stumbling in the gloom.

'Lauren, this is not good!' I groaned. 'I've got a bad feeling about this place.'

This time Lauren didn't slap her hands to her ears and tell me to shut up. Instead she said simply, 'I know, but we can't just leave her here.'

Just ahead of us, a wide flight of stairs led to a landing. Ruby was up them in a moment. As we followed, the voice drifted down to us, clearer, bell-like. This must have been enough proof for Ruby. There was a door on the left, and she plunged straight through it. She probably hadn't even seen the notice emblazoned across it: NO ADMITTANCE – PERFORMANCE IN PROGRESS.

NO ADMITTANCE, the notice said, yet it had admitted Ruby easily enough. Not so Lauren and me. The door was so heavy it took the combined weight of the two of us to move it.

I gasped as we heaved the door open, just wide enough to allow us to squeeze into the faded splendour of the auditorium. 'Wow! What a place!'

The vast dusty space had a sanctified feel. It was as if we'd just burst into a church or cathedral mid-service. Except that there was no one here. No one except for Ruby, of course, looking lost and bewildered on the

102

enormous stage. It was hung about with velvet drapes the colour of dried blood. Everywhere you looked were whorls and ribbons of tarnished gilt and cupids blowing on trumpets. Gas lights illuminated shadowy rows of seating. Again, empty.

I held my breath. The air was so thick, so undisturbed, it was like a velvet cushion pressed to your face. And what had happened to the singing? The singing had stopped.

Lauren cleared her throat nervously. 'Ah-hem! Ruby, did you see the notice back there? It said "no admittance". Ruby, I think we're trespassing.'

This was horrible. Lauren was speaking in her usual voice, yet something about the acoustics transformed it. It echoed dizzily around the auditorium, like a voice in a dream.

'Yeah, come on, Ruby, let's get out of here please!' My own voice didn't sound much better: muffled and croaky, like it was somehow trapped in my throat. As for Ruby's, it had a panicky shrillness to it as she flapped an arm at us. 'No, wait! I heard singing. It was coming from here. I swear it was!'

Lauren and I looked at each other in despair. What could we do? We could hardly drag Ruby out of here kicking and screaming. On the other hand, we couldn't leave her here alone.

But matters were taken out of our hands. It seemed we weren't alone after all. There was someone else here. From the back of the auditorium a man's voice made us all jump. 'The stage is yours, dear girl. Hurry now. We grow impatient.'

Ruby shaded her eyes. Squinting into the dim recesses of the theatre, she hissed at us, 'That must be the producer back there.'

'No, Ruby,' I began, 'I don't think . . .'

But why would Ruby listen to me? Already she was addressing the shadowy figure at the back. 'Excuse me, but there's no microphone or anything.'

This was excruciating. 'She's going to do it,' I whispered to Lauren. 'Oh my God, she's actually going to sing.'

'And there's no music neither,' Ruby piped up.

But even as she said this, an elaborate ripple of piano notes almost made us cry out.

I hadn't even noticed the piano, huddled just below the stage. Surely there hadn't been anyone sitting at it a moment ago? Now, the pianist swept her fingers delicately across the keys. Her back was turned towards us, but I could see the shawl draped over her long white dress. Her dark curls bounced with every note.

'Lauren, it's—'

'I know who it is,' Lauren finished for me; adding below her breath, 'Tell me this isn't happening. Please.'

Without a word, we both just sank into the front-row seats. At least the seats felt real enough. The padded upholstery was rough and itchy against my bare thighs. My fingers gripped the smooth wooden hand rests, as Ruby opened her mouth to sing.

But at the very first line of '*That boy is my des . . . iah*', the pianist launched into a halting melody of her own. Lauren and I winced. The two sounds clashed horribly. Still, Ruby just wouldn't admit defeat. Ignoring the pianist, she strutted about the stage, giving it all she'd got. How she even managed to hold her tune with those piano keys tinkling in the background, I couldn't figure out. But she did. She beamed and pouted and wiggled her bum for all she was worth. She sang better than I'd ever heard her sing before her own mirror at home. Ruby sang and sang. She sang from somewhere deep inside herself. This was what frightened me. It was like the theatre itself had tricked her into doing this. The theatre would swallow her voice and her heart with it. It would trap Ruby's soul, like a piping bird in a cage.

Just when I felt I could bear it no longer, there was the hollow sound of hands clapping from behind us. Ruby stopped singing at once. The piano notes trembled, then fell silent. The pianist fled. I just caught the pale glimmer of her skirts and the flash of her eyes as she did so.

Someone was treading softly down the aisle behind us, towards the stage. Footsteps. Clumpy. Uneven. Followed by a patter of paws; a snuffling sound.

'Bravo, dear girl, bravo!' The poet was still clapping. 'You have the voice of a nightingale.'

'Ron! I mean, er . . . Mr Lord, it's you! I never knew you were doing the auditioning!' Ruby cried out theatrically from the stage, like someone in a pantomime. 'I couldn't quite see who it was back there.'

Lauren and I sank lower into our seats. I suppose we hoped the poet wouldn't notice us.

'Go away!' I glared at Smut, who was sniffing beneath the front seats for morsels. Beside me, I could hear Lauren's breathing, fast and rustly like dry leaves, as if her asthma had come back suddenly.

'To be sure,' Byron was saying to Ruby, 'the stage is but a diversion for me, when I grow weary of scribbling. Indeed, I used to sit upon the committee at Drury Lane.'

'I never knew you had anything to do with the music business, Ron,' Ruby trilled.

How could she be so dense? Didn't she recognize a ghost when she saw one? Couldn't she feel the suffocating atmosphere in this place?

'I am a man of many pursuits.' Byron had perched himself on the back of a seat, across the aisle from where Lauren and I were shrinking. '*Ennui* is the enemy.' He looked down at his hands, as if studying his fingernails.

'On we?' Ruby repeated blankly.

'Boredom, dear girl.' Allowing his gaze to wander over Ruby, he added, 'Sometimes I think I shall fall *violently* in love. *Pour passer le temps.*'

Up on the stage, poor Ruby was looking rather confused. 'I know I'm a bit thick – sorry, but I don't get it. I mean, didn't you audition any other girls? 'Cos I know I've blown it. I've never sung so rubbish in all my life. It was the piano that put me off, it was' – she glanced down at the grand piano, now closed and silent – 'the pianist, she didn't know the tune.'

The poet withdrew a square of emerald silk from his pocket. He dabbed his forehead with it. 'Think no more on it, dear child. You are a nightingale! A butterfly! You are the sun and the moon shining as one in the sky! You shall sing at my estate, at Newstead. I put on a little diversion there, you know, every year.'

'So that's what the audition was for?' Ruby said slowly. 'I see. But what about the other girls?'

Byron waved his handkerchief scornfully. 'Phah! They were all as ugly as virtue. I require a *nymph* for my little diversion. I desire a creature who *walks in beauty like the night*. And you, dear Ruby, are the perfect choice.'

'I am? Really and truly?' Ruby stood, hands clasped to her chest in a gesture of gratitude.

I couldn't help feeling slightly sick. It was odd. A few minutes ago I'd been cringing with horror. I'd felt sorry for poor Ruby, singing herself hoarse for a ghost. But ghost or not, all this nightingale, butterfly and walking-in-beauty-like-the-night stuff was enough to make any girl jealous.

'So, er,' Ruby said, 'when is this, um, performance at your place to be exactly, Ron? Oh, sugar! It's my mobile. 'Scuse me a mo, Ron!'

Ruby bent and scrambled frantically in her bag, as the theme tune from *Star Wars* blasted throughout the auditorium.

Lauren nudged me. 'Where is he?'

Byron had gone. Looking across to the exit doors, I had a vague impression of him and Smut simply drifting through them. You couldn't blame him. Ruby's mobile was enough to scare anyone off.

'Hello? Oh, it's *you*, Mum.' Ruby hadn't noticed yet. Embarrassed by the interruption, she'd turned her back on the seats and was hissing into the receiver, 'No, I can't come now, I'm at an audition. You'll have to get some-one else to babysit. I told you I wouldn't be back till late . . . Yes I did. You don't listen. Mum, I got to go out sometimes . . . But it's important . . . It's . . . Oh . . .'

Her face was all flushed as she turned to apologize.

'Sorry about that, it was— Oh, where's he gone?'

'Dunno, Ruby,' I said, glad to get off the itchy seat and breathe freely again. 'He just left in a hurry, and I think we should do the same.'

Ruby was distraught. How could her mum do this to her? Tonight of all nights? 'He didn't give me any details about that performance of his,' she said, confused, as Lauren and I practically yanked her from the stage. 'I can't understand why he'd go off like that.'

'Oh, you know these arty people, head in the clouds.' I said this just to shut her up. At the same time I realized that sooner or later we were going to have to tell Ruby the truth about her drop-dead-delish poet. And that wouldn't be easy.

Right now, though, I was more worried about getting out of this creepy theatre. Lauren was so keen to escape, she caught her heel in a brass stair-tread and would have fallen down the stairs if I hadn't grabbed her elbow.

'He must be here somewhere.' Ruby was still keeping her eyes peeled for Byron as we blundered back through the passageway. 'Maybe there's a bar? Maybe he's in the bar or something?'

'No,' Lauren panted. 'There's no bar, Ruby.'

'How do you know?'

'She just does, OK?' My one fear, as we reached the foyer, was that we were locked in for ever. Supposing those doors, which had admitted us so reluctantly, would not let us out? I hurled myself sideways against them. Whooh! I must be stronger than I thought. They gave so suddenly, the three of us were launched onto the pavement as if shot from a cannon.

'Wait a minute,' Ruby called, clattering after us in her wobbly heels. 'What's up with you two? What's the hurry? I wanted to find Ron.'

I called out over my shoulder, 'Don't worry, Ruby, Ron'll find *you*. Count on it.'

Behind us the awning of the Free Spirit Theatre shivered in the evening breeze, the gold lettering dulling to invisibility even as we looked.

Chapter Nine

Between two worlds life hovers like a star
'Twixt night and morn, upon the horizon's verge.
How little do we know that which we are!

'If that really *was* Lord Byron yesterday,' Lauren said, as we reached the poetry section of Northgate Library, 'and I'm not saying it *definitely* was, but it won't do any harm to find out more about him.'

It was late on Saturday afternoon, and the library, with its glary expanses of glass, automatic doors and humming computers, was somehow reassuring after the dusty gloom of the music hall.

'Yeah, but where do we begin?' I wondered.

Byron took up two whole shelves to himself. My eyes ran along the well-thumbed pocket volumes, the *Complete Works*, the dry old literary studies by professor types in pebble glasses.

'We begin with the poetry, I imagine.' Lauren wiggled out a pocket edition of *Childe Harold's Pilgrimage*.

'*Childe Harold*? How is that going to help us?'

Lauren sighed at my stupidity. 'Well, if we study the poetry, we'll know where he's coming from, won't we?'

'We know where he's coming from' – my finger paused at the row of flashy biographies – 'he's coming

from the Realm of the Restless Dead, isn't he? Hmmm
. . . this promises to be interesting.'

Staggering to a table, I set down the enormous
tome entitled *Byron's Babes: A Scandalous Life* by Poppy
Pryer.

The book must be recently published. It was fat and
glossy, and packed with illustrations. On the cover, Byron
stared scornfully into the distance. His lips looked much
redder and poutier than I remembered, and he looked
like he might just drop dead with boredom any minute.
Inside, there were reproductions of portraits and
miniatures, sketches of ruined villas, paintings of landings
on romantic shores. Mostly, though, they were portraits
of the women in Byron's life. And what a lot there were!
Quite apart from the string of mistresses, here was a
pudding-faced woman, who was apparently his mum,
and the dreamily beautiful Augusta, his half-sister.

The most famous of his girlfriends was Lady Caroline
Lamb. I held up her picture to show Lauren. 'It says here
that she called him "mad, bad and dangerous to know".
She wasn't far wrong, was she?' Turning the page, I came
upon the portrait of Byron's prim, apple-cheeked wife,
Anabella.

'Poor Anabella. It says that when she was giving birth
to their daughter, Byron spent the night downstairs hurl-
ing soda bottles at the ceiling to disturb her labour.'

Lauren looked shocked. 'Why would he do that?'

I turned the page again. 'Oh . . . my—!' I couldn't
finish my sentence. My throat had gone dry suddenly.
The woman in the portrait wore her hair in black
sausagey ringlets. Her dark eyes challenged me. It was like

she'd been expecting me to come upon her in this book. Like she'd been waiting.

'Oh my God! Lauren, it's *her*. It's only bloody Ringlets.'

'Let me see.' Lauren swivelled the book around to face her.

I almost held my breath as she read aloud from the text: ' "Claire Clairmont, aged twenty-one. This is the only surviving likeness of the girl who pursued Lord Byron from the age of sixteen, and lived to regret it." '

'Why though? Why did she live to regret it?' Lauren wondered.

I grabbed the book back again. So. Claire Clairmont. Now we could give her a name. This was the same woman who had hung about the festival, who had accosted us on Byron Drive, who had played the piano yesterday afternoon to accompany Ruby's warblings. Here were the simmering eyes, the curls, the smug little mouth. As portraits go it wasn't too flattering. The artist had given Claire the fattest neck I'd ever seen. More like a prize bull than a girl.

However, it was the smaller portrait beneath Claire's that drew my eye. The child must be about a year old. Draped in drifts of artfully arranged muslin, she posed against a gnarly old oak tree, carrying a flower basket. The caption beneath read: 'A Portrait of Allegra, Byron's daughter by Claire Clairmont'.

'Allegra! So there really *was* an Allegra.'

Lauren came round to my side of the table and peered over my shoulder. 'The question is,' she said, 'what became of her?'

112

'She must have died young,' I said. 'Otherwise why would Claire be wandering the streets in search of her lost child? And you know what, she reminds me of someone.'

'I know what you're going to say,' Lauren said slowly, 'but I wish you wouldn't.'

'She does, though, doesn't she? She looks exactly like Ruby's baby sister, only without the chocolate stains all round her mouth.'

'Excuse me' – the library assistant caught my eye as she came over to switch off the computers – 'but we'll be closing in exactly ten minutes.'

I looked up from the portrait. It was nearly six. There was a last-minute rush of activity as the assistants thumped books onto shelves and saw the last borrowers out.

I stood up, clutching *Byron's Babes* beneath my arm. 'We'd better go. You don't mind if I take this out first?'

Lauren thought for a moment. 'Why don't I come back to your place, then we can look at it together? We could go to my house, but my mother and Harv-wit are having a majorly stressful time with their mosaic sunken floor.'

'Mosaic sunken floor?'

'Don't ask,' Lauren said.

So I didn't.

Lauren didn't often come back to our flat in Smedhurst Road. It felt quite strange to have her sitting beside me on the bus that night. No doubt my mother would shame me as she always did, I thought. She would probably serve some deeply uncool, pre-war concoction for our tea.

'It could be Potato Jane tonight,' I warned Lauren. 'Or Homity Pie. My mum's got this recipe book which dates back to the last war. Actually, they sound naff but they don't taste bad.'

'Anything'll be a change from couscous,' Lauren said as we got off the bus. 'Anyway, looks like your mother's still at work.'

'What?' I stared along the High Street. My mother's surgery, Feet First, was just a little way along from the bus stop, wedged between a Cypriot greengrocer's and a video shop. Normally at this time the surgery would be in darkness. Why was it all lit up?

'That's odd,' I said. 'She never works later than five usually. So much for Homity Pie, then.'

Actually the meal was the least of my worries. As we drew close to the brightly lit surgery, I had a horrible feeling. The back of my neck began prickling. I clutched the book more tightly beneath my arm. This was not a good sign. The prickling spread slowly upwards, crawling through my hair and over my scalp.

Pushing open the heavy glass door, I actually felt queasy for a moment. No sign of Mum. But there *was* someone sitting in the waiting room. A patient was flicking idly through a copy of *Chiropody Monthly*, a look of revulsion on his face. Not just any old patient. At the sight of the chestnut curls and the green velvet jacket, my heart thumped fast against my ribs.

'No.' I shook my head. 'Please, not here.'

This was definitely out of order. Ghosts materializing

at the festival or in leafy, faraway Hampstead were one thing. But not here, in my mother's own waiting room! So great was the shock that I actually lost my grip on *Byron's Babes*. It slid from my hands and landed just by that lame right foot.

'Now look what you've done,' Lauren whispered.

We gazed speechlessly from the moody, rock-star type Byron on the front cover to the real thing. Or rather, the *unreal* thing.

To our horror, Byron actually retrieved the biography from the floor. He laid it on his knee, smoothing the cover beneath his hand. 'What's this, by God?' He read the title aloud, voice thick with incredulity and disgust: '*Byron's Babes: A Scandalous Life.*'

He stared up at Lauren and me, as if *we* were the authors.

Without thinking, I muttered, 'They have to make the title catchy, don't they? It helps sell books.'

Lauren looked at me, aghast. Her look said, *What the hell are you doing talking to a ghost?* I wasn't sure myself. I should have just recited a prayer or something, or made the sign of the cross.

'Do they still persist in perpetuating these falsehoods?' Byron said. 'The truth is that I am tolerably sick of vice; which I have tried in all its varieties. As for love, hah! Love in my humble opinion is utter nonsense, a mere jargon of compliments, romance and deceit; had I fifty mistresses, I should in the course of a fortnight forget them all.'

Fifty women in a fortnight? I gulped. Obviously that Poppy Pryer had only caught the tip of the iceberg.

With an air of cold nonchalance he continued, 'Still, I have yet to see a finer likeness. What think you, ladies?' The way his fingers lingered over the cover of the book, it was as if he was stroking his own face.

'What are . . . you . . . doing here?' I decided to come to straight to the point.

'Doing here? Ah, and what the deuce are any of us *doing here*?' Byron threw the question back at me. He extended his right ankle slightly, and for the first time I noticed the clumpy built-up heel. He sighed. 'Who would think that a woman might prove so excellent a doctor. Better than that quack, Lavender. Called himself a surgeon. Hah! I can barely describe the torture I was forced to endure as a boy at the hands of that swine.'

'You mean my mother?' My heart gave a sickening lurch suddenly. 'Where is she? What have you done with her?'

'*Done* with her?' Byron's eyelids drooped with disdain. 'Dear girl, I am not such a rogue. Besides, forgive me, but your amiable mama is a little on the plump side for my tastes.' He sighed again. 'I do so abhor a *dumpy* woman.'

I was just reeling from this insult to my poor old mum, when she came scuttling from the back room. 'Here it is! Silly me! I couldn't find the appointment book any-where. So sorry to keep—' She stopped mid-sentence. 'Oh. He's gone. What did you do to my patient, Abigail? I was just about to make him another appointment.'

'What did *I* do?' It was typical that she would blame me, I thought, bending to pick up the book.

'We didn't say anything, Mrs Carter,' Lauren put in. 'He just . . . er . . . sort of left. Suddenly.'

My mother sighed. 'That's very peculiar. I was just closing up when he walked in off the street. "Madam," he said to me, "I beg you to look at my right foot, for every step I take is torture." Well, I couldn't turn him away, could I? Then, when he showed me' — she virtually winced — 'I have never in all my experience seen a foot in such a state . . .'

Usually, whenever Mum started on about people's feet, I'd leave the room. All I could do now was gape foolishly at her.

'The poor man was born with a club foot, it seems,' Mum continued as she rushed around switching off lights and tidying instruments. 'He should have had an operation to correct it. But some doctor who ought to be struck off the medical register, if you ask me, actually forced it into this wooden clasp. It must have been agony. I don't know what his mother must have been thinking of to allow such a thing. Are you all right, Abigail?' She peered at me. 'You don't look well.'

It was lasagne for dinner, something I'd usually have second helpings of. Tonight, though, I had no appetite.

'Still moping after that nice boy Joel, I expect,' my mother confided to Lauren. Taking my half-finished plate to the sink, she added, 'I keep telling her there's plenty of time for boyfriends. I was twenty-eight when I met Abbie's father, and it was another two years before we got serious.'

'Please, Mother, spare us the details!' I prodded a smirking Lauren along the narrow landing to my room. We had to sit down on the bed, there being no room for a chair.

'It's completely gross,' I said. 'Mum looking at his feet. I mean, surely she realized they weren't flesh and blood? They must have been like ice blocks.'

We were silent a moment. It was difficult to imagine a ghost's feet, deformed or otherwise. Lauren was looking a bit furtive, I noticed. She was doing that thing with her plaits, coiling them around her little finger until they looked like Claire Clairmont's ringlets.

'Have you noticed his eyes?' she said at last. 'When he looks at you – I don't know, you feel you'd do anything.'

I knew what she meant. I'd felt that too, just for an instant, back at the surgery. Before he mentioned about my mum being dumpy. When Byron looked at you, it was like a touch. It was like he could see right through to your soul. As if he knew all your deepest secrets and desires.

'You know,' Lauren said slowly, 'when he looked at me tonight, I could understand it, why women swarmed around him like flies.'

Lauren was getting carried away. She was getting on my nerves.

'Actually,' I said, 'in point of fact, it was me he was staring at.'

'You?'

'Yes. When he looked up from *Chiropody Monthly*, his eyes were, like, glued to mine. It was kind of weird. Like being hypnotized or something.'

Lauren laughed. She shook her head. 'Uh-uh. Actually, Abbie, it was *me* Byron was staring at.'

I could barely believe her arrogance. 'He might have given you a cursory glance, I'll admit,' I conceded.

'Cursory glance!' Lauren's eyebrows contorted into a furious mono-brow. 'Excuse me, but his eyes were all over me, from head to toe. Well, I should know. I mean, it was quite embarrassing, his eyes flickering all over me like that. I hardly knew where to look.'

'Sorry, Lauren, but we were standing, like, really close together at the time. I see how you could be mistaken, but that was me he was checking out.' I laughed. 'If you'll forgive me for saying so, Lauren, I'm not completely stupid. I mean, I know when some bloke is hitting on me, OK?'

Lauren shot up from the bed so abruptly the mattress springs twanged. 'Yes, well, I know when a guy is giving me the eye, right? And I can tell you, Abigail Carter, that Lord Byron was definitely giving me the eye!'

'To be honest, Lauren,' I said, 'I really don't think you're his type. I think he liked his women to have a bit more up front, if you know what I mean.'

'At least I'm not dumpy!' Lauren threw back.

'Are you saying I am?'

'I'm not saying anything, but since Joel went off, you *have* been overdoing the chocolate a bit, though I thought it beneath me to comment.'

'Who wants to look like a stick insect anyway?' I snapped furiously. At the same time I drew my stomach in. Lauren had a point actually. Just lately I'd had to undo the top button of my jeans after dinner.

Lauren was no stick insect, but her figure might be described as willowy. For a moment I hated her. I hated the sneer on her face, which almost matched Byron's own, as he gazed out into the distance from the book jacket, utterly indifferent to our quarrel. He was well used to women fighting over him, I guessed.

'I think I'd better go.'

As Lauren gathered her bag, lips pursed, it struck me suddenly how ludicrous this was. Lauren was my closest friend. We'd been through loads together. Now we acted like we were scrapping over a real live boyfriend, when Byron had been dead for over two hundred years!

'Anyway,' I said, making a huge effort not to trade more insults, 'it's Ruby he fancies.'

'Maybe,' Lauren said, like she couldn't care less.

I saw her to the front door. 'See you in town on Monday then?'

I'd just remembered I was supposed to be helping her choose a new outfit for some cousin's wedding.

'Mmmm, expect so.'

What did she mean 'expect so'?

I felt kind of lonely as I closed the door on Lauren and went back to my room.

'See what you've done now?' I said to Byron. Then I stuck the book face down beneath my bed with all the fluff and used tissues and stuff. Just to show him. But not before I'd had a last lingering look into those eyes. Not before I'd visualized them flickering over me.

Chapter Ten

Each kiss a heart-quake, – for a kiss's strength,
I think must be reckon'd by its length.

Lauren and I had never really had a row before. We'd had sulks and sniffs and differences of opinion, of course, but never a full frontal, verbal assault. When Monday came, I couldn't face meeting her in town, and left a message with her mum that I was sick.

'Think I'll just chill out chez Smedhurst Road today,' I told my mother. 'Holiday revision.' I tapped my copy of *Byron's Babes*. Without her glasses on, there was little chance Mum would recognize the patient with the deformed right foot. Those handsome tortured features would be little more than a blur.

'By the way, Mum, if that, er ... bloke with the crushed foot turns up again, you will let me know?'

I said this as casually as I could. However, my mother, who was on her way to the surgery, was instantly suspicious.

'You don't know that gentleman, do you, Abbie?' She frowned at me.

'Um, only by sight. I've seen him limping about the place. He, er, turns up at the festival sometimes. Fancies himself as a bit of a poet. And there's this poor girl who works there, who fancies him. Hah! She's a bit dumb, to be honest.'

'How old is this girl?'

'Not sure. Sixteen, I think, but she's finished school.'

'Well then, he's much too old for her,' my mother declared.

'Only about two hundred years,' I muttered.

'Pardon?'

'Nothing, Mum.'

'Hmmm . . .' my mother said doubtfully. Picking up her little black case, she had a quick check in the mirror. As she stood there, patting her perm, I noticed she was wearing lipstick. Lipstick? My mother? To my knowledge, my mother possessed only one orangey-coloured lipstick which she'd had for about a hundred years, and only wore for the annual chiropodists' dinner dance. I couldn't help wondering as she blotted her lips together whether she too had fallen under the great lord's spell. That would be too disgusting!

As if answering my question, she said, 'I think that poor man must have had a very sad childhood. He strikes me as a lonely person.' In a brisker tone, she added, 'Anyway, I certainly hope he will be back, because he left without paying yesterday.' She smoothed her tweedy skirt over her hips. 'I'm sure it was an oversight though.'

'Oh yeah. I'm sure it was,' I reassured her.

Once my mother was safely out of the way, I put on a CD and microwaved myself a pile of maple syrup pancakes. Then I plumped up the sofa cushions in the sitting room and settled down comfortably with *Byron's*

Babes, turning first to the chapter about Claire Clairmont.

Funny, I'd always thought that girls doing the running and asking boys for dates and that was a twenty-first-century thing. But Claire had practically laid siege to her hero, hanging about outside his London home like the original groupie for hours on end. Claire's dodgy poems, stories and letters were rattling through his letterbox every day. Finally worn down, Byron read some of her stuff, declared she showed 'promise' and invited her in. Whereupon she charmed the pants off him with her piano playing. Literally! Next thing you know, Claire is pregnant, and Byron is doing the time-honoured love-rat thing and running a mile. Well, several hundred miles actually, because he took off for Europe. Not one to be cast aside like an old boot, Claire followed.

A cold chill ran through me suddenly as I read. The letters and poems, the staking out of Byron's pad – wasn't that exactly what Ruby was doing now? Was Ruby somehow following in Claire's footsteps? And if she was, wouldn't it all end in tragedy? Unless, that is, Lauren and I could convince her that her drop-dead-delish poet had actually dropped dead a very long time ago. A trickle of syrup rolled down my chin and onto the page, forming a perfect teardrop in Claire Clairmont's eye.

I really needed to discuss all this with Lauren. Difficult, because Lauren was obviously still sulking about our row. It was the last night of the festival, and the gallery was packed with Northgate's very own wannabes, bearing their works of genius to read out on stage. Lauren stood taking tickets, dressed in slinky black with one eye on the doors. I knew *who* for.

'I see you've dragged yourself from your sickbed for tonight,' she murmured nastily as I passed.

'I was studying actually,' I snapped back.

'Studying? Oh, let me guess, it wouldn't be a book called *Byron's Babes*, would it, by any chance?'

Ignoring her, I pushed the café doors open and groaned inwardly. I could see this evening was getting off to a great start. Ruby had only brought her baby sister along to work with her! She was standing jiggling Rosie on one hip, watching Nathan Daly spread an *A-Z* of London out on the bar. Sounded like they were arguing about something.

'Ruby, there's no such place, I tell you. They tore the old music hall down back in the eighties. I can prove it. It's all in our records office at *The Buzz*.' Nathan was scratching his head over the map.

Ruby sighed. 'No offence, Nate, but it doesn't matter what your records say, does it? I know 'cos I was there, wasn't I? And I saw it with my own eyes. Oh hi, Abb.' She glanced over her shoulder at me. 'Tell Nate, will you, that you were there too. And Lauren. I mean, we can't all be bloody dreaming, can we?'

I stared at Nathan. 'You're saying that we were running around a building that doesn't even exist? Oh my God, it's worse than I thought.'

'Of course it exists, Abb!' Ruby insisted. 'We were *there*, weren't we?'

Ignoring her, I spoke to Nathan. 'It was all musty and dusty, like it had been shut up for a million years. And *he* was there.'

'Our mystery poet?' Nathan swivelled round on the stool to face me, arms folded, a hungry, intrigued look in his eyes. I'd like to flatter myself the hungry look was for me, but I knew it was for the 'story'. 'Hey, I don't know what kind of trip you girls were on that night, but I could take you there now, to that street. They built a health and fitness centre on the site. My sister even went there a few times for step aerobics.'

'You've got the wrong street, Nate,' Ruby snapped, exasperated. 'Just 'cos you work for a newspaper doesn't mean you know everything, does it, Abb?'

Seeing me staring at Rosie, she looked sheepish. 'I had to bring her with me, didn't I? My mum's got a date tonight. What could I do? I couldn't leave her at home with the other kids. She's got this thing about the baby-sitter. Screams her head off whenever she sees her.'

I sighed. 'Your mum's got a date? Ruby, that's unbelievable.'

Rosie grizzled as if she agreed with me. Watching me warily, she gnawed on her dummy like it was a bone. Grubby tears tracked her scarlet cheeks.

'She's tired out,' Ruby said. 'Aren't you, babe?'

Ruby looked pretty knackered herself. I noticed her make-up was smudged; a butterfly hairclip dangled over one ear.

'I had to come.' There was a frantic look in her eye as Rosie's grizzles grew louder. 'I need to catch Ron. Have you seen him anywhere yet? I've asked Lauren to keep an eye out at the desk.'

'There's no saying he'll show up tonight, Ruby,' I warned her gently.

Rosie let out a sudden wail. Grabbing her pink sun bonnet, Nathan stuck it on his own close-cropped head. 'Hey, Rosie, nice hat. How do I look?'

Rosie stared at her hat, astonished. She giggled. The dummy loosened from her jaws and fell slop into a sugar bowl, trailing a thread of dribble.

'She likes you.' Ruby smiled with relief, forgetting about the nonexistent theatre for a moment. 'Thanks, Nate.'

'Think nothing of it,' Nathan said. 'Must be my magnetic charm. All the girls like me, big and small' – he winked at us – 'don't they, Rosie, yeah?' Another few moves with the hat and Rosie was in hysterics.

It was lucky for Ruby that Nathan was proving so good with babies, because there was a sudden rush on in the café. Ruby and I were kept busy, scurrying about the tables. It was a good half hour before the café emptied for the final event – some incredibly depressing war poet who read in a kind of mumble and sounded as if he had serious sinus problems.

'I think I'll just take a look in the gallery while Rosie's quiet,' Ruby told me. 'See what's going on.'

I went over to the bar, where Nathan was still gamely entertaining Rosie.

'Ruby'll be back in a minute. She's looking for him – you know who I mean. It's terrible. He's invited her to sing at his estate up north and everything.' I told Nathan all about the ghostly audition at the theatre which didn't exist, while Rosie sucked on a rusk, watching me darkly. 'She thinks he's going to make her famous. I don't know how to tell her the truth about him. I don't know where to begin.'

Nathan drained his coffee cup and wiped his mouth with the back of his hand. 'It's a tough one. You could try the old "he's no good for you" line, I suppose.'

I laughed. 'That wouldn't get me far.'

Nathan was silent a moment. I noticed for the first time that his eyes were a light green colour, like new leaves unfurling.

'You know,' he said, 'I've been doing a bit of research about our friend. It's interesting that that theatre should be in Hampstead. He lived in Hampstead at one time. His funeral procession would have passed right by the theatre.'

'Funeral procession?' I shivered.

'Yeah. Byron always wanted to be buried in Greece. His exact words were, "I trust they won't think of pickling and bringing me home to Clod or Blunderbuss Hall." Reckoned his bones wouldn't rest easy in an English grave. Said the very thought would drive him mad on his deathbed.'

'And is he?' I said uncomfortably. 'Buried in England?'

'In the family vault at this little church in Hucknall, a few miles from Newstead Abbey.' Nathan chuckled. 'So much for last requests, eh? But the real joke was the funeral. All Byron's old toff friends felt they ought to pay their respects, but they couldn't do it in person. I mean, the shame of being associated with this guy who had screwed half of London! So what they did was send empty carriages with the family crests on the side. The carriages turned back at the Hampstead Road, while the carriage with Byron's body trundled on to Nottingham.'

127

'Empty carriages?' Just like in my dream. At the memory of those beetle-black coaches rattling over the cobbles, my blood ran cold.

'Empty as Byron's body.' Nathan scratched his head. 'Did you know that the Greeks held onto his lungs for—'

'Do me a favour!' I turned away. 'I don't want to hear the gory details.'

I felt Nathan's hand on the back of my neck. 'Sorry. Didn't have you down as the squeamish type.'

I shivered suddenly. Funny thing – I wasn't sure why. It could have been anything really: spooks, body organs; it could have been – Face it, Abigail Carter, I told myself – the touch of Nathan's fingers brushing against my skin. But that was ridiculous. When I was totally off men.

I was about to tell him how squeamish I actually was, and how my mother was a chiropodist and how *feet* were my worst thing in the whole world, next to people's innards and bodily organs and stuff. But just as I opened my mouth, it kind of met his mouth. And there we were, me and Nathan Daly, kissing. I won't call it 'snogging' because it was definitely 'kissing'. I mean, very gentle and kind of questioning, as if our mouths weren't really sure of each other.

When Nathan's hand slid about my waist, drawing me closer to his stool, I almost forgot I was supposed to be at work. I almost forgot about Rosie, until I heard the yell from behind us.

'What the bloody hell d'you think you're doing?' Ruby was shouting.

At the sound of her voice, Nathan and I jerked apart so fast, my elbow knocked a glass flying. I couldn't figure it out. Why would Ruby yell at us like that? Then, turning, I saw with a strange thrill of horror who it was she meant.

A minute ago Rosie's highchair had been pulled right up to the counter. While our backs were turned, someone had moved it. Someone had shifted both baby and highchair over to the corner table, where the fake banana plant rustled its silken leaves.

The woman removed her bonnet. Shaking free the black curls, she held out her gloved arms to Rosie: 'Come, sweetheart. Come to Mama!'

'No you bloody don't!' Ruby was sprinting around the tables. 'Get your paws off my sister, you weirdo!'

Nathan jumped up from the stool. 'That's not who I think it is, is it?'

I nodded. 'Claire Clairmont, Byron's girlfriend. I can't believe it. I can't believe this is all happening again.'

But Nathan didn't hear me. He was at the highchair in an instant. 'Hey, lady! Back off. You're upsetting the kid.'

What scared me most wasn't Claire herself, but the expression on the baby's face: a look of utter incomprehension as this strange, pale woman bent over to lift her from the highchair. Instead of holding up her chubby arms to be lifted, Rosie held tightly onto the tray of the highchair and screamed her lungs out.

A scream which brought Lauren and Giles and the war poet and half the audience in to see who was being murdered. I tried to imagine how it would look to them. As the ghost of Claire Clairmont melted away into the

129

shadows, all they would see was Ruby, grabbing handfuls of thin air and yelling dementedly, 'Who d'you think you are? You're not her mum, she's not *your* baby. You're one of them child-snatchers, you are. I'm reporting you, I am. To the police!'

Later, Giles said he'd been sadly mistaken when he took Ruby on as a waitress, and she needn't think of applying for a job with the festival next year. In the meantime, perhaps she'd care to apologize to the war poet for ruining his act with her 'theatricals'.

Poor Ruby. There was another hour of the performance to run, but she was asked to leave immediately.

'This is a poetry festival, Ruby, not a day nursery,' Giles snorted.

'Supposing Ron turns up at the last minute?' Ruby seemed close to tears as Giles flounced off, and she tried to soothe her little sister.

I glanced uneasily at Nathan. 'Don't worry. If he does . . . turn up . . . I'll tell him you, er . . . I'll, er . . .'

'She'll tell Ron to give you a bell, OK?' Nathan came to the rescue. He rattled his car keys. 'Listen, I was about to shoot anyway. I'll give you a lift, Rube, if you like.'

It was really kind of Nathan. But as he swung Rosie up in one arm, and looped the other round Ruby's shoulder, I couldn't help feeling the tiniest smidgen of jealousy. I touched the inside of my lips with my tongue. That kiss just now — it was over almost as soon as it began. I couldn't help wondering if it had happened at all. And if it had, did it mean anything?

As if he knew what I was thinking, Nathan looked

over his shoulder at me, and winked. 'I'll call you to-morrow, Abbie.'

'Oh yeah. Right.'

'I wouldn't have thought he was your type,' Lauren remarked as we walked back through the park together that night.

'Who?'

'Who, she says, who? I mean Nathan Daly, of course – Northgate's answer to the paparazzi. I thought you were supposed to be pining for Joel. All that stuff about "Oh, I'll never look at another bloke again" . . .'

'So? I can't help it if a bloke looks at *me*, can I? Oh no . . . I mean—' I broke off. Not *that* argument again.

But Lauren managed a half-hearted snigger. 'Let's not get into that again. Look, I'm sorry, I was stroppy the other night. It's just that . . . well, maybe I imagined Byron was looking at me.'

'Maybe he has cross eyes.' I shrugged. 'Let's forget about it. Anyway, now that the festival is finished, maybe Byron is too. I mean, it was like the poetry thing brought him here in the first place. Hopefully we'll never see either him or Ringlets again.'

It was a faint hope. My words sounded hollow. It seemed as if the stifling Northgate night smothered them before they were out of my mouth, and threw them back at me. As if someone out there was laughing at me.

Chapter Eleven

Some reckon women by their suns or years;
I rather think the moon should date the dears

The poetry festival was over. As the Beardies and Bead Chokers departed Northgate, I wondered if we had seen the last of Byron and Ringlets. It was all so confusing. My lips were still burning from Nathan's kiss; I could feel the rasp of his cheek on mine, yet still I secretly longed for one last glimpse of the poet. Was this two-timing, or a simple case of total insanity? And Ringlets may or may not have wafted on back to the Other Side, but we certainly hadn't seen the last of Ruby Blagg.

It was Ruby, of course, who was the most upset over the festival ending. How would she get to see Ron again? She was going to miss me and Lauren too – a helluva lot, she confessed.

''Cos we were good mates, weren't we, us three?'

To placate her, Lauren and I agreed to meet her on Hampstead Heath the following Sunday. We would go for a walk and, well, have a bit of a chat. We'd decided it was time to educate Ruby in the Ways of the World of the Dead. She had already made a fool of herself at the local police station, giving the police a description of Claire Clairmont. Clearly this couldn't go on. Any more visits from Claire, and the police would be mounting a nationwide woman-hunt.

'Sunday? That'll be wicked!' Ruby gushed when we suggested it. 'I might have to bring Rosie though.'

'Yeah, OK. Whatever,' I said, hoping she wouldn't end up bringing her entire family with her.

The Friday before our arranged walk, Nathan Daly phoned.

'Oh? Nathan?'

'Yeah, it's me,' Nathan said. 'Who were you expecting? Lord Byron? Aren't you glad it's me and not him? I mean, there's no contest, is there? Old Byron just doesn't have my fatal charisma.'

I couldn't help smiling to myself. 'Don't know about that, but he definitely hasn't got my phone number. Anyway, we haven't set eyes on him since he turned up in my mum's chiropody surgery.'

'He what? You are kidding me!'

'I tell no lie. My mother actually treated his lame foot, like he was a real patient. Which is revolting. I mean, can you imagine cutting a ghost's toenails?'

Nathan said he'd rather not, and we discovered we had a mutual repugnance for other people's feet. Suddenly there were all these things Nathan and I had in common.

There was a pause, then Nathan said, 'I was wondering – are you doing anything on Sunday?'

'Sunday? Well, er . . . actually, yes. Lauren and I are going to meet Ruby for a walk on the heath. We think we need to, you know . . . enlighten her about one or two things.'

'Enlighten the poor girl, eh?' He chuckled. 'Tell you what, I'll come with you. Moral support.'

I wasn't so sure about the moral support bit, but secretly I was pleased Nathan was coming with us. I just liked him. *As a friend*, I told myself. I'm totally off men.

Sunday turned out to be fine. On the heath, kids rode their bikes along the wide gravel tracks, and joggers in headbands whooshed past.

'Isn't this fun!' Ruby burbled happily, as she negotiated the buggy over bumps and potholes. 'All of us together again. Like old times.'

Nathan laughed. 'Old times? Come on, Rube, we saw each other only a few days ago.'

'Well, you know what I mean.'

We must have made an odd group. There was Ruby tottering along in her killer heels and micro skirt; Lauren, cap tugged down over her plaits, eyes peeled for dog poo; and me in combats and old T-shirt. I was hoping the combats would make me look tough, and not some kind of bimbo that a boy could snog whenever he felt like it. Nathan had a lot going for him: apart from being a great laugh and having this wicked grin no girl could resist, he was sensitive enough to believe in spirits. Also, I had to admit, he looked pretty fit in that beaten-up denim jacket, throwing sticks for his labrador, Barney. But Joel going off had left me feeling kind of wobbly and uncertain about myself. I wasn't sure I wanted to get into another lurve-thing just yet.

Still, if I wasn't sure what I wanted, at least the baby,

Rosie, was. Wagging her starfish fingers at Nathan, she repeated her mantra: 'Me want. Rosie want.'

We all laughed. Whether Rosie wanted the sticks, or the dog, or Nathan himself, no one could figure out.

As we trudged deeper into the heart of the heath, Ruby began chuntering on about her latest poem. 'I wrote it specially for Ron. I sat up late last night after the kids were in bed, just scribbling away, like I was in this dream.'

Lauren cleared her throat awkwardly. 'Ruby, actually, we've got to tell you something about Ron. I mean, Byron . . .'

'Yeah?' Ruby's smile faltered a fraction. 'What is it then? Oh no, don't tell me he's married. You've found out he's married with six kids. Oh well. Just my luck, eh?'

'He's not married, exactly,' I began. 'Well, he was once. But he, er . . . isn't now.'

'So? He's divorced then. No problem.'

'The thing is, Ruby, he's had more women than you've changed nappies,' I burst out.

Ruby smirked. 'That doesn't surprise me. Anyway, I like a man with experience. I've always been one for the older man.'

'Not *that* old though,' Nathan muttered.

'He's not that much older than you, Nate, come off it. Twenty-two – maybe twenty-three. Hardly drawing his pension, is he?' Ruby frowned as she bumped Rosie over the ruts in the path. 'I don't understand why you lot are trying to put me off him. Ron is a gentleman. I've never met anyone like him before.'

By now we'd walked quite a distance. The paths we'd

taken twisted through a shrubby undergrowth of gorse and brambles. Rosie reached out for the clusters of fat, dusty blackberries. 'Rosie want!'

Scooping Rosie out of her pushchair, Nathan carried her off to pick the fruit.

'Sorry, Ruby, but you should know the truth,' Lauren said in a pious tone. 'I mean, there must be dozens of children.'

'Dozens?' Ruby's eyebrows shot up.

'At the last count,' I said.

'Oh, come on. You're kidding me! I'd never have taken Ron for a dad. He doesn't seem the type.'

'Exactly,' I said. 'He wasn't much of a dad actually.'

'In point of fact' – Lauren struggled gamely on – 'there was one child in particular – Allegra.'

'Allegra . . .' Ruby said thoughtfully. 'That name rings a bell.'

'It should.' I was practically jumping up and down. 'Remember the other night in the café? That woman who took a fancy to Rosie? That's Claire Clairmont. And Allegra was her and Byron's daughter.'

We sat down on a bench that had a couple of slats missing, and DEBS AN LEE FOR EVER carved on the back.

'It's like this,' I said bluntly. 'Your Ron Lord isn't Ron Lord at all. Know how he signs everything – by *Ron Lord*? Turn it round and what have you got? Ruby, Ron is really Lord Byron – Byron, practically the most famous poet since Shakespeare. And I know you won't want to hear this, but Byron died over a hundred and fifty years ago. He died, Ruby, in eighteen thirty-six.'

Ruby crossed her legs to examine the heel of her shoe

where the leather was peeling off. 'You two – honestly,' she said vaguely. 'You two have got some imagination.'

'I know it's hard to believe,' Lauren persisted, 'but that's why Claire is, like, a restless spirit. Byron said she was too poor to look after Allegra properly, and he forced her to give the baby to him to bring up.'

A little voice sang out suddenly. 'Rosie want. Rosie want.'

Nathan was striding back towards us, his hair ruffled into peaks by baby hands. Ruby's eyes settled fondly on her little sister. 'That's stupid. As if you'd give up a kid, just because you were poor.'

'It was the law then,' I said. 'Byron kept Allegra at his villa in Italy until he got bored. Then he stuck her in a convent, to be brought up by nuns.'

'What about her mum? Surely she must've visited at least?' Ruby's eyes were still on Rosie, as she decked Nathan's hair with leaves.

'Byron forbade her to go there,' Lauren said, 'even when Allegra became ill with fever. She died at that convent without either of her parents. She was just five years old.'

For a moment we were silent, picturing that convent with its chanting nuns, where a child not much older than Rosie had died.

'That's a terrible story,' Ruby said. She sat, hands folded between her knees as if to warm them. 'But I still don't get why you're telling me this. I mean, you say it all happened hundreds of years ago—'

'Yes!' Lauren and I said together. We sat staring at Ruby, willing her to understand.

'But what's it got to do with me then? Or Ron?'

137

This was too much. Sticking my face right up close to hers I said, 'For God's sake, Ruby, we've told you a million times. Ron isn't *real*. Get it? Ron is really the poet Lord Byron who . . . who . . . Oh' – I stared fixedly into her puzzled blue eyes – 'Ron isn't the man you think he is. He isn't a man at all. He isn't human. Ruby, listen to me, Ron is a *ghost*!'

The revelation that her hero wasn't made of flesh and blood like the rest of us must have come as a bit of a shock to Ruby. We waited in silence for this news to sink in. Nathan settled the baby back on Ruby's lap, while Barney sniffed at a Kentucky Fried Chicken carton beneath the bench.

The evening was still warm, but kind of tired and dusty, as if it was dragging itself towards the night. The sky smudged crimson to the west. It looked like someone had daubed a bloody thumbprint across the rooftops of Hampstead. A magpie swooped low over our heads, chittering in that harsh mechanical way, like an old typewriter.

'Birdie laugh,' Rosie interpreted.

'A ghost?' Ruby stroked the baby's red-gold hair. 'Ron is a ghost? Is that what you lot brought me here to tell me?' Her face was soft with wonder. 'This is some joke, right?'

Nathan stuck his hands in his pockets. 'No joke, Rube.'

'You're mad,' Ruby decided, sensing a conspiracy. 'All of you.' She began tucking a protesting Rosie back in the pushchair. 'My baby sister's got more sense than you lot, and she's not even two yet. I mean, you expect me to fall for this rubbish? I don't believe in ghosts. There's no such thing.'

Lauren sighed. 'I used to say that. But just because you don't believe in them, it doesn't mean they don't exist.'

Impatiently, Ruby rammed the baby's bonnet on her head. 'And you lot are supposed to be clever – hah! How could a man we've all seen with our own eyes, and spoken to, be a ghost? Answer me that!'

But the dog, Barney, answered for us. Or growled, rather.

'What's up, Barn?' Nathan crouched to scratch his dog's ears. Barney ignored him. He went on staring intently into the dusky clearing among the birches. There was nothing to see. Leaves crunched. Twigs cracked. Barney growled again. The labrador didn't have much of a coat, but what he *did* have was standing on end. The sleek black fur stiffened about his collar. His ears were laid back almost flat. Every muscle tensed. Suddenly the growls gave way to a piteous whining.

'Hark at him,' Nathan said softly. 'Some guard dog he is. Scared of his own shadow.'

'Not his own shadow,' I murmured. 'Something else's shadow. Look.'

At first it was just another dog trotting out of the brambly undergrowth. Then I saw it wasn't just any old dog. The bulldog was headed straight for us. As it trotted through a bank of dry, whiskery grasses, I could hear it snuffling like a pig.

'Woof woof!' Rosie yelled. 'Rosie want!'

Ruby turned, shielding her eyes against the lowering sun. Her face lit up suddenly. 'Hey, look! It's Ron's dog. It's Smut! Hi, Smut, over here, come to Ruby!' She began to wave wildly, like somebody on a TV game show.

'Where's your master, eh, Smut?' Fishing in her beaded purse, Ruby slicked on a fresh coating of lip gloss. Lauren and I looked at each other. So much for our little speech just now!

And here he was, Smut's master, limping through the trees towards us.

Beside me, I heard Nathan draw in his breath sharply. 'Speak of the devil. The great man himself.'

My heart jolted. Not again. I was really hoping we'd seen the last of him. That somehow he was confined to the café; to the festival. And yet . . .

'Abbie, does my cap look stupid?' Lauren whispered harshly in my ear.

'Not if you're into the garden-gnome look.'

'Thanks.' She whipped off the hat so fast, one of her plaits unravelled. It dangled like a crinkle-cut chip about her face.

'Is my nose shiny?' I whispered back.

'Yes, but no different to normal.'

'Thanks a bunch.'

Why were we so worried about our appearance suddenly? Did it matter what Byron thought of us, ghost or not? He might have drifted right on past, if Ruby hadn't planted herself and the pushchair in his path.

'Hi, Ron. Fancy us bumping into you like this!'

My stomach twisted as Byron looked up from the book he was holding open in front of him.

'Ah, the fair Ruby and her friends. Well, well. A good day to take the air, is it not?' He greeted us with that half-stern, mocking look that made the blood rush to my head.

140

Ruby giggled and said she liked it hot herself. 'What's that you're reading, Ron?'

Byron's sulky mouth twitched slightly. 'This, dear girl, is my masterpiece, *Don Juan*. Or my *Don Jonny*, as I sometimes prefer to call him.'

'*Don Juan!* Omigod.' Lauren seemed to forget all about our lecture to Ruby on the dangers of getting too chummy with ghosts. 'A work of sheer genius, in my opinion.' She clasped her hand to her throat, and gazed gooey-eyed at his lordship.

Encouraged, Byron held up a gloved finger for silence. 'I have been amusing myself composing these few lines. Listen to this, dear friends:

'Some reckon women by their suns or years;
I rather think the moon should date the dears . . .'

Ruby stood confused, yet eagerly smiling. 'That's totally brilliant, Ron. Isn't it, you lot?'

Ignoring her, Byron turned to Nathan in a confidential, man-to-man sort of way. 'Tell me this, is it not Life, is not the Thing? Could any man have written it who has not lived in the world? And tooled in a post-chaise? In a hackney coach? In a gondola? Against a wall? In a court carriage? On a table? And under it?'

'Oh brilliant, wicked!' Ruby exclaimed, clapping her hands.

Byron gave her a disgusted look. 'Dear Ruby, that was not the *poem*. That was *about* the poem.'

'What's "tooled" mean?' Lauren whispered.

'Put it this way,' Nathan said; 'he's not talking about leathercraft.'

Lauren glared at him. 'Trust you to make something dirty out of it. That's just the kind of thing you expect from the gutter press.'

Mortified that she'd misunderstood his poem, Ruby gushed, 'Oh Ron, I'm so chuffed I bumped into you, 'cos we got so much to talk about . . .'

She nudged me hard as she said this. A signal for me to take the others and leave her and 'Ron' alone, I imagined. I ignored it. Leaving Ruby alone with a spirit would be irresponsible – and anyway, I had a thing or two I wanted to discuss myself.

'Yes, I'm really glad we bumped into you too.' Ignoring Lauren's withering look, I went on, 'My mother was talking about you only the other day.'

'Is that so?' Byron plucked a stray hair from his velvet jacket. 'The whole world talks about me, and most of what they say is scandalous cant.'

'Actually, she was talking about your bill – you know, for your, er . . . problem.' I hardly liked to mention his foot. 'You forgot to pay her,' I finished.

At last I was worthy of a glance from the Great One. I almost fainted as his eyes swept imperiously over me. How could I mention a chiropodist's bill at a time like this? How could I even think of my mother and Byron together?

'Please assure your mother that I fully intend to pay my dues,' Byron said loftily. 'I have been, shall we say, unlucky at the gaming tables of late. When I sell my estate at Newstead, then I shall settle with my creditors.

Your amiable mama will be the very first upon my list.'

'Your mum?' Ruby looked at me askance. 'What's all that about?'

'She's a chiropodist,' I explained.

Ruby looked blank. It struck me she didn't even know what a chiropodist was!

Determined to get back on track, she blurted out, 'While I've got you here, Ron, you remember about that audition? You know – the other night, at the theatre?'

'Audition?'

'Remember? I sang. And you said afterwards I was exactly what you were looking for.' For one awful moment I thought she was going to break into song again to remind him.

'I did? Ah yes,' Byron recalled lazily. 'And so you are, dear Ruby. Exactly what I want.'

Hearing her favourite word again, Rosie wriggled her small body into a contortion of anger beneath the confining straps. 'Rosie want!'

'Only I need the dates and everything,' Ruby blurted. 'See, you have to give six weeks' holiday notice at Pizza Pronto, otherwise you get the sack. And I can't afford to—'

'Sack. I have some fine sack in my cellar at Newstead,' Byron said. 'When you come, you shall taste it.'

'I shall? Oh yes, I'd love to. But when?' Ruby said hopefully. She began rocking the buggy roughly to quieten Rosie.

Ruby was getting a bit pushy. Byron must have thought so too. He didn't so much beat a hasty retreat towards the trees as melt gradually into the background.

143

Somehow the distance between us had expanded. The green of his jacket merged with leaves and grass. His voice drifted back to us, a faint promise: 'I shall send a carriage for you. And bring your pretty friends along – the more, the merrier. Come, Smut.'

These were his last words, and Ruby was left to make the best of them.

'But ... Ron? Where's he gone now?' She stood gazing into the thicket of birches and brambles. 'I wish he wouldn't keep going off like that. What does he mean, "carriage"?'

Nathan whistled softly. 'Girls, we have just witnessed what it is given few mortals to see.'

'Oh, speak English, will you?' Ruby turned on him, her face flushed and shiny. 'No offence, Nate, but leave the poetry to the experts, eh?'

'That was some manifestation,' Nathan said, shaking his head.

'Mani— what? Oh, you're not still on about ghosts, are you?' Ruby gestured towards the trees. 'You lot and your ghosts. A ghost doesn't invite you back to his place, now, does he?'

Nathan smacked his hand against his head. 'Shit! If only I'd brought my camera.'

'Why is it so important to have your camera?' I asked him.

He scratched his head. 'What does one usually use a camera for?'

'To take a photograph?'

'Correct! Miss Carter, tonight you walk away with the star prize holiday for two in Barbados.'

'What is he on?' Ruby said, as we began walking back in the direction of the pond.

'It didn't work the first time,' Nathan was saying. 'But then I didn't have the right equipment. You've got to use a really fast shutter speed.'

'Oh, shut up with your stupid ghost story!' Ruby yelled.

Ignoring her, Nathan went on, 'There was that famous Victorian one of the psychic oozing ectoplasm, but that turned out to be a fake. The Victorians were big on communing with the dead. They were big on fakes too.'

'You're a fake,' Ruby declared. 'A flaky fake, hah!'

'We might even get old Byron to pose,' Nathan said. 'He'd love that, wouldn't he? He hated his portrait painters. They never made him quite gorgeous enough.'

'And what,' Lauren said stiffly, 'would be the point of this exercise?'

'Point? Point?' Nathan leaped around, slapping his thighs and groaning at our stupidity, while Barney snapped at his heels, trying to rip pieces out of his jeans in a mock attack. 'You girls are slow to catch on, aren't you? We get a picture and sell it, of course. Make a fortune. Imagine the headline – LORD BYRON: BACK FROM THE DEAD – We'd make a killing – sorry, a fortune . . .'

'Shut up, Nathan' – I nudged him – 'you're upsetting Ruby.'

For Ruby had had enough of this talk. She was already stalking off ahead of us, bumping Rosie over ant hills and tree stumps. 'I'm going on home!' she yelled over her shoulder. 'Got to get Rosie to bed.'

I made to go after her, but Nathan caught hold of my wrist. 'Let her go. She needs to think over what we've just said.' He turned to me. 'Listen, Abbie, this is what you do. Next time his lordship comes mincing along, you give me a call, right? No matter what time of the day or night. I'm going to get some special equipment together and we'll do the business. All right?'

'All right,' I said.

Nathan smiled. I got the feeling he would have made a move on me again, had it not been for Lauren standing there.

For once I didn't mind about Lauren getting in the way. Nathan was nice, but he could wait. Like Ruby, I just wanted to be alone. I just wanted to think about Byron receiving us in his stately pile. He would hold out his hand to help me down from the carriage, and as he did so, he would gaze deep into my eyes. His gaze would penetrate deeper, into my very soul. He would see that Ruby was a silly shallow little thing, and that Lauren had unfortunate taste in headgear. He would recognize a kindred spirit when he saw one.

In place of Nathan's naff headline, I imagined a different one. It would go like this:

ABIGAIL CARTER AND LORD BYRON: THE LIVING AND THE DEAD — UNITED IN LOVE.

Chapter Twelve

Man's love is of a thing apart
'Tis woman's whole existence

I suppose you couldn't blame Ruby being mad for Byron. Dead he might be, but he was still *hot* all right. As I raced through the pages of *Byron's Babes*, it became clear to me. All the girls of Byron's time agreed he *had* something. What it was he had, they couldn't be sure.

Was it the poetry itself? Maybe it was that look of cold disdain? Or was it the plummy voice drawling drop-dead clever witticisms? No one could say for sure. Yet all over the country respectable young ladies were swooning over his verses and sending him locks of their hair.

Obviously death had done nothing to dampen Byron's sex appeal. In the days that followed our walk on the heath I began to wonder who was haunting who. Instead of booking the nearest priest for an exorcism, or investing in crucifixes, or painting pentagrams all over the place, we couldn't wait for our next visitation. This in itself was deeply weird. I was hung up on a ghost! I of all people knew the dangers, didn't I? Yet scared as I was, I just couldn't help myself.

Ruby had no such fears. Still convinced her hero was mortal, she practically wore her killer heels down to stumps as she tottered over the heath in the hope of bumping into Byron again; and, as she put it, settling on a date.

Nathan meanwhile was on red ghost alert, camera and several rolls of film at the ready. 'Seen his lordship yet?' He rang me almost every day, mainly to ask me out. I warded him off with excuses.

'Sorry, Nathan, but I'm a bit, like, distracted right now.'

'Well, don't forget – minute you set eyes on him, give me a bell, right?'

Then there was my mother, enquiring after 'that gentleman with the limp'. 'If you see him, dear, you will tell him he needs another appointment? That poor foot of his requires an extensive course of treatment, in my professional opinion.'

Whenever she said this, she'd have a crafty check of her appearance in the mirror over the gas fire, wondering aloud if she needed another perm just yet.

As for Lauren, she was campaigning to replace that old duffer Wordsworth with Byron on the school syllabus. Now that we were back at school again, every lunchtime would find her in the school library, half buried in Byron's *Complete Works*. Normal conversation with her was no longer possible. When I mentioned something about missing Joel, all I got in the way of sympathy was: 'Well, Abbie, remember, "*Man's love is of a thing apart, 'Tis woman's whole existence.*" Isn't that just so true?' She would sigh, a faraway look in her eyes.

Actually, I had to agree with those lines. Love had certainly become my whole existence. The problem was, I really really liked Nathan. Nathan was good fun, he was sensitive, he had the kind of mischievous sex appeal any girl would go for. You could say that Nathan was full of life, whereas Byron . . . well, Byron was full of death. It was Byron who dawdled alongside me as I trudged from the bus stop to school each morning, twirling his red silk neckerchief, tempting me to turn back with the words, 'Abigail, why waste your youth on this wretched place? In my opinion a girl should read neither poetry nor politics. A little music, drawing, dancing and cookery maybe . . .'

Poor Nathan! With a rival like Byron, what chance did a mere human stand?

Even at meal times, Byron hovered close by. Every time I indulged in a second helping of Mum's apple crumble and my jeans button popped open, I heard his voice drawling scornfully in my ear, 'I do detest a dumpy woman.'

Once, when I had a crafty session with my tarot cards, it was Byron who shuffled them between elegant gloved fingers, declaring them a feeble kind of game. 'Is there anything in the future,' he wanted to know, 'that can possibly console us for not being always twenty-five?'

On Saturday nights, when Lauren and I slouched in front of a video at her house, the current Hollywood heart-throbs would simply morph into Byron before my eyes.

But the real test of my obsession with Byron came when a letter postmarked Sydney, Australia, plopped through the door. My long-awaited letter from Joel, informing me that he'd met a girl at some youth hostel who was going on the same dig, and well, sorry, but hopefully we could still be friends.

Instead of beating my breast and refusing food for a month, all I could think of was how much more, like, *eloquently*, Byron could have put it. What was happening to me? Here I was, doing the very thing I kept warning Ruby against: I was mooning after a ghost! But even though my brain told me that this was madness, there was another part of Abigail Carter that just wasn't getting the message. It was like there was some swooning, besotted girl inside me that I had no control over.

Three weeks had passed since our day on the common when I got a call from Ruby.

'I'm so-oooo excited, Abb, I can hardly wait to tell you! In fact, I will . . . no, I won't. I'll save it. Oh look, can you and Lor come round tomorrow night? My mum'll be out at her mate's house. Puh-leeeese!'

Another visit to Warren Road wasn't something Lauren and I looked forward to. On the other hand, if there was news of Byron, then we couldn't afford to miss it.

'Do you think she's actually seen him again?' Lauren said in a piqued tone as we knocked at the door.

'No idea.' Nervously I glanced up at the upstairs window, just to make sure it wasn't raining oven chips again. Someone, probably Rory, had scraped the word PANTS on the blistering paintwork of the front door.

It was Roxanne who opened the door to us. She was wearing what looked like the net curtains. 'I'm getting married, I am.'

'Do tell me, who is the lucky bridegroom?' Lauren said. She was no good with children.

Ruby darted at us and almost hauled us into the house, as if it was dangerous to leave the front door open. 'Quick! Come in! We're in the front room. I been trying to get the kids to bed before you came, but it's hopeless. Sit down then.' She shoved a pile of comics off the sofa to make a space for us.

'So!' I said brightly. 'What's all this about then, Ruby? Why the urgency?'

'Urgency? Oh, urgency . . .'

The TV sat on an old chest of drawers. Ruby began scrabbling frantically in one of these, while Rory and Ritch cursed her for blocking their view of *The Rugrats* video. Finally she found what she wanted.

'I thought for a moment I'd lost it.' She fanned herself with the letter, as if with relief. 'That would have been the end.'

You could see at a glance it wasn't just any old letter. The envelope was stippled and creamy, like woodchip wallpaper. The handwriting was faded and slanted. Instead of a stamp, there was a seal the consistency of toffee sauce.

'How it got here without a proper stamp, God knows,' Ruby said. 'But there you go – good old post office, eh?'

'Rosie me want.' Rosie made a grab for the letter, but Ruby was too quick for her. She tossed it over to land in my lap.

'Go on. Read it.'

Feeling the rough grain of the envelope between my fingers, I felt a quiver of excitement. Swiftly followed by a stab of jealousy. I could guess who this was from. But why Ruby? Why would the greatest literary genius since

Shakespeare waste his efforts on a girl who only read silly magazines?

'Go on then,' Ruby cried impatiently. 'Read it aloud. It's not personal or nothing.'

The paper inside was thin and delicate, like tracing paper. I smoothed it flat on my lap, heart quickening. Then I cleared my throat and read:

My dearest Ruby,

You will forgive me for not writing sooner. Sadly, I find that my forebear, whom some call Wicked William, has left my estate in a near ruinous condition. To render my mansion habitable has been a task of Hercules, I assure you. Yet fear not, dear Ruby, these past weeks I have been fitting up drawing rooms and bedrooms with Brussels carpets and superb draperies. My plan is to offer you and your companions my proudest chambers. So be assured that I have your comforts foremost in my mind.

As for the production, I am currently devising a diversion to entertain my friends, in which you, fair damsel, will most certainly shine.

Do not concern yourself with travelling arrangements. A coach leaves Victoria for Newstead Abbey at eleven o'clock on the morning of October 21st. A Saturday.

In the meantime, please convey my compliments to your pretty young friends, and assure them of my eagerness to receive you all as my guests.

Fondest Regards

By Ron

Ruby was watching me all the time I read, cheeks

aglow, eyes shining. 'See!' she cried triumphantly. 'I told you Ron was for real. All that stuff about him being a ghost – ha! I don't know of any ghost that can write letters. Anyway, what d'you think? The twenty-first. That's four weeks away. You two will be able to make it, won't you? Pizza Pronto won't like it.' She frowned. 'I'll probably get the sack, but who cares?'

At the sound of the front door slamming, Ruby's face kind of closed up, the way flowers do on a cold night, petals just shrivelling into tightly furled buds. 'What's *she* doing home early?' Ruby spoke as if to herself.

Something about that slamming door sent shock waves through the whole house. Ruby's mum teetered into the room, muttering something about her friend having a headache. 'So much for our one night out of the week, eh? Y'all right, girls?'

We nodded dumbly. So transfixed was I by the sight of her that I didn't notice Roxanne creeping stealthily up on me. I didn't notice, until she snatched Ruby's letter out of my hand.

'Look, Mum, I'm getting married, I am. An this is my wedding indication.' Jumping up and down in her net curtain, Roxanne waved the letter at her mother.

'Oh yeah? Listen, our Roxie, take my advice 'n' stay single.' Ruby's mother shot Lauren and me a wry, worldly look, as if we were all pals. 'Let's see, what's this then?'

Probably she thought it was some little scribble that Roxie had done herself on her Barbie stationery set.

'Mum, that's mine.' Ruby seemed almost beside herself, as her mum squinted at the handwriting through mascara-smudged eyes.

153

'I can read, you know. What's this then, Rube, a love letter?'

'Mum, that's private. Give it to me, please.' Ruby's voice sounded weird, like glass breaking. She held out her hand impatiently.

But it looked like her mother had no intention of giving it back. 'Bet you girls know all about it, don't you?' She gave Lauren and me a conspiratorial wink. 'Got an admirer, has she? Here, budge up, girls!'

Lauren and I shifted stiffly so that Ruby's mother could fling herself between us. Ignoring Ruby's protests, she began to read Byron's lines in a kind of muttering disbelief, before exclaiming, 'Blimey! Who is this geezer, Rube? Is he taking the mickey or what?' You couldn't tell if she was laughing her head off or having some kind of coughing fit. Both together, I thought. At least, her eyes were streaming with tears as she choked out Byron's endearment: '"Fair damsel"? He's calling my Rube a damsel! What is he, some kind of perv? Oh, leave it out, Rube, for God's sake, I'm only having a bit of a laugh – God knows I need one.'

Lauren and I edged our bottoms to the sofa edge, ready to make a discreet exit. It was painful to watch Ruby trying to snatch back her letter, while holding a screaming Rosie in her arms. Her mother dodged and teased. To get the letter back she would have to fight for it. For a moment I feared it might come to that.

'Wait a minute,' her mother's tone changed suddenly. 'What's this about the twenty-first of October? A coach from Victoria?'

At once the laughter, the teasing stopped. You could

feel the change in atmosphere, focused and tense. As though sensing this, Roxanne began sobbing half-heartedly beneath her net curtain. The two boys huddled closer to the TV. Rory clamped his hands over his ears, as if he knew what was coming next.

'I was going to tell you anyway,' Ruby said wretchedly.

'Tell me what, Ruby?'

Suddenly dumping Rosie on the carpet, Ruby grabbed the letter out of her mother's hand. 'That's my own private letter, addressed to me.'

Ruby's mum stood up so abruptly that Lauren and I were almost pitched off the sofa. 'Now you listen to me, madam. I don't know what all this is about, but you can just forget it, OK.'

'But—' Ruby began.

'Don't "but" me, Rube. I don't care who this bloke is, or how posh he is, or how big his blinking mansion is, OK? I don't care if he wipes his bum on rose petals. I don't care if it's Prince William himself inviting you to his country pile, understand? You can't just go swanning off whenever it suits you and leave me with this lot.'

Behind her back, Lauren and I looked at each other. I could tell she felt the same as me: torn between wanting to escape and thinking she should stick up for Ruby. But how could we? One look at her mum, roughly yanking Rosie up from the floor, and my nerve failed me.

But as we both stood up, Ruby's mum turned on us. 'I suppose you two know him, this Ron character?' she demanded.

'No. Well . . . er . . . sort of . . .' Lauren mumbled.

'Make up your mind, love. *Do* you know him or *don't*

you? I take it you two are the "pretty young friends" the old devil's drooling on about, so you *must* know him.'

We nodded miserably. If only we could tell her! If only she knew she was fighting over an invitation from a ghost, and this whole thing was a fantasy. After all, how could Byron really make the abbey ready for us? The invitation was no more than a ghost-scribbled dream, yet it didn't make Ruby's mother's behaviour any more excusable.

'Well, you two can tell this toffy-nosed toff from me, all right?' She fixed us with her cross, bleary eyes. 'Tell him my daughter won't be going nowhere. So he can just fix up his "salons" and his "draperies" for some other dopey girl. Tell him from me, she's got responsibilities, right? Tell him—'

'Mum!' Ruby pleaded. 'Leave my friends alone. Let them go.'

She sounded tired. Defeated. I couldn't understand this. Why didn't Ruby fight back, for heaven's sake? Why didn't she tell her mum the kids were *her* problem, that she had her own life to live? Instead of just standing there, wringing her hands, flushed and miserable, while Lauren and I snuck out of the door.

'Some mother!' Lauren said, as soon as we were out of sight of the house. 'And I thought mine was bad. I'll never complain about her again.'

'Too right,' I agreed.

I have to confess, though, that it wasn't poor Ruby's family we talked about the rest of the way back to Lauren's house. It was the poet. We just couldn't talk about anything else. The thought of Lord Byron decorating his ghostly ruin with carpets and draperies in honour of our arrival was just too incredible. *Our* arrival!

Could he really be waiting for us at Newstead Abbey? According to my book, the abbey was now owned by the council and was open to the public. I imagined Byron, wandering through the empty galleries, unseen by the tourists. Setting things to rights, devising diversions, waiting for his guests to arrive. Just thinking of this, I shivered suddenly. What was I thinking of? How could we even think of accepting an invitation from a ghost?

'We won't go of course,' I said to Lauren finally, as we reached the High Street.

But this was what worried me. Lauren just looked at me. And she said nothing. Nothing at all.

Chapter Thirteen

Death, so called, is a thing which makes men weep,
And yet a third of life is passed in sleep.

Four weeks later and we were standing on the bleak tarmac of Victoria Station coach park. It was almost eleven in the morning and on such a morning, with the heavens chucking everything they'd got at us, including hailstones, this had to be madness, didn't it?

'You do realize,' I said to Lauren, 'that we must be, like, *totally* off our trolleys?'

'Speak for yourself,' Lauren sniffed. 'I am in full possession of my mental facilities, thank you very much.'

'Oh yeah?'

I wasn't so sure about Lauren's mental faculties myself. I mean, she'd actually taken out her plaits so that her hair fuzzed about her face and shoulders in a dense brown cloud. Also she'd abandoned her cap for a sleek fake-fur creation.

'What's with the fur, by the way?' I said. 'Is that your Snow Queen look or something? I hope we don't get the weather you're expecting.'

'In case you've forgotten, I suffer with my ears,' Lauren said, buttoning her new plum velvet coat to the neck.

'And I'm not risking an ear infection at a time like this either.'

I was a bit annoyed. She might have warned me about this style-makeover thing, when here was I, in my jeans and zip pullie as usual. I stood glaring at the coach to Newstead, which was already waiting at the stop. The doors remained firmly closed while the driver swigged tea from a polystyrene mug. We wouldn't be allowed on, he'd told an anxious old lady, until eleven a.m. precisely.

In any case, Ruby hadn't arrived yet. I kept glancing over my shoulder towards the terminal. 'Ruby's late.'

'So what's new?' Lauren sighed. 'She's always late.'

'You don't think her mum went crazy and locked her in her room or something?'

'Well, if she *has* locked her up,' Lauren said com-placently, 'we'll just have to go without her, won't we? You can't expect the driver to change his schedule, after all.'

From her smug tone and the look on her face, I guessed this was exactly what Lauren wanted. You didn't need to be a genius to figure out why. Without Ruby to steal the limelight, there'd be less competition. It would be down to me and Lauren to battle it out for the attentions of his gracious lordship.

But wait a minute. What the hell was I thinking of?!

I lowered my bag to the tarmac and folded my arms. 'Lauren, this is mad. I mean, what happens when we arrive there this afternoon? The house is closed to the public at dusk. What happens then? Where are we going to stay the night?'

'How should I know?' Lauren shrugged.

'But Ruby's expecting a sumptuous four-poster with velvet draperies and brekkie on a tray, for heaven's sake. And very likely her precious Ron in his silk dressing gown. She'll be lucky if she gets one night in the local youth hostel.'

'There is no youth hostel near there' – Lauren yawned – 'I checked.'

I stared straight at her. 'Oh, you checked? Well, Lauren, you seem remarkably cool about sleeping rough tonight. Because, call me a wimp, but personally I don't much fancy a night under a hedge in this weather.'

Lauren sighed and pointed out that we'd discussed all this before, like, a thousand times. 'You said yourself, if the invitation came from the spirit world, we can't just ignore it. And anyway, this is a unique opportunity for us, Abbie. Think about it. We have privileged access to the mind of a poetic genius.'

She had a point. Even Nathan thought we should go when I'd told him. He'd wanted to come with us in fact, until I pointed out that he hadn't been invited. 'What's that got to do with anything?' he had said, adding that it was a sod that he had to work on an assignment for *The Buzz* this weekend. He looked really upset at missing out. Worried even. 'You look out for yourself' were his last words to me, when we met briefly in the pub one night. 'Tell that randy poet to keep his hands to himself, OK?' He was just honing in for another kiss when his mobile rang and he had to rush off to cover an accident in Northgate High Street. All of which left me feeling more confused than ever. Was Nathan just that kind of touchy-kissy, friendly guy. Or did he really fancy me?

160

And how did I feel about him? His concern for me made me feel all kind of warm and glowing inside. Yet every time I thought about Nathan, the image of Byron crept between us, like a shadow.

'I just wish Ruby would believe us about Byron,' I said to Lauren. 'It's going to be a terrible shock when she sees the portraits of him at the abbey. Mind you, I tried to show her *Byron's Babes* but she wouldn't even look at—'

'Shhh,' Lauren warned. 'Here she comes, and— Oh no, I don't believe it. Look who she's brought with her.'

'Yoo-hooo! Hey, Abb, Lor . . . sorry I'm late!'

I turned to see Ruby stumbling out of the station terminal, a vision in mock-croc heels and suede coat. The coat had one of those fake furry collars that looks like a small lion hanging round your neck. A lava-flow of fiery hair tumbled down to her waist. Such a sight she was that the queue at the coach stop all turned to stare. As for the bus driver, he set down his cup and opened his doors at once.

Not that it was Ruby's looks we were interested in. It was the baggage she'd brought with her.

To our absolute horror, it looked like Rosie was coming too. Rosie, cute as a button in her pink pixie gear, the pushchair hung with carrier bags bursting with babyfood jars, plastic toys, toiletries and enough nappies to keep her dry for a year.

Lauren murmured uncharitably, 'She can't be serious. Not that wretched kid again.'

'It's her mum,' I decided. 'Told you she'd be awkward. She's only gone and dumped the baby on Ruby at the last moment.'

161

'Hi, can you help me with this lot? Reckon I've got the kitchen sink here!' Breathlessly, Ruby folded the buggy, shouldering bags and babe at the same time, as if she'd done this many times before.

Lauren gaped. 'Ruby, you're not bringing your sister to Newstead with us?'

'What else can I do? Mum won't have her. She's not well again.'

'But Ruby,' I broke in, 'that's *her* problem. You've got to have your own life, your mum can't—'

'Look, she can, OK?' Ruby cut me short. 'It was either bringing Rosie or staying at home. Now, are you going to help me with her, or not?'

Half an hour later the coach had cleared the outskirts of London and was hurtling north up the motorway. The drab scenery slid past: airfields, farms, orange-brick towns and Welcome Breaks. Neither Lauren nor I felt much like talking. Ruby prattled on enough for both of us.

Eventually I muttered something about being knackered. I bent my head against the dingy window, pretending to be asleep. Actually I was thinking hard. I couldn't help feeling angry that Ruby had ruined this adventure for all of us, just because she couldn't stick up for herself. If the worst should happen, the three of us might have been able to rough it for one night, but how could you sleep rough with an eighteen-month-old child? Ruby must be off her head.

But then I remembered: as far as she was concerned, we were honoured guests, about to be cosseted in the

162

luxury of Ron Lord's mansion. Oh God. What were we getting ourselves into?

It seemed like I sat there for ages with my eyes closed. I could hear Ruby wittering away to a monosyllabic Lauren, and beyond that the tinny jangle of Walkman headphones. The voices of the other passengers merged with the engine roar into a deep rumbling drone that made me sleepy.

Then, gradually, a different sound took over. Sharp. Metallic. A clatter of hooves. The rumble of great wheels crunching over cobbles.

I opened my eyes, expecting to see the passengers' heads lolling on the upholstered neck rests. But there *were* no passengers. There *was* no coach. There was only me, walking along an empty street, and, weaving its way up the road behind me, that long line of carriages I vaguely recognized. A kind of fear gripped me. I tried to think logically: what was it that was so creepy about the carriages? Perhaps the way they gleamed in the lamplight? Or the way they wiggled like one single creature, black and shiny as a centipede scurrying up the hill?

When the first few carriages drew level with me, I couldn't resist looking in the windows. I knew I shouldn't. I knew this was the last thing I should do. *Don't look*, my little voice told me. *Don't look or you'll regret it.*

Still I couldn't resist. Here was a carriage rattling right past, with the driver sitting up front in his coachman's livery, the gleaming black horses plumed and trotting like old-fashioned showgirls. Yet when I looked in through the windows, all I could see was my own scared white face reflected back at me.

The carriages were empty. Except for one. As the very last carriage disappeared round the corner of the street, I noticed that the coach at the front had pulled into the kerb just ahead of me. It sat motionless. The coach driver sat staring straight ahead like a waxwork. The six black horses stamped and snorted. Their ostrich plumes swayed gracefully with every jerk of the reins.

Don't look, that voice said again. *Walk right on past.* I thought I was going to do just that. Don't look. Just walk. Just keep setting one foot in front of the other. Then, as I drew level with the coach, my head just swivelled round, as if of its own accord, and stared right in.

A face stared back at me. Not my own, this time. A man's face, sulky, scornful, framed by chestnut curls. The eyes were like melted toffee, trickling over me, up and down. Oh.

'May I offer you a ride?' The door clicked open. It was as if he'd been expecting me. Still I hung back. 'I don't know,' I said. 'If you're going my way . . .'

With a careless gesture, Byron waved his silk scarf. 'Not *your* way dear girl, but you are going *my* way, I believe. They all do.' He sighed. 'All mortals do go my way. In the end.'

I stepped up into the carriage, surprised at how high it seemed from the ground. Inside, the seats were upholstered in burnished leather. There were so many cushions, tassels, brocades and velvets I thought I might suffocate. As soon as I was inside, Byron tapped the roof of the coach with a gold-tipped cane and we lurched forwards.

'We have many miles to go' – he waved the cane at me

– 'so tedious. I beg you, make yourself as comfortable as you can. This cursed thing is a bone-shaker.'

'I think I've lost my friends,' I heard myself saying. 'I think I should get out and find them.'

It was exciting, being alone with the poet, his scornful eyes brooding over me. I also knew there was something horrible, terrifying about it. Something wrong. But I couldn't remember what it was.

'Haven't we all lost our friends?' Byron sighed. 'Not one of my so-called friends could bear to show his face. Empty carriages, they send, hah! Can you imagine such cowardice? Such hypocrisy!'

He looked so angry I dared not answer. It didn't matter whether I spoke or not. Byron talked and talked, and read aloud his poems until my head nodded. After what seemed an age there was a different motion in the carriage, a bumping and jolting, as if we were out in the country and jerking over the rutted mud roads.

'These roads are the devil, are they not?' Byron complained. 'Had I not already left my internal organs behind in Greece, I swear they would be jolted out of me.'

When he smiled, his sulky mouth was like a wet poppy. I couldn't help staring at it. Then I wished I hadn't. Out of the corner of Byron's beautiful, sulky, wet poppy mouth wiggled a live worm.

I screamed. Screamed until there was nothing else in the world but my own screaming.

Something was shaking me.

'Wake up! For God's sake, Abbie, wake up!' Lauren, her hair tickling my nose as she bent over me, was practically shaking my brains out of my skull. 'Everyone's staring at us. You practically caused the driver to skid off the road. We nearly had an accident.'

I opened my eyes to find myself under scrutiny. Most of the passengers must have got off the bus at Nottingham. The remaining few were straining their heads to check out the crazy girl at the back.

'Oh God. Ouch. I think I've twisted my neck. Why didn't you wake me before?' I struggled upright.

'We didn't like to, did we, Lor?' Ruby said. 'You were dead to the world. You've slept all the way to Newstead.'

'Newstead?'

'Yeah, we're here at the abbey!' Ruby held up Rosie to the window. 'Look, Rose, look at all the lovely trees. We're in the country now.'

The country. I looked out of the window as far as my stiff neck would allow. The coach was rumbling slowly up a long, endlessly twisting driveway. Dense woodland crowded either side of the drive. The bumps, which I'd imagined to be the carriage in my dream, were actually pedestrian humps to slow the tourist traffic. I glanced at my watch. It was three thirty. It wasn't long till dusk. Then what would we do?

Ruby was looking puzzled. 'I can't understand what these other people are still doing on here.' She looked around at the three middle-aged couples who remained. 'I thought they'd get off at that village we just passed. I mean, I know the abbey's a big place, but Ron can't have invited them all, can he?'

Rosie, looking for noses or hair to pull, leaned over the back of the seat and snatched in Lauren's direction. 'Rosie want.'

166

'Rosie can't have.' Lauren scowled.

Just when you thought the twisting would never end, the bus pulled into a car park to our right. The woodland here was the tame kind that goes with stately homes. Little stiles and signposts and litter bins, and notices telling you to keep dogs on the lead. We couldn't see the house itself yet.

'All right, ladies and gents,' the driver announced. 'There's a bus passes back this way in three hours' time. Anyone gets left behind, watch out for the ghosts, ha ha . . .'

Ha ha, indeed.

'We need our heads looking at,' I grumbled to Lauren as we shuffled off the bus. 'What're we going to do now?'

'Look over the abbey, of course. What else?'

'Yeah, and what's Ruby going to say when she finds we've got to share the place with a bus load of tourists? Uh-oh . . . looks like trouble already. Ruby isn't looking too happy.'

Ruby had struggled off the bus ahead of us; an elderly man was helping her with the pushchair. Now she stood in the centre of the coach park, clutching Rosie to her chest. She didn't have to tell us who it was she'd just seen. I knew. Just from looking at her face.

'It's that woman!' Ruby pointed along a dusky track through the trees. 'She must have been on the bus all the time, right at the front. Can you believe it? That bloody crazy woman, following us everywhere, waiting to get her hooks into Rosie!'

So Claire Clairmont had decided to invite herself along too. Lauren and I followed Ruby's gaze into the trees. We couldn't see her. But that didn't mean she wasn't there of course. Lurking. Watching. Waiting.

Ruby clutched at my arm. 'Abb, d'you reckon I should call the police?'

'Are you sure it's her?' Lauren said coolly.

'Course I am,' Ruby said, indignant. 'Could hardly mistake a screwball like that, could I? Doesn't exactly blend in with that outfit of hers, does she?'

'No,' I agreed. 'She doesn't. But we can't call the police. She hasn't actually done anything after all.'

'Not yet, she hasn't.' Ruby buckled Rosie into the pushchair so tightly the poor thing could hardly breathe. 'Supposing she's just waiting her chance? The minute I turn my back, she could snatch her, just like that.'

Lauren shook her head. She laid a hand on Ruby's shoulder. In her kind-to-lesser-beings voice, she said, 'Ruby, will you trust me, please?'

Poor Ruby. She nodded dumbly at Lauren. 'Course I will, Lor.'

'Will you trust me when I tell you that this woman is just a poor sick creature, a mere shadow of a human being. That she can't actually hurt Rosie. I promise you, she can't.'

Ruby frowned. 'I don't know what makes you so sure.' As we turned towards the house, she added, 'Anyway, I tell you – if she comes within an inch of that buggy I'm calling the police, and I don't care what anyone says. In fact, I've got a good mind to tell Ron. He'll have security people, won't he? Place like this.'

It took a while for Lauren and me to calm her down. Actually I felt far from calm myself. As I glanced into the

168

shadowy depths of the trees I began to seriously wonder what we were getting into.

The abbey was an ancient monument. It was known to be haunted. Supposing the ghosts of Byron and Claire were stronger out here? Supposing Claire was trailing us now, shadowing the buggy? Waiting her chance.

Chapter Fourteen

Between two worlds life hovers like a star
'Twixt night and morn, upon the horizon's verge . . .

You couldn't actually see the house from the car park. We tramped along behind the other passengers around one last bend in the drive, and there it was, Byron's place.

'Wow!' Ruby's mouth dropped open. 'It's practically a castle! I never realized it'd be that big.'

We stood gazing at the vast expanse of mushroom-tinted stone, the row upon row of mullioned windows.

'Yeah,' I murmured. 'It's got the wow-factor all right.'

It wasn't just the sheer *size* of the place that made us stand there, drooling. Byron's pad had everything you'd expect of a stately pile. There were parapets and battlements, there were pinnacles and urns and gargoyles, their grizzly faces erupting from the stone the way a tree sprouts nodules. On either side of the main building the gothic arches of the original abbey framed puffs of cloud. Now that the rain had stopped, sunshine dripped like melted butter onto the grimy stone.

'I can't figure it out – why Ron never told me it was open to the public.' Ruby craned her head back to peer at the row of uppermost windows. 'Can you see him anywhere, Abb?'

'Who? Ron?'

'Well, who else? He must be looking out for us. After all, we're not the general public, are we? Don't forget, we three are here by *special invitation*.'

How could I forget? As we drew near the entrance, I began to feel edgy. Would Ruby get hysterical when she realized the truth? I had visions of fainting fits, and emergency trips to hospital, while Lauren and I were saddled with Rosie. After all, she wasn't experienced like us. She hadn't had to fight off the attentions of Henry VIII; she hadn't been to hell and back with the Witchfinder General. When Ruby came upon her beloved 'Ron' gazing down from a portrait at her, she was very likely to lose her marbles altogether.

'This is stupid,' Ruby was complaining now, as we shuffled into a dark panelled reception hall. 'I know the invitation is in here somewhere.' She began rummaging in the bag that housed the portable nursery and enough stage make-up for the entire cast of *Cats*.

'Don't get it out here!' Lauren hissed, laying a restraining hand on her wrist.

'Why not?'

'I just don't think you should flash it about. It's a rare document.' She nodded at a couple of tourists exclaiming over a suit of armour. 'Some of these Americans would pay a fortune for it.'

'I don't see why. It's nothing to do with them.' Ruby glanced up the wide curving stone staircase opposite the front door. 'It's too bad of Ron not to come and down and meet us. We could go straight up, I suppose. And surprise him.'

'Yeah. Great surprise,' I murmured. 'Anyway, look, we have to buy a ticket.'

A woman with big glasses was sitting behind a counter laden with leaflets and tour guides.

'Rubbish!' Ruby fumed. 'I'm not buying a ticket. Why should we? We're Ron's personal guests. You don't invite someone round and charge them entrance fees – come off it, you two.'

'One adult, is it, dear?' The woman at the ticket office smiled automatically. 'That'll be five pounds, and the little one goes free.'

'No thanks.' Ruby beamed back at her. 'I don't want a ticket. I just want to know where the private apartments are.'

'Private apartments?' The woman faltered, puzzled. 'Do you mean the staff quarters?'

'No, not the staff. I mean Ron Lord. The owner.'

How could we stop her? Behind Ruby's back, Lauren and I cringed in utter embarrassment and dismay.

'Owner?' The ticket woman's expression had changed from blank to downright suspicious.

'Of this house.' Ruby waved her arms dramatically to indicate the hall in which we stood, with its gift shop, heraldic shields and suits of armour, its vaulted ceiling and wide curving staircase. 'Mr Ron Lord,' Ruby repeated happily. 'The famous poet.'

A look passed over the ticket woman's face. A we've-got-a-right-nutter-here kind of a look. She cleared her throat. 'Look, dear, could you just have a word with my colleague over there for a moment? Only I'm not quite with you. And we don't want to keep these people waiting.'

Already the rest of the queue were shuffling and raising their eyebrows at one another. Ruby had little choice but to let them pass, with a sigh. She turned to Lauren and me. 'Hear that? I don't think that woman's very bright. Acted like she'd never heard of Ron. Says I should speak to her colleague.' She fished in the carrier bag again. 'If only I could find that blessed invitation . . .'

Not looking forward to a repeat of the scene we'd just had, I glanced over at the colleague. An old bloke dressed in a tweedy waistcoat stood guard at the foot of the staircase. The idea of engaging him in a conversation about Ron and private apartments was enough to make me want to run back to the bus. But Ruby had no such qualms.

'Excuse me, but could you show us the way to the private apartments please?' Already she had one tottery heel planted on the bottom step.

'Why? Got an appointment with his lordship, have you?' The man sniggered softly as he took tickets from the visitors tramping past us.

'Yes,' Ruby said, sticking her chin out. 'Yes, we have, as a matter of fact.'

The man winked. 'Still got an eye for a pretty girl after all these years. Got to hand it to him.'

'I beg your—' Ruby began, just as Lauren returned, thrusting our tickets at the attendant. 'Hey, what are you doing with—?'

'It doesn't cost much,' Lauren said quickly. 'Anyway, it'll be fun to do the tour.'

173

'Yeah,' I said. 'We'll probably bump into By— I mean, Ron, on the way round.' When Lauren and I took hold of the pushchair between us and carried Rosie up the staircase, Ruby had no choice but to follow.

'Give him my regards when you see him,' the attendant quipped sarcastically. Or maybe he wasn't being sarcastic at all? Maybe he knew something we didn't?

My uneasy feeling grew stronger as we began our 'little tour'. At the top of the stairs was a baronial hall with nothing much in it but some stained-glass windows and various heraldic crests. Our footsteps echoed across the polished floorboards. There was a strong smell of wax furniture polish and soot, which was strange, because obviously no fires had been lit here for a very long time. A plaque told us that Byron had been a bit strapped for cash, and hadn't been able to furnish this hall. Ever inventive, he had used it for pistol practice instead.

Ruby wasn't much interested in plaques or ancestors. She looked a bit dazed as we wandered through a gloomy, confusing jumble of rooms. 'Ron must be loaded,' she kept repeating over and over. 'He must have pots of dosh. It must cost a fortune just to furnish a place like this.'

The furnishings were a mish-mash of Regency chairs, Victorian chamberpots and lion-skin rugs. Only Rosie was unimpressed. She began to kick her fat little legs and scream, 'Rosie want walk now! Rosie want out!'

'Rosie's not the only one who wants *out*,' I murmured to Lauren.

Ruby responded by unpeeling a banana and sticking it

in Rosie's mitt. 'She'll be wanting her tea soon. If that Ron doesn't turn up in a minute, I'm going right on up to the private apartments – and just let anyone try and stop me!'

We'd just reached Byron's library, a long, panelled room stuffed with bookcases of carved oak. Here, displayed in glass cabinets, were some of Byron's most precious possessions: a pair of boxing gloves, a curved sword in a brass scabbard, a green velvet jacket that looked like it would turn to dust if you touched it.

'Look,' Lauren was sighing, 'this must be the very ink-stand Byron used to write with.'

'All this history stuff is boring.' Ruby wasn't listening as she bent to wipe banana mush from Rosie's mouth. As she straightened, something caught her eye. She pointed at a portrait above our heads. 'Look, you two, if that isn't the spitting image of Ron's Smut, I'd like to know what is.'

We held our breath as she read the plaque beneath. Aloud. 'Oh. That *is* Smut.' She turned to us, eyes shining. 'Another Smut, that must be. Like an ancestor.'

'Oh yes, of course,' Lauren said, raising her eyebrows at me. 'The dog's family name.'

Opposite the portrait of Smut was his master, a bit younger and chubbier of cheek than the image Byron chose to manifest himself in, but still undeniably Byron.

Ruby spun on her heel and gasped. Her hand flew to her mouth. 'That' – she pointed an accusing finger – 'that looks the spit of Ron. Would you credit it? There's a real family likeness, isn't there?' She bit a lip, puzzled a moment. 'So this Byron fella was Ron's ancestor then? That must be where Ron gets his poetry from. It's like my singing. Mum says I get that from my great-aunty Barbara. She was a backing singer at the London Palladium—' She broke off. 'Why are you two looking at me like that?'

We shrugged. But perhaps she knew what we were going to say, for she suddenly turned her back on us. 'Oh look, I'm fed up with staring at all this ancient old stuff. I'm taking Rosie up them stairs at the end of the gallery, and I'm going to find Ron, OK?'

Ruby didn't hang around to argue. She flounced off before we could say anything. She must have broken into a run. We could hear her heels clacking on the tiled floor of the gallery, the pushchair wheels whirring.

'Shouldn't we go after her?' I wondered aloud.

Lauren shook her head. 'She won't go far. She'll be back in a minute.'

We hung around the library for what seemed an age, while Lauren oohed and aaahed over letters and lockets and locks of hair. Personally I was finding it hard to concentrate. Supposing Ruby had barged into the private staff quarters raving about Ron? Wouldn't she be seen off the premises pretty smartly? Still, to go searching for her now would be hopeless. This place was such a maze of corridors and stairways and galleries we'd never find her in a million years.

But Ruby didn't come back to find us. Eventually even Lauren got tired of sighing over Byron's bits and bobs, and we decided to move on.

'Where the hell is she?' I murmured, as we walked

through the East Gallery. A clock was chiming the hour in the distance. The visitors seemed to have thinned out suddenly. Attendants dawdling about by the glass cases began to fidget and check their watches.

Through the gallery windows I could see shadows lengthening across the lawns. A deep pink stain spread across the sky. All the lights were on in the abbey, yet there was a kind of buzzy uncertainty about them. As if the darkness waited. As if something was waking deep within the bowels of this house, shaping itself out of the gloom.

At the end of the gallery a woman attendant was standing in front of a marble bust, some grumpy-looking ancestor of Byron's.

'Excuse me' – I turned to her as we passed – 'you haven't seen a girl with red hair go past, have you? She's got a baby in a pushchair.'

The attendant looked thoughtful. 'There was a girl with a pushchair a while back, asking about someone called Ron—'

'Yes, that's her,' Lauren said, rolling her eyes at me.

'She seemed to think he was living here. I'm afraid I couldn't help her. But that was quite a while ago.'

'Did you notice which way she went?' I asked.

The attendant shook her head. You could see her point. Who could be sure of anything in this labyrinth?

'I'd better warn you that we close in half an hour,' she said, looking at her watch.

'How could anyone need so many rooms?' I grumbled as we whirled through an ornately swagged drawing room, and something called the Charles II Dressing

177

Room, in hot pursuit of Ruby. 'They had rooms for every blooming single thing.' I reeled them off, despairing as I did so of ever finding Ruby again. 'Rooms for writing letters in, rooms for putting your togs on, music rooms, prayer rooms, withdrawing rooms — what does that mean, by the way?'

'After dinner,' Lauren informed me, 'the ladies used to "withdraw" so the men could chat about, you know, important things.'

'Huh. So they could get drunk and tell each other dirty jokes, you mean. They certainly had enough bedrooms,' I added as we glimpsed yet another magnificent bed with gilt eagles and scarlet draperies.

Lauren threw me a scornful look. 'You have to do things in style when you're an aristocrat. You could hardly expect someone like Byron to live in a flat in Smedhurst Road, could you?'

Suddenly I wanted to punch Lauren. 'Why are you being such a snotty cow all of a sudden? And another thing, I think you could be a bit more concerned over Ruby. I mean, if she doesn't show up soon, we'll miss the bus back to London.'

We halted a moment. From somewhere deep within the house, a bell was tolling. I peered out of a casement window. Far below, visitors — some I recognized from our bus — were already spilling out onto the forecourt. Footsteps clattered softly in the passages as staff began checking and clearing rooms.

'We'd better go down then,' I said to Lauren. 'We'll probably meet up with Ruby in the forecourt or somewhere.'

Lauren just tossed her hair and loped slowly along behind me like she had all the time in the world. I realized she wasn't a bit bothered about the bus, or Ruby, or getting back to London.

'Hurry up, Lauren, for God's sake!' I led the way past the empty rooms, following the EXIT signs. That seemed the most obvious thing to do, after all. Exit meant way out, didn't it? I was expecting the signs to lead us back down to the ticket hall where we'd first come in. Instead we went down narrow flights of steps, so worn and twisty I began to wonder if we'd taken a wrong turn. At the foot of one of these flights, a new sign pointed to the CLOISTERS.

'Cloisters?' I turned to Lauren. 'What the hell . . .? This is meant to be the gift shop.'

'Oh, fabulous!' was all Lauren said. 'We *must* see the cloisters before we leave.'

'Must we?'

'*Naturellement.* This is the original part of the abbey.' Lauren's voice echoed back at me as she set off along one of the four stone walkways. 'You know, where the monks would go to pray and meditate.'

'Really? Well, I'm going to say a few prayers myself if we don't get out of here in a minute.'

The walkways surrounded a small inner courtyard on four sides. Peering out through one of the arched latticed windows set in the wall, I could see mossy cobbles lapping about a fountain. The fountain was hardly beautiful – a squat crenellated stone column with a lion's-head spout, decorated with strange, gargoyle-like animals. Their faces, blunted by centuries of wind and rain, grimaced straight at me. The only human figures were the ugly fat cherubs, embracing each other at the very top. They looked as if they had made some suicide pact and were about to hurl themselves into the greenish slush below.

I shuddered. There was a strange atmosphere of tainted calm. As if the prayers had somehow turned sour. As if too many people had loitered here — those ancient Byrons maybe — hatching evil, brewing plots.

Quickly I caught Lauren up. 'Where is everyone anyway? The staff, I mean. We haven't even seen an attendant since that woman we spoke to.'

'There's someone.' Lauren nodded towards the far end of the passage. Then she hesitated. 'Oh no, it's that totally obnoxious old man with the leer.'

The man was leaning against the wall, arms folded, as if waiting for us. Great. A human being at last! Not much of a human being, it was true, but still, I was pleased to see him.

'Excuse me, but is this the way out?' I thought he'd be only too glad to get rid of the stray visitors and hustle us to the nearest exit at once.

Instead he said in an oily tone, like he was in no hurry whatsoever, 'It's *one* way out, dear.'

As his grey eyes slid over us, I realized with a sickening jolt what he reminded me of. His face was like one of those stone gargoyles on the fountain back there, the features all blunt and weathered, scarcely recognizable as human. His skin was the same dingy yellowish colour as the stone.

'I thought you wanted to find your friend, though. That pretty girl with the red hair.'

'Have you seen her?' Lauren demanded in her haughtiest tone.

'I might have.' The man nodded over his shoulder, back in the direction we'd just walked in.

'Ruby,' I sighed. 'Thank God.'

She hadn't actually come into view yet. Still, you couldn't mistake the clack of her heels on the stone flags, the rattle of buggy wheels, the shrill tones of her voice . . . and . . . I drew in my breath sharply. Something else. Another step. Heavy, uneven, clunking.

Then, 'There they are!' Turning a corner, Ruby hurtled towards us, waving frantically as if we might miss her. Rosie waved too. The man limping behind them didn't wave at all.

'Byron!' I heard Lauren sigh beside me.

'Yoo-hoo, you two!' Ruby shrieked. 'S'all right. We don't have to leave. Told you I'd find him. I found Ron!'

Chapter Fifteen

Thought that it might turn out so — now I know it,
But still I am, or was, a pretty poet.

When Byron, poet, love-rat and sixth lord of Newstead, came limping out of the cloister shadows, one part of me wanted to run screaming for the exit. The other part was like all those other daft girls who had swooned over their poetry books and sent him their tresses in sealed envelopes.

'Abigail, Lauren . . . Welcome to my humble home.'

At the sound of his velvety tones, my knees went weak. It was like being touched, kissed in places so secret you didn't even know you had them. Also he was so massively gorgeous it almost hurt you to look at him. Who would imagine what tight white breeches and spurred boots could do for a bloke? The burgundy jacket strained tight across his shoulders; the shirt was undone at the neck, allowing a glimpse of foxy chest hair. I opened my mouth to speak, and a kind of rusty squeak came out.

Luckily no one noticed.

'What a lucky fellow I am.' The gorgeous one spread his arms wide, as if to scoop us all into them like fish in a net. 'Not one, but three fair damsels under my roof. I am astonished at my good fortune.'

Even as he spoke, there was a sound of doors banging closed, the rattle of great bolts being drawn. The house – the house was closing. I glanced around for the seedy attendant, but he too had disappeared.

Were we shut up then? Alone? With Byron? Something about the house itself had changed, I noticed. The air had a dank, undisturbed feel. In places, the cloister walls gleamed emerald with moss. The stone slabs beneath our feet were chipped and broken. The scent of waxed furniture polish and air freshener was replaced by a rank animal scent, which reminded me of the big cat cages at the zoo. Or maybe it was coming from the dog – not Smut this time, but a great shaggy wolf-like creature.

'I don't believe you have met Boatswain yet?' Byron said. 'My most loyal friend. His only fault being that he cannot play a tolerable hand at cards.'

'Woof-woof!' Rosie leaned over in her buggy in an effort to get a fistful of ghost-fur.

'Two woof-woofs!' Rosie shrilled, as Smut also came snuffling out of the shadows, instantly snorting up the brown banana mush that clung to one of the pushchair wheels.

Just as we were foolishly staring at the dogs, something roared. A great bellowing animal sound echoed through the stone corridors.

'Bloody hell!' Ruby gasped aloud. Rosie's little face froze in utter bewilderment, then creased. Her screams would have been enough to wake the dead – if they weren't already awake, that is.

'Oh shush, shush now!' Ruby whipped her sister out

183

of the buggy to comfort her. 'It's all right, Rosie Posy, it's only a . . . It's only a . . .' Stumped, she turned to Byron. 'Er . . . what is it, Ron?'

Byron smiled faintly. He beckoned to us. 'Follow me, ladies, if you will.'

'Do we have to?' I hung back, but Lauren prodded me from behind.

'Remember that motto?' she snapped at me.

'What motto?'

'The family motto, of course. Didn't you see it over that marble fireplace in the dining room? *Crede Byron.*'

'Well, what the heck does that mean? I'm not exactly an expert on Latin, am I?'

'*Trust,*' Lauren declared. 'It means "Trust in Byron". You don't think he's throwing us to the lions, do you?'

'Who knows how he gets his kicks?' I muttered. I was trying to show Lauren that, unlike her, I wasn't a pushover for Byron's charm. But who was I kidding? I probably would have followed him into the lion's den, had there been one.

Whatever it was, the creature was big. As we followed Byron along the passage, the roar came again like a mighty yawn.

'Allow me to show you the chapel,' Byron drawled over his shoulder. 'It was here that my ancestors said their prayers – and God knows, they needed too.' He pushed open a door to the left of the cloister, and I felt a whoosh of fetid air. The 'chapel' was more like a cave, the windows furred up with grime, the stone walls dripping with damp.

Byron waved his hand. 'As you see, I have put it to

excellent use. It serves very well for my dear dumb friend.'

Naturally I'd seen bears before – at the zoo, on wildlife programmes – but never such a bear. Never such a great hulking, bear-like bear with its alien meaty stink and shaggy, matted coat. The animal appeared to be anchored to one of the pews by a long rusting chain attached to its ankle. It seemed more sad than savage as it lumbered ceaselessly down the aisle of the ruined chapel, nosing its great snout into an empty bucket. The brass spiked collar we'd seen displayed in the library was clamped about its neck.

'Ah, poor thing!' was Ruby's response. 'That's an unusual pet you've got, Ron, but doesn't he, you know, get a bit lonely?'

'Handsome brute, is he not?' Byron drawled. 'He made a most stimulating lodger at my rooms in Cambridge.'

'But doesn't that chain hurt his leg?' Ruby said, as if she was about to remove it herself.

Byron looked at her with interest, amused by such concern. 'Dear Ruby, such a soft little heart you have. I shall loose him presently. He roams freely about the grounds, but the ladies do love to scream and faint at the sight of him, and call him savage.'

We all stood there, staring at the beast as it rummaged and snorted, dragging the bucket clanking across the chapel floor. Then Byron laughed at us, and said this might be the place for pious old monks with their hair shirts, but it was no place for girls with roses in their cheeks.

'Come into the house. The rooms are prepared.

The fires are blazing. The beds are warmed. Follow me.'

Beds? Were we to spend the night here then, in the abbey? None of us protested as a shadowy housemaid, who introduced herself as Lucy, led us back along the gallery and up a short flight of stairs to one of the sumptuous rooms we'd passed earlier. It was one of the state bedrooms, awash with scarlet hangings and throne-like chairs; the great pillared bed was adorned with golden eagles.

Even Ruby seemed a bit disconcerted as she laid Rosie on the richly embroidered quilt. 'Bloody hell. How am I going to change her nappy on this thing?'

'You're not.' I dumped my rucksack on the Turkish carpet. Funny how I could only think clearly when Byron wasn't around. In his presence it was like part of my brain had fallen asleep. I was his to do as he liked with. I could have hung out for eternity at Newstead Abbey like some cobwebby doll in the attic. Shuddering at the thought, I turned to Lauren. 'We can't stay here. Lauren, did you hear me? This isn't real, for God's sake. We can't stay the night here.'

Ruby frowned. 'What are you on about, Abb? We were invited, weren't we? Where d'you expect to sleep, under a gooseberry bush? Sometimes I just don't get you.'

'You realize we have to dress for dinner.' Lauren was gazing into a great walnut-framed mirror and fluffing out her hair. 'If only I'd brought my green velvet dress – you know, the one I got from Oxfam the other week? It would have been perfect.'

At the foot of the bed was one of those chaise longue things women used to recline upon. I flopped down onto it in despair.

'Lauren, I don't believe you.' I held my nose as Ruby wrestled a dirty nappy from Rosie. 'You're waffling on about dressing for dinner. Think about it, Lauren – dinner? Ghosts don't eat dinner, do they?'

'You've got ghosts on the brain, you have,' Ruby chirruped.

I sighed. This was hopeless. I'd suddenly realized we couldn't just waltz out of here, even if Byron let us go. As soon as we slid back a single bolt, the security alarm would go off. There were sure to be video cameras too, watching our every move. How would we ever explain our presence here to a security guard?

While Ruby and Lauren fussed over their hair and make-up, my fingers closed over my mobile. Perhaps I could ring Nathan? He'd know what to do. He was the only outsider who had any idea what was going on. Yes, why not? Suddenly I longed to have Nathan here with me. However, as I punched in the number, my mobile bleeped feebly at me. Weird! I was sure I'd charged it before leaving home. Now it was telling me my battery was dead.

Ruby was squirting herself with clouds of her favourite perfume, Passion. 'It's not just his money, Lor, don't get me wrong. He's so handsome, isn't he? And different to the other blokes I've met. A proper gentleman. Not just after one thing. And he's got proper conversation. And those long words he uses, it's like everything he says is a poem – know what I mean?'

Clearly Lauren didn't know what anything meant any more. Only Rosie, it seemed, was free of Byron's spell as she tottered about the room, pawing priceless ornaments with her sticky fingers.

'Rosie got hat, hat!' Lowering the blue china wash-bowl over her head, she beamed at us.

'Give that to me!' Ruby whisked it off just in time. She replaced it on the ebony washstand with a sigh. 'Oh, Rosie,' she said helplessly, 'whatever am I going to do with you, eh?'

At once a voice said, 'I'll take her for you, madam.'

Even Lauren stopped brushing her hair and stared. Where had she come from, this plump, smiling girl in the long grey dress and starched cap? She held out shapely, capable arms. 'We'll look after the little poppet, won't we, my angel?'

Rosie gurgled in Ruby's arms and held out her plastic teething ring. Obviously this was a gesture of friendship.

'Ruby, I don't think you shou—' I began.

But Ruby was already passing her little sister over, into the arms of the ghost nurserymaid.

'Are you sure?' Ruby said, unable to believe her luck. 'She can be a right little handful, this one.'

The girl jiggled Rosie in her arms. 'I been dandling babies since I was nine years old, miss. We shall be snug as two bugs in the nursery, won't we, little one? There is eggy-peggy and rice pudding with strawberry jam for our tea.' As a dinner gong rang out from below, she added, 'You go on down and enjoy yourself, miss. The master's dinner table is no place for infants.'

'Ruby, you can't— I mean, she's not—' I began, but already Rosie was snuggled contentedly into the ghostly arms. As she was carried off we could hear

188

her chuckling all the way down the passage.

Ruby stood staring after the nurserymaid, a bit dazed. 'Cool or what? I never thought there'd be nannies and stuff to look after the kids. This is the life, eh?'

The life, Ruby said. When actually it wasn't life at all, but death. What should I do? I agonized a moment over whether I should run after that servant, offer to take Rosie myself. So why didn't I?

It occurred to me that this whole thing was different to what Lauren and I had been through before. Before, the ghosts had intruded into *our* world. Now they were drawing us into *their* world. They were the masters here. They knew the game plan, and we just had to fall in with it.

And fall in with it we did. First the dinner gong, and then the maid, Lucy, appeared to take us to the master's dining room – the room we'd seen earlier with its ornate fireplace and the Byron motto – *Crede Byron* – now lit by silver candelabras, the crystal sparkling on the white cloth, a fire crackling.

Byron was already at the table, pouring claret. Not into a glass, but something that looked like – oh God – a human skull!

'What think you of my drinking vessel?' He raised the skull cup to us. As he did so he repeated the lines from 'Lauren's' verse:

> *'Quaff while thou canst: another race,*
> *When thou and thine, like me, are sped,*
> *May rescue thee from earth's embrace,*
> *And rhyme and revel with the dead.'*

It was that 'quaffing' poem again. I shivered as I saw the words inscribed on the side of the skull cup. That's what we were doing, weren't we? Revelling with the dead?

'One of our little discoveries whilst digging beneath the abbey ruins,' he continued. 'I was hoping to find gold – some treasure to furnish this place and pay my debtors – but all we find are the bones of monks. Thank you, Lucy, for bringing my guests. Dear Lucy, she is commander of all the makers and *unmakers* of beds in this household!'

Thereupon Lucy vanished into the shadows, leaving us three timidly standing there. Byron chuckled. 'You should have seen the maidservant when I took over this place from my uncle. Such a flat face and squeaking voice, I cannot tell you. Argh!' He shook his head, and told us to be seated. 'Though I warn you, these cushions might be filled with peach stones, so uncomfortable are they.'

Ruby giggled as she sat down. 'I don't know how you can drink out of some poor bloke's skull, Ron, I really don't.'

'Oh, it's damnably easy,' Byron said. 'One simply puts it to one's lips and' – he demonstrated, draining the skull and refilling it to the brim – 'and quaffs, like so.'

Disconcerted, Ruby gabbled, 'This house of yours is fantastic, Ron. Really. I feel like I'm in a dream.'

The dark red wine in the decanter gleamed like Ruby's hair, I noticed. Byron poured a glass for her. I watched her as she took a sip. Always fiery, now she positively crackled. The candlelight flickered on her skin, dashing sparks from her hair. I expected Byron too would be transfixed by Ruby's glow. What ghost wouldn't? But then, unexpectedly, he turned to me.

'And you, Abigail? Is this how it feels to you, like some dream?'

His eyes fixed on mine as he poured the wine, dark as blood, into my glass. My breath seemed to catch in my throat as I watched my glass fill. If I opened my mouth, a silly little squeak would come out, like that ugly banished maid of his.

Ruby answered for me, her own voice clear as bells. 'Excuse her, Ron. Abbie's a bit gobsmacked. You won't believe this, but she reckons you're not, like, a real bloke 'n' that.' Ruby tittered to show how ridiculous she thought this was.

I could hardly bear to watch Byron's face, the singular raised eyebrow, the drooping lids. 'Not a real fellow? She thinks me a woman, then? Is it the hair, perhaps? The mouth? Do tell, Abigail.' He seemed amused, mocking me. I felt myself colour redder than Ruby's hair. What had she got me into now?

'Oh, she doesn't think you're a woman, Ron,' Ruby roared. 'She thinks you're a ghost!'

Oh. I held my breath. Ruby had said the unsayable. A ghost. *You are a ghost.* I closed my eyes. When I opened them again, the scene would shatter like broken glass. No more Byron. But when I did so, he was still there, still gazing at me in that mildly amused way of his.

'So, you think me a spectre, do you, Abigail? Ha. I have been called many things. A vampire, some would have me.'

'Oh no, Ron. A vampire!' Ruby shrieked. I noticed she'd already glugged a whole glassful of wine and had started on another. 'Why would anyone call you a vampire when you don't look anything like one? Does he, Lor? He hasn't got the teeth, for a start.'

Byron sighed and said he had no idea where the rumour originated. 'For myself I have a personal dislike to vampires. And the little acquaintance I have with them would by no means induce me to reveal their secrets.'

Our first course had arrived. I hadn't been aware of anyone serving it, but here it was, a slice of rosy watermelon in a gold-rimmed dish. Ruby took a forkful, red juice dripping down her chin.

Somehow I found my voice. 'A ghost is a completely different thing to a vampire,' I said.

When Byron looked at you, it was like his eyes were just drifting, searching for something in your face. His voice was so soft it seemed to stroke the air as he said that ghosts and vampires were much the same.

'For me, I sometimes think that life is death,
Rather than life a mere affair of breath.'

Ruby thought this clever and repeated it until it made no sense at all. Lauren, toying sulkily with her melon until now, came to life herself. 'I think your lordship is absolutely right. I mean, we could all be ghosts for all we know. Nobody really understands consciousness – what it is, I mean.'

I began to feel dizzy. Lauren, nibbling on her melon, looked to me like a drowned girl, as if I could see her through a silky skein of water. Ruby dazzled my eyes so much I had to look away.

If I squinted my eyes against the candlelight, I could almost make Lauren and Ruby disappear. I imagined how that would be. Byron and me. Alone. Drinking each other up with our eyes. It was a weird, scary, horrendous thought, and yet . . . Sometimes when his eyes drifted across my face like that, like feathers stroking my skin, well . . . He could take me down into his cold mildewy vault for all I cared. He could lay me in his great oak coffin with its velvet pall, and I would be his love beyond the grave.

But wait a minute. What was I thinking of? Ruby's voice prattling on brought me back to myself.

'If I could just get on TV — just once,' she was saying; 'prove myself, you know? Give it everything I've got. Maybe you know some people in the business, Ron? Are any of them coming to your — what did you call it? — die . . . die . . . ?'

'Diversion.' Byron supplied the word, his eyes lingering regretfully on Ruby's face. Maybe he too was wishing she would shut up. I glared at her. There was such a thing as going too far.

'Diversion. That's it. What I was wondering, Ron, was — when is it exactly, the diversion? And, er . . . who else is performing? I like to know the competition, 'cos—'

'Competition? My dear Ruby, I promise you, you will shine like the morning star.'

'Oh . . .' Ruby sighed. 'D'you think so?'

Shut up, Ruby, put a sock in it! I was sending her this message with my eyes, brain, everything I'd got, but still she wittered on. The more she talked the redder her cheeks got. Maybe it was the fire. Or the wine. Whatever it was, Ruby was scarlet to the roots of her hair.

'Phew!' She actually stopped talking for a second to dab her forehead with an embossed linen napkin. 'It's a bit hot in here, isn't it? I feel like I'm burning up. I feel . . . oh . . .' Her eyes swam about strangely as if they'd ceased to focus. 'I feel a bit strange, to tell you the—'

Then *flump*! And that was it. Ruby couldn't tell us anything. She had crashed forwards onto the table, scattering china and glass as she fell, a sliver of melon peel like a funky slide in her hair.

Chapter Sixteen

Be hypocritical, be cautious, be
Not what you seem, but always what you see.

Back in our gilded bedroom, we somehow managed to manoeuvre the unconscious Ruby beneath the quilt.

Lauren rubbed her shoulder. 'Ouch. I think I've twisted something.'

I sighed. 'Yeah, Ruby's heavier than she looks. And Byron wasn't a lot of help, was he?'

Thinking back to the scene at the dinner table, I felt pretty confused. One minute Byron had been gazing into my eyes, the next Ruby had fallen into her melon. What happened after that? Byron hadn't exactly fanned her feverish face or kissed her back to consciousness. I remembered how disgusted he looked. He even made some scornful comment about sickness in women and how *dreadfully tiresome* it was.

Later, as we'd climbed the stairs, Lauren and I half dragging Ruby between us, I thought I heard pistol shots in the Great Hall, and the sound of men laughing. It was just like I'd read about in the book, and on the plaques. Byron liked nothing better than to hang out with his mates, shooting tops off bottles.

'She's dreaming about him now, just listen to her' –

Lauren eased herself onto the edge of the four-poster, as far away from Ruby as she could get – 'Ron this, Ron that . . .'

'I suppose it's in her blood,' I said. 'You know, wanting to be the centre of attention.'

'Yes, well, it didn't work this time,' Lauren said smugly. 'Lord Byron is a man of taste and refinement after all.'

'Is he? That's not what it says in *Byron's Babes*. It says he wasn't too fussy when it came to women. Posh totty or tarts. Made no difference to him.'

'Mmm . . .' Lauren settled her head upon the pillow and stared dreamily up at the carved eagles. 'I can understand why women were said to faint in his presence. I almost thought I'd faint myself tonight. The way he kept staring at me. Well. It made me feel quite swoony.'

Actually I felt a bit swoony myself. What on earth was in that wine? And anyway, how could you get drunk on spirit wine? All I knew was I needed to get horizontal. Fast.

'Don't worry about me, Lauren,' I sniped. 'You just make yourself comfortable on the bed, won't you?'

'Mmmm . . .' Looked like she already had. Her eyelids were closed, and from the smug little smile flickering on her face I guessed that she too was dreaming of Byron.

'Don't worry about me,' I mumbled into the silence. 'I'll just prop myself up on the chaise longue all night.'

The chaise longue had surely been designed for midgets to recline upon. I couldn't believe that any woman with a normal-sized bottom had ever snuggled up on its taut padded surface. Yet, to my surprise, it wasn't half as uncomfortable as it looked. Once I'd pummelled

196

one of the antique cushions into shape and covered myself with Ruby's coat, I felt myself drifting into that sweet nothingness that precedes sleep.

Not for long though. It seemed like I'd only been asleep ten minutes when I was woken by the sound of a baby crying.

Baby? I pushed the hair out of my eyes, blinking into the darkness. What baby? It took me a few seconds to remember. Rosie! My heart went cold suddenly. For a moment, and this was a dreadful thing to admit, I'd almost forgotten about poor little Rosie, carried off into the ghost world while her big sister dreamed on.

Oh, but the crying was horrible! There was something about it that sent prickles of fear zizzing along my spine. I cupped my hands over my ears. Perhaps it wasn't Rosie at all? Wasn't there something a bit yowly, a bit cat-like about it? Then the cry came again, and it was just the lonely wail of a child who knows no one is going to comfort it.

I glanced over to the bed. Somehow the sound must have penetrated Ruby's dreams. 'Must go . . . find Rosie . . .' she whimpered. Yet still she showed no signs of waking. Her eyelids, smudged with green glitter, fluttered, her lips twitched. She flung out her arms, kicked off the covers.

What should I do? If I tried to wake her up now she'd be a liability, flopping all over the place. She might even be sick after all that wine. As for Lauren, judging from the way she was snoring, rousing her would be like raising the dead.

Raising the dead. Oh God. I shuddered as I pushed

Ruby's coat off my legs. The thought of leaving this room, of venturing out alone into the labyrinth of corridors, made me feel physically sick, but I had no choice. I couldn't just leave Rosie to cry all night, could I?

Rubbing the sleep from my eyes, I forced myself to be calm, to think logically. Rosie was in the nursery, wasn't she? And the nursery was usually at the top of the house. I remembered seeing something about these big old houses on a documentary once – how the nursery was always miles away, so the parents weren't disturbed by the kids when they were giving their dinner parties.

Tugging my zip cardigan around my shoulders, I reached for the lighted candle, which the maid had left us.

'Here goes then,' I whispered aloud. 'Don't worry, Rosie. I'm coming.'

Finding the nursery was a lot more difficult than it sounded. In the day time the abbey had been well lit. Busts and works of art were illuminated with spotlights. Now, of course, everything was in pitch darkness.

As I crept down the stairs from our room and into the draughty space of the East Gallery, I couldn't stop shivering. My candle almost flickered out. This was hopeless. You can't exactly hurry with a candle in your hand; you have to glide really smoothly, like you're a ghost yourself.

I turned right towards the staircase. Apart from the guttering flame, all I had to guide me was Rosie's crying. Yet this was deceptive. The cry seemed to come at me from every direction. Sometimes it seemed to echo from deep within the cloisters, bouncing off the stone walls, gurgling like water in old pipes. Now it sounded so faint and far away, it might be carrying on the wind from a distant village. Now it was close enough to make me jump; as if it came from the far end of the gallery, from the West Wing and Byron's own personal quarters.

I swung round, uncertain which way to go. 'Where the hell are you, Rosie?'

It struck me suddenly that Rosie couldn't just be lying ignored in her cot after all. The way her cries kept changing direction, someone must be carrying her around with them. But who?

Suddenly a pistol shot rang out of the darkness. Voices whooped like a crowd at a football match. Wherever these mates of Byron's were, they were having a hell of a time.

'Don't you lot *ever* sleep?' Muttering to myself like this made me feel a bit less alone.

It didn't help, though, when beneath the laughter I heard another sound. The hollow barking of a dog. Could be Boatswain, I reasoned. Or Smut. Or even that bear, rummaging in its stinking chapel? Now I was shaking so much I had to hold the candlestick with both hands to steady the flame. Perhaps Rosie was back in our room after all? Maybe I should just . . . go back . . . and check?

Coward, I told myself. Think of that poor little kid. If *you're* scared, think of how terrified she must be!

This time, when Rosie's cry sliced through the darkness, I didn't hesitate but allowed it to draw me on, deeper and deeper into the unknown heart of the house.

Thanks to the candlelight I could only see a few feet

ahead of me at a time. Beyond the light, shadows reared – such fantastic shapes that I had to keep telling myself, It's just a vase, a plant stand, a suit of armour, that's all. Sometimes my feet padded across thick carpet, then stone floors, the damp rising into my bones. Once I saw the light of my candle reflected like a star in a great mirror. Once I thought I saw something swift and black like a great wing flapping at the end of a passageway.

'What the——?' I slammed my back so hard against the wall, the candle jolted. Scalding wax dripped over my thumb. It must be one of the monks in his black robes. The abbey booklet mentioned that Byron himself had once seen the ghost of a monk in one of these rooms.

My throat tightened in sheer terror. What kind of a place was this? Spirits piling up through the centuries like jumble in an attic. Ghosts haunting ghosts.

I began to whimper pathetically to myself, 'What am I doing here? How am I gonna get back to that room? Flipping hell, I wish——'

Rosie's cry was even fainter. It had a smothered sound. As if someone was holding a cushion to her face. As if she was giving up.

At once I doubled back, retracing my footsteps, or trying to. Had I been up this staircase before? I couldn't think. I clung to the cold shiny rail, spiralling round and round, until I sensed I was in a new, larger space, and Rosie cried out so loud and close I almost dropped my candle.

Looking round, I realized where I was. The library.

There were no glass cases in this library, just endless shelves of dusty books. I stood staring, eyes adjusting to the shadows. Sometimes those deep, high-backed chairs gave you a start. They looked like people were sitting in them. Then you looked again and saw that no, it was just a chair. Wasn't it? I blinked and held my candlestick higher, so that the shadows drooped like cobwebs on the walls.

Then I saw her. There was a woman sitting in one of those chairs by the marble fireplace. She looked like someone who's been sitting in a doctor's waiting room; as if she had waited a very long time. The baby on her lap was trying to stand up, hands clutching at her sausage curls.

'Rosie want Rube-Rube . . . Rosie want . . .'

I drew in my breath sharply. My hand trembled so much the candle flame shuddered. 'Rosie!' I whispered.

The woman who bounced Rosie on her knee was not the plump little maid who had carried her off for her eggy-peggy. Claire's black ringlets mingled with Rosie's spaghetti curls as she bent her head protectively over her charge.

Without thinking, I took a step towards her. 'Give her to me. She's not yours. She's not Allegra.'

Byron's dumped girlfriend didn't even look at me. She crooned to the baby, 'Give her up, the lady says. Haven't we just plucked you out of your cradle, little one? Left to cry in this great house while his lordship shoots his pistols and cavorts with his wicked friends? Left to cry her little self to exhaustion, were you not, my pet? My lambkin . . .'

To my amazement this crooning seemed to have a good effect on Rosie. She began plucking at the lace

201

collar of Claire's dress. 'Mummmumumym . . . Rube–
Rube . . .'

I held out my arms. 'Give her to me and I'll take her
to her sister.'

Claire responded by taking hold of Rosie's hands and
clapping them between her own. '*Pat-a-cake, pat-a-cake,
baker's man, bake me a cake as fast as you can . . .*'

What the hell could I do? Gentle persuasion was
hardly going to cut it. Perhaps I should just grab her?
Could I do that? Could I wrestle a live human child out
of a ghost's arms? I was just thinking how to go about
this when Claire seemed to twig. She wasn't sitting in the
chair any more but standing against the fireplace, Rosie
secure in her arms.

'Do not ask me. I will never ever give the child to *him*.
Never.'

'I won't give her to Lord Byron, if that's what you
mean,' I said. 'I'm giving her back to her sister, that's all.
She's not Allegra. She's not your child. Her name is
Rosie. Rosie Blagg.'

The mention of Allegra only made things worse
though. You could actually *feel* Claire's grief, the raw ache
of it, stealing over the room.

'He took my Allegra.' Claire spoke with icy calm. 'He
said I was not fit. I was too poor. I had no home of my
own, no husband to care for me. He took my Allegra to
his villa. What a pretty doll she was, to be played with and
caressed until he grew weary of her.' Her eyes burned
black upon me, as I struggled under a weight of tears.
'The stories I heard. Allegra's nurse reported such things.
One time he threw our child into the lake to see if she

202

might swim. 'Twas a wonder she did not drown.' Clutching Rosie tighter, she said, 'I shall not part with her again.'

'But she's not Allegra, she's Rosie Blagg!' I tried again. Then I thought of another tack I might try. 'Listen, your Allegra is dead. She needs you, doesn't she, on the Other Side? I can hear her calling you now—'

'No!'

I had planned to make a grab for Rosie. I'd forgotten one vital thing though. When you're carrying a lighted candle, it's a good idea to set it down before you decide to arm-wrestle someone. Instead of which, I lunged forwards, candle flying out of my hand and fizzling out in the fall.

I'd completely missed the spook mother and child. The gloom gathered around me like a blanket, as if shielding them from my sight.

'Rosie! Rosie?' I called.

I might have heard something. The faintest hint of Rosie's babble echoing from God knew where. Then nothing. Even her voice was snuffed out, as if it had never existed. Claire Clairmont had gone. And she'd taken Rosie with her.

Chapter Seventeen

. . . for I wish to know
What after all are all things — but a show?

Someone was knocking on the door. I opened my eyes to find myself lying on the Regency chaise longue. Ruby's coat was thrown over me and the antique cushion was stuffed beneath my head.

'Wakey, wakey then, young ladies. Rise and shine!' The creepy attendant had just pushed open the door and sidled right in, uninvited. Hands clapped roughly. 'Chop-chop. It'll be more than my life's worth if they find you in here.'

I sat up at once, clutching the cushion to my chest. How had I found my way back here last night? My head felt muzzy. Vaguely I remembered the baby's cries, luring me through the sleeping house to the library; Claire Clairmont with Rosie on her lap. Flipping hell! Rosie . . . Where was she now?

I glanced over to the four-poster bed, where Lauren and Ruby were only just stirring. Did Claire really have Rosie in her clutches? I scratched my head. Supposing I'd dreamed the whole thing? How could I tell Ruby, and risk sending her into total hysterics over a dream?

The attendant stood in the doorway, rubbing his hands

together. 'Bit of a heavy night, eh?' He winked horribly at me. 'Burning the candle at both ends, was you?'

'You . . .' I began. 'You knew. I mean, you left us here. You locked the doors . . .'

The man shrugged. 'We do our best to clear the place, but sometimes people get left behind. Bed comfortable, was it?'

Lauren propped herself up on one elbow. 'What on earth are *you* doing here?'

Anyone would think she was Lady Byron already, the way she stared scornfully at the attendant through a cloud of hair.

'Yeah, what *are* you doing here?' I echoed her. Was this man somehow in league with Byron? Maybe it was a habit of his, procuring young girls to entertain his lordship throughout the night.

The man didn't bother to explain himself. Crossing the room, he wrenched back the drapes. A thin sunlight flooded in. Daylight! The outside world! My heart leaped. I didn't know about the others, but I for one couldn't wait to breathe fresh air, to see real live people again. Almost at once I felt guilty. What about poor little Rosie?

Then, seeing my cardigan draped over a chair where I'd left it last night, I began to favour the it-was-all-a-dream scenario. How could it be otherwise? I mean, traipsing through this house in the middle of the night? Alone? Even thinking about it gave me the wobbles.

'I asked you a question,' Lauren persisted. 'I said, what are you doing here?'

At the windows the man turned. Caught in a shaft of

205

sunlight, he seemed insubstantial suddenly, like a ghost himself. 'Just doing my job, miss. I'm the caretaker. I *take care* of things, if you know what I mean. I could have thrown you girls out last night. But I could see you had nowhere to go, couldn't I? I let you girls have this room for the night 'cos I'm soft hearted, see. Too soft hearted for my own good, I am.'

'Very kind of you, I'm sure.' Ruby sat up at last, shaking out her hair. 'But as a matter of fact, we were invited to stay here by the owner, Ron Lord. And we're not going anywhere until Ron tells us we're no longer welcome, OK?'

The attendant folded his arms. He shook his head ruefully. 'How I do like a young lady with a bit of *spirit*. The thing is, miss, his lordship don't keep normal hours, as you might say. His lordship, see, he retires at dawn and rises just before dusk, when the house closes.'

'That's OK' – Ruby rubbed her bare arms – 'we can amuse ourselves until he gets up, can't we, Abb, Lor?'

'Certainly,' Lauren agreed. 'And frankly, Mr . . . *whoever* you are, I don't think his lordship would care for the way you treat his guests.'

Slipping Ruby's coat over me as I stood up, I said, 'Yeah, he might think you're a dirty old pervert barging in here without even knocking.'

'Please yourselves.' The man picked a gob of wax out of his ear and examined it as if it was far more interesting to him than we were. 'But I should warn you, we're expecting a coachload of Americans from the Byron Society any minute now. Course, if you really want to be gawped at by a lot of strangers while you're getting . . . er, hem' – he cleared his throat – 'dressed, and, er . . . titivating yourselves or whatever you young ladies do in the mornings, then that's up to you. On the other hand, I could just call security and have you thrown out of here.'

'This is outrageous!' Lauren exclaimed, already reaching for her clothes. 'You can be sure that his lordship will hear of this.'

'Yeah, and he'll most likely sack you on the spot,' Ruby joined in. 'I'm supposed to be giving a performance tonight,' she added, as if that made all the difference.

'Tonight? Excuse me, miss, but here's me thinking you're giving a bit of a performance already. Well then. Twenty minutes then, young ladies. I'll put the rope up to keep the visitors out in the meantime, and I'll be waiting for you at the end of the gallery, all right?'

The doors were wide open now. Securing the crimson plaited rope with brass catches, he disappeared, leaving us to struggle into our clothes.

'Bloody cheek!' Ruby combed out swathes of auburn hair with her fingers. 'Not even a cup of tea on offer. Ron'll be livid when he finds out.'

I reached for my clothes. As I wriggled into my sweater, Claire Clairmont's posh, piping voice sang in my head . . . *Pat-a-cake, pat-a-cake . . . baker's man . . .* At once, the vision of Rosie, her little hands held between Claire's, flooded back to me. I paused, one empty sweater-arm dangling. Could a dream be that vivid? Supposing it really *had* happened? Supposing Rosie was never seen or heard of again? Supposing I was the very last person to hear her cries before she was borne away into the world of spirits?

'Ruby,' I began, 'what about, er . . . Rosie?'

'Rosie?' Ruby changed out of the dress she'd slept in and into jeans with a glittery butterfly appliquéd on the back pocket. 'She'll be fine. She's in good hands.'

'Um, shouldn't you check though, Ruby? Just to make sure?'

Ruby looked at me as if I was stupid. 'I did check. Last night.'

I shook my head. 'Sorry, Ruby, but you were dead to the world last night. You were knocking back that wine like it was going out of fashion. You passed out in the dining room. Don't you remember?'

Ruby looked devastated. 'I did? Oh no, you're kidding me!'

'No kidding,' I assured her.

'Abbie and I had to practically carry you upstairs.' Lauren gave her shoulder an experimental waggle. 'It wasn't easy. In fact I think I may have dislocated my shoulder.'

Ruby hid her face in her hands. 'Oh no. What did Ron say? Was he, like, totally disgusted?'

I shrugged, as I struggled to button my own jeans. 'I don't think so. He just went off with his mates. I heard them shooting their pistols, laughing in the Great Hall. Anyway, Ruby, you've got more important things to worry about than what Ron— I mean, Byron thinks. Like Rosie.'

Ruby sighed. 'I told you. I woke up in the night. Well, I thought I heard her crying. You and Lauren were flat out, so I went up to check on her.'

208

I looked at her, astonished. 'And . . . er . . . what did you find?' I hardly dared ask.

Ruby's face lit up suddenly. 'Oh, Abb, you should see the nursery! It's fantastic. Just like you see in old films. It's got a rocking horse with a saddle and a real horse's mane and everything. And there's this fantastic doll's house with every room beautifully furnished, and real little velvet curtains and wallpaper and stuff.'

'Nursery. You found the nursery?' I held my breath.

'Yeah. It's right at the top of the house, in this huge, like, attic place.' Ruby sat before the mirror, and began defining her generous lips with cherry lip-liner.

I gaped at her. 'And Rosie . . . was . . . OK?'

'Like I said, more than OK. She was sound asleep in this gorgeous cradle. It was all hung with white lace, I tell you, fit for a princess. That's what she looked like. A princess—' Ruby broke off, gazing into the distance. It struck me suddenly that she was probably thinking of that other cot, back in Warren Road, with the paint all scratched and the creaking hinges.

'But won't she be upset if you don't go and see her? I mean, being among strangers and everything?'

Ruby considered a moment. Then she said brightly, 'If I go up there now, she'll only get upset, see. And then she'll want to come with us, and God knows what we'll do with her if we've got to hang around the grounds until dusk. Anyway, I spoke to that nurse or nanny or whatever she is last night, and she said she'd be only too happy to look after her for the day.'

Ruby seemed like she was trying to convince herself. 'And then I've got to practise for tonight. I can't practise

209

with Rosie to look after. It'd be cruel to take her out of that nursery. She's got that nanny to make a fuss of her and tell her rhymes and that. Tell you what, I bet she's on that rocking horse right now, having the time of her life.'

Still, as we shoved the last of our belongings into our bags, Ruby paused in the doorway. She looked confused, as though torn between the nursery and her career.

'Ruby, I . . . last night . . .' I began.

'What about it?'

I hesitated. 'Oh, nothing.' What could I say? If Ruby claimed she'd seen her baby sister happily sleeping in her cot last night, then clearly *one* of us had to be dreaming. I just hoped it was *me*.

In any case, Ruby had made up her mind. She was already flouncing ahead of us along the gallery, sweeping right past the attendant who waited by the EXIT sign. At once he lurched forwards to intercept her.

'This way please, young ladies' – he beckoned to us – 'you'll have to go through the back, by the servants' stairs. Mind you don't trip, that's it.'

The stairs were steep and narrow and smelled of cats. Our footsteps clattered on the shiny green lino. The doors at the bottom were arched like doors in a church. I noticed the attendant's wormy white fingers as he slid back the bolts.

'Remember, no admittance,' he said as if reciting through some rule book. 'Not until five thirty. Be good girls now. Don't do anything I wouldn't do.' His wheezy laughter followed us out into the daylight. The door slammed behind us.

'Well,' Ruby said, 'he's got a nerve!'

'Revolting little man,' decided Lauren. 'I thought Lord Byron said he'd got rid of the bad faces when he took over the abbey.'

'I don't think he cared about the men having bad faces,' I said. 'Only the women.'

Ruby giggled and flapped her arms against her sides. 'Well, what do we do for the next eight hours?'

'Don't know,' I said. 'But we could start with breakfast. That melon we had last night wouldn't keep a flea going.'

We crossed the grass, still silvered with dew, in search of a café. A good thing the gates hadn't opened to the public yet. There hadn't been time to investigate the grounds yesterday; now we had them to ourselves.

'Must be hundreds of acres Ron's got,' Ruby kept saying, as we took in the sweep of lawns, the glittering rectangle of water. Beyond these were smaller gardens hemmed about by dark box hedges. Through iron-grilled gates we glimpsed stone fountains and statues. Peacocks were strutting about, their thin piercing cries reminding me horribly of Rosie last night. A dream, I told myself once again; that's all it was. Still, I felt horribly guilty as we followed the signpost to BOATSWAIN'S CAFÉ. Who really was looking after Rosie? And what on earth would *her* breakfast be? We followed a pine-scented path shaded by giant cedars. To the left of us, tracks plunged down to soupy ponds clogged with weed. There was a scent of late honeysuckle and cut grass in the air. The sun shone through transparent veils of cloud, warm enough for me to roll my sleeves up.

Boatswain's Café was housed in the old coach house.

Inside, it was cosy, with a hissing tea urn and pictures of Byron's favourite dog on the walls. A woman in a nylon overall served us rolls and marmalade. Not quite what I had in mind for breakfast but better than nothing. I poured tea from the metal pot and tipped in a snowstorm of sugar just to cheer myself up.

Ruby sat fiddling with her hair slides, unclipping then repositioning them, a long stray red hair looping itself in the marmalade. She didn't seem her usual sunny self suddenly.

Spreading her roll with butter, she said, 'She'll be all right. Rosie, I mean. I bet she's getting a better breakfast than we are in fact — eggs and stuff. That nurse I spoke to, she said she'd come from a big family herself. Funny how Rosie just seemed to take to her . . .'

Lauren nibbled the edge of her roll, as if she suspected it of being poisoned. 'To think I was expecting smoked salmon and scrambled egg. That seems like a Byron-ish sort of breakfast, don't you think?'

'Seeing as he never got up till about five, I don't suppose he bothered with breakfast,' I said. 'It was probably straight down to the claret and roast partridge and that.'

A vision came to me suddenly of the poet sprawled on his silken sheets, dark curls tumbling, quill and inkstand by the bed for those moments of inspiration. It was horrible. Even in daylight, in this café with a radio burbling in the background and the clink of china, I could feel Byron's hold on me. It was weird how, while I longed to feast my eyes on his total gorgeousness again, at the same time I couldn't wait to be out of here.

Ruby's chatter brought me back to the present. 'Did I tell you it's going to be a solo performance? Just little ol' me. Imagine' – she giggled – 'Ron's invited some of his mates. He told me they have a wild time up here, dress up as monks and get totally plastered. That skull he drunk out of last night that he dug up from the abbey ruins – well, he's got several of them, and—'

'How do you know all that?' Lauren interrupted crossly.

Ruby looked confused a moment. She stroked the lucky rabbit's foot charm around her neck. 'I don't know. He must've told me last night. Yeah, I think it was after I went to the nursery to find Rosie.'

'You saw him after that?' I cupped my hands around my mug to warm them.

Ruby put a hand to her head. 'Yeah. Well, I must've done. I saw him with his mates – bit of a wild bunch, drunk as skunks. He offered me a drink from one of them skulls.' She gave a little shudder. 'It was all right. Just a bit of a laugh, you know.'

'Hilarious,' I mumbled into my teacup.

'You might have caught something,' Lauren said. 'Probably that monk died of some terrible disease. It might have been the plague.'

'Ha ha,' Ruby laughed. 'Plague. Honestly, Lauren. The skulls are all cleaned up and mounted – he didn't just dig it up from the ground and fill it with booze.'

Lauren frowned doubtfully. I guessed she wasn't concerned for Ruby's health. She was just jealous that Ruby had some private meeting with Byron. This was all getting out of hand. Byron couldn't do this to us, could he? Set us against each other? He wasn't even alive, for heaven's sake! How could a ghost make us lose our reason with one scornful flip of his eyebrows. It was crazy.

I took a last comfortless sip of lukewarm tea. Somehow I had to get Lauren on my side. I had to get her thinking straight. Then we might stand a chance of rescuing Rosie and getting the hell out of this place.

'Well anyway,' Ruby declared, 'I'm alive, aren't I? In fact I feel great, on top of the world. Know what, I reckon Ron's planting some sort of talent scout in the audience. Someone from the TV world maybe. Between you and me, I heard the abbey was going to be the venue for the next *Pop Idol* contest. No, really. So all I need to do is get my act together.' She glanced out of the window to the grounds, already filling up with tourists and coaches. 'I got to find somewhere in the grounds to rehearse. Somewhere quiet. You guys can tell me what you think. I want it to be perfect for tonight.'

Lauren and I almost ducked beneath the table as she suddenly broke into song. Hurriedly, we stood up, scraping back our chairs.

'OK, Ruby, let's find somewhere quiet then,' I said.

We left the café and turned left at a sign pointing to THE WILDERNESS, which Ruby decided would be perfect for her private rehearsals. As she sashayed ahead of us, humming tunes to herself, I prodded Lauren lightly in the back.

'Lauren, we've got to stop this.' By 'this', I meant Byron, the abbey, us being here at all.

But Lauren just batted a fly away from her face and

said she couldn't see why. 'If you want my opinion, Ruby's about to make a complete fool of herself.' She shook her head. 'That girl is so sad. Doesn't she realize that's all she is to him? A bit of cheap entertainment?'

I gaped at her open-mouthed. 'Is she? Then what are *we* to him, Lauren?'

She gave me a long meaningful look. At least, it would have been meaningful if I had understood what it meant. 'I can't answer for *you*, Abbie,' was all she said.

'Well, answer for your flipping self then.' I was beginning to lose my cool – not that I ever had much.

Lauren gave one of her exasperated sighs. 'Look, face it, Abbie, we're talking about *souls* here. And if you want my opinion, Byron's soul and mine are like that . . .' She folded her hands over her heart.

'Like what? What's with the heart thing?'

'I mean, we are eternally bonded – you know, like, we recognize each other from a former life. Well, you've heard of soul-mates . . .'

'Soul-mates? But Lauren, he's dead and you're alive. At least, if you have a soul it's still in your body somewhere, and his is, well, it's somewhere else . . .'

I was confusing myself now. No wonder Lauren lost the thread and hurried to catch up with Ruby – pretending to be her friend, when all she wanted was for Ruby to make a total divvy of herself. It made me feel sick. Why wouldn't anyone listen?

As I trailed miserably after the two of them towards the thickening trees of the 'wilderness', I was aware of the abbey, the great stony bulk of it. As if the house itself was gloating over my efforts to warn the others.

215

All those endless rows of windows watching us like eyes.

Some distance behind us, a coachload of people were trooping up the gravel driveway and heading for the entrance. I glanced back over my shoulder. They must be the American members of the Byron Society the attendant had warned us about. They wore white sneakers and baseball caps; cameras bumped around their necks. If only I could be part of that crowd! Ordinary. Safe. Mooching about looking at pictures, then home to tea with a souvenir pen and a postcard.

If only . . . I hesitated, still gazing back at the crowd.

'Abbie!' Lauren was calling. 'Are you coming, or what?'

'In a minute.'

Someone in the crowd caught my eye suddenly. Wasn't that . . . ? I watched as he stood back, gazing up at the abbey. Even then, it wasn't until he focused his camera on the ruined arches that I knew.

Nathan!

Nathan turned towards me and waved.

I looked back at Lauren. 'You two go on if you like!' I shouted, hardly able to believe what I saw. 'Nathan's here.'

Chapter Eighteen

He turn'd his lip to hers, and with his hand
Call'd back the tangles of her wandering hair;
Even then their love they could not all command,
And half forgot their danger and despair . . .

The minute he saw me, Nathan threw his arms out wide. And guess what? I went hurtling straight into them. In fact you could say we threw ourselves at each other so hard, it was more like a head-on collision than a hug. Even Nathan seemed a bit taken aback as he staggered slightly under my weight.

'Hey, hey, I know you're pleased to see me, I have this effect on all the girls, but watch out for the goods, yeah?'

His camera equipment, he meant, which I'd very nearly knocked flying. I pulled myself free of his arms, embarrassed. What could I be thinking of? This was so not the way to behave when I was totally off men.

'Don't get the wrong idea or anything,' I said, 'but, well, it's nice to see, you know, a friendly face. Anyway, what is all this gumph? You look like a one-man film crew.'

Nathan spread his arms and grinned. 'I *am* a one-man film crew.'

He glanced up at the upper windows of the house

glittering in the thin sunshine. 'Is his nibs about then? D'you reckon he could spare me a few minutes of his valuable time?'

I looked away at the tourists milling about the entrance. 'Nathan, it's not funny. What's happening here, I mean.'

'Where are your mates then?'

I glanced back along the path where I'd left Ruby and Lauren. Now there was no sign of them. Curious. I'd expected they'd at least come over and interrogate Nathan about what he was doing here.

I shrugged. 'They must've wandered off. We'd better catch them up.'

Nathan shook his head. 'Was it something I said?'

'Listen, don't take it personally. They're both so besotted with Byron, they'd hardly notice if Robbie Williams himself were to show up.' I winced inwardly at my hypocrisy. I mean, there I was, talking as if I were totally immune to the poet's ghostly charms, which was *so* not true. But I didn't want Nathan to know this.

As we walked back towards the wilderness area, I began telling him what had been going on. How the attendant had fixed it for us to spend the night in the abbey. How we had 'dined' with Byron and met his tame bear; how I'd tracked down Rosie in the library and found her in the arms of Claire Clairmont.

'Although that might have been a dream. It must have been, 'cos Ruby reckons she heard Rosie crying in the night, and found her tucked up in her cot in this nursery, with—'

'Wait a minute,' Nathan interrupted me. 'You mean the kid is still in there, in the house?'

'Yep. It's so awful, I can hardly bear to think about it. The trouble is, we just can't get through to Ruby. She actually spoke to this weird spook nursemaid, and now she thinks Rosie's in good hands, being cared for like a princess. And anyway, she's so full of herself over this performance tonight. She thinks it's her big chance. And as for Lauren, she's totally lost the plot. Seems to think she'll be the next Lady Byron.'

Nathan shook his head. 'Sorry, but this is all a bit hard to swallow. As spirits go, this guy is a bit over the top, isn't he? I mean, throwing dinner parties, and laying on the dancing bear entertainment. I told you, my gran was a psychic, but this lot would have done her head in.' He paused. 'If only I could get it on camera. What a scoop.'

I groaned. 'I've heard spooks don't photograph well. Anyway, does your paper know you're here?'

'They sent me, didn't they.' Nathan looked pleased with himself. 'Told Bob, my editor, this local girl had won an audition to sing at Newstead. Convinced the old bugger she was the next Britney Spears, and he fell for it.'

'Clever.'

'Yeah, well, I had to feed him a line. Couldn't tell him I was planning an "At Home" feature with Lord Byron, could I? Still, if my cunning plan works, it's goodbye to *The Buzz* and hello Fleet Street—' He broke off. 'Abbie? What's wrong?'

I was silent. I concentrated on the path, scraping lines in the gravel with the toe of my trainer. It had struck me suddenly that Nathan was as bad as Ruby. All they could think about was the big break, the lucky chance, the scoop. Hardly anyone, it seemed, had given a thought to how we might rescue a live human baby from a ghoul.

'Nothing,' I said. If he didn't know, there was no point in my telling him. But then, unexpectedly, he reached out and took my hand.

'I know what you're thinking. You're thinking I don't care about Rosie. I do. Listen, that kid's not going to come to any harm. Sod the pictures. If I get them, great; if not . . . I'm here to help you, Abbie. It was *you* I came up here for, not Byron.'

'Was it?' I hardly knew what to say. It was so strange, the effect of Nathan's hand on mine. It made me safe but excited at the same time. How warm it was. How human! I imagined how Byron's hands would feel if they touched you, limp and cold as dead fish. I shuddered.

'You OK?' Nathan said.

I smiled at him. 'Yeah. I'm OK. But I really think we ought to go and find the others now.'

The sign to the wilderness area led us through an ancient yew walk. The trees here were so old their roots dug in like clenched toes. The air was dim and soupy. The unseasonable October warmth had brought out the flies in huge swarms, bashing into our hair and eyes, crawling over my bare arms even as I beat them off. The flies had a repulsive reddish glitter to them, as if they'd been feasting on blood.

I flapped my arms in panic. 'Get off, you little bastards!'

Nathan laughed. 'They must think you smell nice. Come here a minute.'

'What?'

'You've got one in your hair.'

'Ugh!'

How did I ever fall for that old trick? Still, when Nathan kissed me, I forgot all about flies. All I could feel were his lips fluttering over my face, the warmth of his hand on my lower back as he pressed me closer. Just when I was getting to like this a lot, he pulled away with a sigh, like it took a real effort.

'Don't worry, I haven't finished with you yet.' His voice sounded all thick and husky. 'But we'll have to pick up where we left off some other time. If we're going to find Rosie, we should get a move on, preferably before his lordship wakes up.'

'Yeah. Right. Of course.' I knew Rosie should be our priority. Even so, I couldn't help feeling a bit dazed as Nathan tugged me on down the path, right into the clearing where Lauren and Ruby sat.

Lauren glanced up reluctantly from her copy of *Don Juan*. She greeted us with a cool, 'Oh, it's you.'

Nathan grinned. 'How's it going, Lauren?'

'Well, everything *was* going fine,' Lauren said. 'Although what the press are doing here, I can't imagine.'

'Hiya, Nate!' Ruby waved, then carried on doing her exercises. At least I assumed they were exercises. She was doing some strange waggly thing with her arms, and breathing in so hard, her chest expanded to eye-goggling proportions. I glanced sideways at Nathan to see if he'd noticed this. Maybe he had. Already he'd whipped out his camera and was snapping dementedly away in Ruby's direction.

Ruby left off exercising at once. 'Hey, do you mind?

221

Put that camera away. I've hardly got any make-up on.'

'You don't need it, Rube,' Nathan assured her. 'A face like yours, you'll knock Ron dead. I mean, you would knock him dead if he wasn't dead already.'

Ruby stood, hands on hips, rolling her eyes at Lauren and me. 'What is he like? And if you don't mind my asking, Nate, what're you, like, *doing* here?'

Nathan tapped his camera. 'Isn't it obvious? Heard you were going to be the star turn up here. Can't miss a moment like that, girl. You want pictures for your portfolio, don't you?'

Ruby looked unsure, then pleased. 'Yeah, s'pose I do. Oh, well anyway, thanks. But please, Nate, no more pictures till I say so, eh? One bad picture can ruin a girl's career – know what I mean?'

Lauren snorted. 'You don't imagine his lordship will let *him* into the abbey tonight? It's by invitation only. And the press, as far as I know, are not invited.'

I groaned. 'Oh lighten up, Lauren, do. It's only Nathan. It's not the paparazzi.'

Nathan slipped the camera back in its case. 'No problem, Ruby. Whatever you say. Although getting a bad picture of you would be next to impossible.'

Ruby denied this, but glowed with pleasure all the same. Poor Ruby. Did she really think Nathan had come all this way to take publicity shots? If only she knew his real quarry was her precious 'Ron', and that even now his eyes were scouring the back windows for a sighting.

'Tell you what, Rube,' Nathan said, really casual. 'Where's that little sister of yours? Now I got my stuff, I

222

could use up some film on her, playing in the gardens and that . . .'

Ruby's manner changed at once. She nodded uncertainly towards the house. 'Better leave her where she is for now. Didn't Abb tell you? She's got a whole nursery to herself – nannies, nursemaids and that. Ron thinks of everything. I'll look in on her around teatime, when the gates close, to say night-night.'

When nobody spoke, Ruby added defensively, 'Well, it's hard work, you know, lugging Rosie everywhere, keeping her amused.' She sank down on the bench next to Lauren. She looked wretched suddenly, picking at the glittery logo on her jeans pocket as if she couldn't look us in the eye. As if she was really torn. 'I know she's my sister and that, and I love her to bits. I do really. But sometimes . . . well . . .' She sighed. 'Sometimes it's just good to think of yourself for once.' She stared defiantly into our faces. 'You don't know. You've got no idea what it's like.'

'But Ruby,' I said, not for the first time, 'you shouldn't have to lug your sister around. It's about time your mum stopped dumping her on—'

'She's not dumping her!' Ruby almost bit my head off. 'I mean, sorry, Abb, but you just don't understand, OK? Let's leave it at that, shall we? Anyway' – she laughed, embarrassed by her outburst – 'don't look so worried, you lot. My Rosie's probably up there right now, pulling the mane out of that rocking horse and giving the nurses hell. "Rosie want . . . Rosie want . . ." Drive them round the bend, she will.'

Nathan and I glanced uncomfortably at one another.

This was our first task. Somehow we had to get the baby out. We had to hope to God she was all right.

As the day wore on and the abbey grounds filled with tourists, we grew more and more desperate. At one point Nathan had the idea of joining the coach trippers in a tour of the house, to see if he could find the nursery or catch a glimpse of Rosie. But a couple of hours later he was back again, reporting nothing but portraits and antiques and waffling tour guides.

'Just look at her,' I murmured to Nathan as Ruby went happily on with her lung-expanding exercises. 'She has no idea of the danger Rosie's in.'

'Hey,' Nathan said, chucking me under the chin. 'Have faith in me, right? We'll get it sorted.'

I wished I could be so sure.

The clock on the tower struck five, and Nathan and I were still no closer to rescuing Rosie. We were all getting impatient as we gulped a final mug of tea in the café.

Ruby drummed her pearly fingernails on the tabletop. 'I need to get inside and do my make-up and have a bath. I need to see the stage too. I don't get Ron really. 'S'all right for him, snoring his head off all day while we freeze to death out here. I mean, why doesn't he let us into his private quarters? Those rooms upstairs aren't open to the public, are they?'

Ignoring her, Lauren glared at Nathan. 'Oh, and by the way, Nathan, let's get this straight — I don't want you flashing your camera around when he appears, and spoiling things.'

'Me? Spoiling things?' Nathan looked innocent.

'You might frighten him off with that thing,' Lauren said.

'Nah. He'll love it. A poseur like him — are you kidding?'

Lauren folded her arms on the table. 'Don't think I'm stupid, Nathan. I know what your game is. And it won't work.'

'It won't?'

'All the so-called spirit photos have been spoofs.' She flung back her hair. 'Spirits only appear to the most sensitive people. You don't imagine they cavort around saying "cheese" for the camera, do you?'

'What *is* all this?' Ruby cut in irritably. 'I'm sick of all this talk about spirits and spooks all the time.'

Lauren went perilously on, 'Don't you think if it was possible someone would have done it already?'

'Oh, they have,' Nathan said easily. 'In fact if you want statistics, Lauren, ninety-five per cent of spook pictures have been proved fake. Mostly double exposures, that kind of thing. That leaves five per cent unaccounted for.'

Ruby had scraped back her chair and stood looking at us with the expression of someone who's been pushed too far. 'Spirits. Ghosts. You know, sometimes I wonder about you lot.' She clenched her fists. 'You're all meant to be intelligent. Staying on at school, taking all those exams and that. Me, I'm meant to be the thick one, just because I work at Pizza Pronto, because I never passed an exam in my life. Well, if that's what being clever is all about, I'm glad I'm stupid, that's all I can say . . .'

She clutched at her throat suddenly. 'And I shouldn't

even be shouting like this, it stresses the vocal cords. I should be resting my voice for tonight. Look' – she regarded us all – 'you lot stay here if you want, but I'm going back to the house right now. I'm going to *demand* they let me in. Now!'

Chapter Nineteen

. . . a monk, array'd
In cowl and beads and dusky garb, appear'd,
Now in the moonlight, and now lapsed in shade,
With steps that trod as heavy, yet unheard . . .

Ruby didn't head straight for the front entrance, but doubled back across the lawns, which led around to the back of the house. Did I say 'lawns'? The grass round here must grow quickly. The manicured rectangles had given way to whispery tangles of reed-like grasses. What was going on here?

I hesitated. 'We're going the wrong way, aren't we? How long does it take for grass to grow?'

'My dad reckons it grows as soon as he looks at it,' Nathan said. 'What is this, *Gardener's World*?'

I shook my head. 'This was a lawn a few minutes ago. Now it's like Florida swampland. Either someone's just sprinkled it with instant-grow fertilizer, or something weird is happening.'

Nathan glanced around. 'Yeah, and where *is* everybody?'

The visitors, he meant. One minute you were falling over the Happy Families; next, there was nothing but empty vistas of overgrown parkland. The sky took on a strange metallic glint. A solitary crow flapped overhead croaking like a duck.

'I expect they've all piled into the café,' Lauren said in withering tones. 'Stoking up with tea and buns before they get on their silly little bus.'

We stood watching as a flock of geese took off, skimming the surface of the lake, the sound of their wings like curtains ripping. The lake looked smaller, murkier, its edges fringed with clumps of yellowy reeds.

I rubbed my Bump of Wisdom, confused. Sometimes it really is hard to believe the evidence of your own eyes. Had there really been a well-kept parkland here? Or were the lawns and flowerbeds and signposted scenic routes just a fake? Maybe the real Newstead was actually this tumbling wilderness, the house itself swamped by ivy, spreading like gloved fingers across the stonework. Only the gothic arches of the original abbey were as before. Except that the clouds they framed belonged to another time. I was sure of that.

'What the . . . ?' Nathan pointed his camera at the trees. 'What the hell is that?'

We stared. The neat yew walk we'd strolled through earlier was now a rambling forest of rotting branches and bracken. A dark shape was moving among the trees, in and out of the shadows. It had a slow, lumbering walk. As it passed, branches snapped, bushes trembled.

Nathan adjusted his lens and clicked. 'Bloody hell, what is that thing?'

'Byron's bear,' I said slowly. 'It used to roam freely about the grounds. He told us. The house must have closed. The house has closed, and Byron's woken up at last. We're back in *his* world.' I turned to Nathan, once again relieved he was with us.

He reached for my hand. 'Come on, we'd better catch up with Ruby.'

Ruby might have reached the house by now if it hadn't been for her footwear. Stiletto heels are not the best things for wading through prairie grass after all. But the change of scenery was the last thing on Ruby's mind as we caught her up.

'There he is!' She nodded at the man watching us from the raised terrace. The attendant. He was standing in front of that door he'd ejected us from earlier. I had the feeling he'd been watching us for some time.

'It's that miserable old duffer who turfed us out,' Ruby said. 'I'm going to ask him straight what's going on.'

The last thing I wanted to do was go back inside that house. But I knew we had to. We had to get Rosie out. All Ruby seemed concerned about, though, was tonight's performance.

'Well, are you going to let us in now, or what?' She confronted the caretaker, arms folded. 'I'm supposed to be the star turn at Ron's concert tonight, and if you don't mind, I'd like to change into my costume.'

The man looked her over approvingly. 'Want to glam yourself up a bit, do you, dear? Better put something warm on then. Didn't his lordship mention? It's to be an open-air concert, as it were.'

'Open air?' Ruby cried. 'You've got to be joking.'

Nathan stepped forward suddenly. 'Look, cut the crap, mate, and let us in, eh?'

At the sight of Nathan, the attendant's mood changed.

Holding out his arm to bar him from passing, he said, 'Oh no you don't. The young lady can go and make herself beautiful for tonight, if she wants. She won't be needing her friends to help her. By the way, sir, I'd be obliged if you'd leave your camera equipment with me. For safekeeping.'

While he and Nathan argued about this, the door in the wall creaked open and Ruby immediately ducked inside. The attendant slid behind her at once, shutting the rest of us out.

'Charming!' Lauren declared. 'If you want my opinion, that man's behaviour is totally out of order.'

I stared at the closed door. 'Everything's out of order, in case you haven't noticed. I know one thing – I wouldn't want to be Ruby, in there alone with him.'

The attendant, I meant, though it crossed my mind that Byron might be up and about, prowling the corridors, eager to advise Ruby on her costume change. It was funny: only yesterday I might have felt jealous about this. Now I couldn't think of anything more hideously freaky than being alone with the dead poet. I had to admit this could have had something to do with Nathan. His hand rested lightly on my hip as we turned away from the house.

'So, what do we do now?'

I thought for a moment. 'There's not much we *can* do. If we force an entry, we'll set off the alarms and get ourselves arrested. We need to convince Ruby these people she's talking to aren't real. We can't save Rosie until she gets that idea into her thick head. Sorry, I don't mean she's thick exactly . . . Oh well, you know what I mean.'

'Dense?' Lauren supplied the word. 'Totally insensitive to psychic vibrations?'

But Nathan interrupted her train of thought. 'Hello, what's this? Don't tell me it's the chorus.'

The three of us had been wandering back through the long grass, towards that part of the wood where we'd seen the bear a few minutes ago. When the tall dark figure emerged suddenly onto the path, I almost screamed. For a minute I'd thought it was the bear walking on its hind legs, doing its sad, lumbering dance. But it wasn't the bear. Others swiftly joined the figure; their faces hidden by great hoods, black robes fluttering like a flock of raggedy crows. They turned away from us and drifted towards the lake, their voices chanting eerily in the silence.

Lauren stared after them. 'They must be the abbey monks.'

'Some monks,' Nathan said. 'They're pissed as newts. Look at them.'

The monks had given up their chanting and were staggering about. I heard that same cruel, raucous laughter I'd heard last night in the Great Hall, when the shooting was going on. Several of the monks were carrying bottles; one fell to the ground and, shrieking with laughter, attempted to tug off the robe of the monk in front. They looked like such a rabble; again I was reminded of crows descending to squabble over the entrails of some road kill.

'I don't think they're real monks,' I said. 'They're Byron's mates. They liked to dress up as monks for a joke. Then they'd have orgies in the grounds, drink out of

231

skull cups, swim in the lakes. Oh hell . . . that's not what Byron's "little diversion" is all about, is it? That's not Ruby's audience — a bunch of drunken monks.'

Thinking of Ruby, we glanced back at the house. In the dusk, the back windows glittered black. There wasn't a light to be seen. What on earth was Ruby doing in there?

We didn't have to wait long to find out. Only about ten minutes had passed when there she was, stumbling down the back steps like she couldn't move fast enough.

We crossed towards her. 'What's wrong? Ruby, what's happened?'

She had grabbed hold of my arms like she'd fall over if she didn't hold onto someone. 'It was there. It was there last night. I saw it!'

'What was there? Ruby, calm down, please.' For a minute I thought she meant something stupid, like her eyelash curler.

'You don't understand. I can't calm down!'

I looked into her eyes, glazed with horror, impatience. And then I knew.

'Hey, Rube' — Nathan put his hands on her shoulders — 'tell us slowly, OK? What happened in there?'

'Nothing happened,' Ruby said faintly. 'That's just it. The nursery. The nursery isn't there. But — how can it just vanish? That's what I want to know.' She stared at me like I might have the answer. As if the nursery was hiding from her, or she'd got the wrong wing of the house or something.

'I saw Rosie. I told you, I saw it all — the rocking horse,

the doll's house. I had a chat with that nurse, for God's sake!'

'Rosie,' I whispered, my heart turning to stone. 'You can't find Rosie.'

This might be stating the obvious, but I hardly knew what else to say. Ruby's expression was so terrible, it hurt me to look at her.

Nathan gave her a little shake. 'Come on, she's in there somewhere, right? She's in the house somewhere. Probably you just forgot where the nursery is, that's all.'

Letting go of her shoulders, Nathan sprinted up the steps. He banged on the door with his fist. 'Hey, you! You've got a child in there. Let us in! Oi . . .' He must have pummelled until his fist was sore. It looked as if it would never open again.

'Oh my God, what've I done?' Ruby held her hands to her face. Her voice had faded to a squeak. 'Rosie, baby, what have I done to you?' She began swaying, like she was going to faint.

'Ruby, sit down a minute.' I tugged her down onto a stone bench, cushioned with moss. 'Don't worry. We'll find her. She can't be far. What happened exactly, when you went to find her?'

'I went in to change, like I said,' Ruby hiccupped. 'That caretaker bloke just disappeared, so I was trying to find our room again, the one we slept in last night. I left my stuff in there – my outfit and everything. Then I thought, No, I'll just go and up and see if Rosie's OK. Just a peep, 'cos I know how clingy she gets when she sees me . . . and so' – her voice seemed on the verge of breaking – 'I found the staircase, the one that leads to the nursery. Or I thought I did.' She stared at me. 'Abbie, it's completely weird in there, all those long corridors, and I could hear voices, like girls singing – lullabies and stuff. So I tried to follow them, and it was like all those great empty rooms were just swallowing up the voices. There was no door, no nursery. I called and called. I found a bell. I pressed buzzers. I went down to the entrance where we got the tickets and yelled my head off. But there's no one there. I don't understand,' she said. 'What about the servants? That nanny who took Rosie yesterday? What happened to her?'

I sighed. How could I ever explain to a girl who didn't believe in ghosts? As I tried desperately to think of a way, Ruby's expression lightened. She snapped her fingers. 'Wait a minute, maybe . . .'

'Maybe?'

'Ron. Maybe Ron's got her, just taken her off to see the lights by the lake . . .'

'Lights?'

'Looks like they're gathering over there.' Lauren nodded in the direction of the lake. Sure enough, I could see the flare of torches. The faint trilling notes of music drifted on the air, along with a smell of roasting meat. Dark figures clustered at the water's edge.

'That must be where the concert is.' Ruby started up from the bench. 'I'll bet you anything Rosie's there, enjoying the show.'

Even if she was, that didn't explain what had happened to an entire nursery. But what was the use of pointing this out? Sooner or later Ruby would have to face the bizarre fact that her baby sister had been spirited off by a bunch of spooks. There was nothing more we could do except follow her as she stumbled across the grass towards the lighted torches, the voices and the music, to find Byron.

Chapter Twenty

So, we'll go no more a-roving
So late into the night,
Though the heart be still as loving,
And the moon be still as bright.

The full moon was tarnished like an old copper penny. As it sailed over the trees, the parkland was drenched in a sinister rusty light. Lauren gazed up at it in a transfixed kind of way, as if little green-cheese men were beaming down messages that only she could tune into.

'It's a harvest moon,' she murmured. 'I don't think I've ever really seen a harvest moon before.'

I grunted. 'Some harvest! Harvest of the dead, I suppose you mean.'

I couldn't help wondering if this same moon was shining over Smedhurst Road right this minute. Somehow I didn't think so. This moon was a fake. It was only a rusty imprint of the real thing, shining down on the world of the dead, on Byron's world.

We waded on through marshy grasses, damp air licking our faces, when somewhere, from deep within the trees, an animal howled. The kind of long, low, lonely sound that makes the hairs stand up on the back of your neck.

'What the heck is that?' Ruby gasped. She caught hold of Lauren's elbow to balance herself as she tugged off her stilettos. 'It sounded like a werewolf.'

'It must be Byron's wolf.' I drew closer to Nathan. 'It used to roam the grounds like the bear. Remember we saw a portrait of it in the house?'

Nathan scanned the blurry edges of the trees. 'Didn't keep tigers as well, did he?'

'It was a tame wolf,' I said hopefully.

'There's no such thing as a tame wolf,' Nathan murmured, sliding his arm around my waist.

'If Rosie hears that she'll be scared out of her wits.' Ruby hooked her shoes over her fingers and stumbled on ahead of us. As we drew closer to the lake, she cupped a hand to her eyes. 'Oh my God, that's never Ron, is it?'

I couldn't see Lord Byron. Not at first. Ahead of us was the dull glitter of water, the flare of torches, a spiralling cone of dark smoke from the fires.

'Got the barbie going, I see,' Nathan said. We paused, like people do when they're not sure if they're invited or not.

I shivered. I remembered seeing a picture once of dancing devils, skinny black figures with jabbing pitch-forks. This was how the monks looked. They had been joined by girls in long gauzy dresses, their hair flying, their faces masked, whirling so fast, my eyes blurred. There were shrieks, and sounds of water splashing as the spook revellers jumped into the lake. At times it seemed like the lake itself was shrieking. The whole scene had a dull coppery glow like an evil dream.

Even with Nathan beside me, my heart was pounding

237

fast. Funny how, among the dead, you felt more alive than normal. As if every sense was unbearably sharpened. The pulse of blood in my veins, the raw sting of my skin where some fly had bitten my arm earlier, were almost painful. Watching the servants flitting about, bearing enormous platters of food, my stomach churned. The sight of the pig's head, a roast peacock, pyramids of glistening fruit, bowls of cream, caskets of ruby wine made me feel sick.

'What d'you think?' Nathan said. 'Should we gate-crash?'

'Do we have to? I'm not really, you know, a party animal. Anyway, I don't know anyone here, except good old Ron, of course – um . . . where is he?'

My eyes shifted from one group to another. It was like one of those classical paintings: so cluttered you hardly knew what to focus on. Then, as if filling in the vital piece of a jigsaw puzzle, I saw him at last, enthroned among the rabble, a vision in gold and crimson.

'Shit!' Nathan's arm edged me forwards. 'No one told me this was fancy dress.'

'Come off it,' I said faintly. 'Byron's always in fancy dress.'

Not *this* fancy though, I had to admit. What had happened to the green velvet jacket, the white frilled shirt casually open at the neck? The curls were hidden beneath a striped silk turban; strapped to the front of the gold-trimmed robe, the ceremonial sword glittered.

'What's *he* come as then?' Nathan said. 'Don't tell me, Lawrence of Arabia.'

Lauren, who had been unnervingly quiet up until now, turned on us. 'Is the commentary, like, totally necessary, Nathan? His lordship looks utterly fabulous in that outfit, if you want my opinion. He looks like a prince. I'd like to see *you* get away with wearing something like that,' she added sarcastically.

Nathan laughed. 'Would you now? Well, no chance, babe.'

'And don't call me babe.'

It might have broken into a row, if Ruby hadn't reminded us what we were here for. 'I want to know what's going on, Ron!' She had placed herself squarely in front of him, folding her arms across her chest. 'You should be ashamed, the way you've treated us. We've been locked out of that house all day, and now Rosie's gone. Where is she, Ron? Is she here somewhere? I want to know.'

Byron chose to ignore this question. It was like he had more important things on his mind – his appearance, for example. 'Ah, Ruby, tell me, do you like the costume? Is it not *magnifique*?' His fingers stroked the gold trimming of his gown.

'Oh yes, yes!' Lauren almost pushed Ruby into the lake in her effort to stand closer to her hero. 'It's *très très magnifique*, in my opinion, your lordship. In fact, it's totally amazing.'

'A little item I picked up on my travels in Albania,' Byron said smoothly. 'The crimson flatters me, I believe.'

Ruby stood before him, clenching her fists. 'I don't believe you! My baby's gone, and all you can talk about is costumes!'

Baby. *My* baby? I whispered to Nathan, 'Did she say *my* baby?'

Byron seemed to acknowledge Ruby at last. He clapped his hands lightly together, the rings chinking. 'Why here she is, my little nightingale. Ruby, dear precious jewel, what do you think of our little diversions, hmmm?'

'I've just been inside the house, Ron.' Ruby's voice was growing shriller by the minute. 'I've looked all over the place. Where are all the servants? Where's the nursery gone? I want to know where my Rosie is. What have you done with my baby?'

Byron sighed, as if Ruby was just another hysterical bimbo swooning over him. 'See how it is. All my loves go crazy and make scenes. Dear Ruby, will you not oblige us with a song? The stage may not be so fine as at Drury Lane, but you have it entirely to yourself.' He indicated the jetty, lit by at least a dozen flares.

Ruby looked at it and almost squeaked in disbelief. 'You expect me to sing, with Rosie God knows where? You've got to be joking, Ron. If you won't tell me where she is, I'm calling the police, right now.'

'Dear girl, the child is quite safe.' Byron tapped his fingers on the arm of his chair. 'Did I not see her with her nursemaid only a few moments ago?'

'Where? Which nursemaid? Where did she go?'

He looked thoughtful. 'I tell you what, Ruby, you shall give us a song, and I will tell you where the baby is. Is that not fair?'

I held my breath. For a moment I thought Ruby was about to grab him by the neck and shake the information out of him. Instead she seemed to crumble suddenly.

'No, it isn't fair, Ron. It isn't fair at all.' She looked

around wildly at the revellers. 'You said it was a concert, not some weirdo fancy dress party. I thought the press were going to be here. Famous people, talent scouts. Not that I give a toss about any of that now . . .' Her voice sounded wobbly, as if she was on the verge of tears.

I took hold of her arm. 'Ruby, maybe you should just give it a go? One little song? I know it's a cruel game to play, but if he tells you where she is . . .?' What did I know? Did ghosts keep their promises?

'The shortest song you know, Ruby,' I urged her. 'A couple of verses.'

At first she looked at me as if I was mad. 'You expect me to sing in this state? I can't even think straight!'

Then Nathan said, 'I think Abbie's right. We've got to play it his way if we want Rosie back. Try it, Rube. A couple of verses, and if it doesn't work, we call the police, OK?'

Something in Nathan's voice must have persuaded her. Ruby positioned herself in the centre of the jetty. She hugged herself with her arms and shook her head. 'It's no good. I can't think! Everything I prepared – it's gone out of my head.'

We waited in silence. Finally we heard this frail, reedy voice that was nothing like Ruby's normal gutsy vocals.

'Who's that gir-rl – na na na nah, na na na na nah . . .'
Who's that gi-ir-irl . . .?'

She was off key too. In fact, had this been a real concert she would have been booed off the stage, never to sing again.

'Some nightingale,' Lauren whispered in my ear. 'More like a crow with sinusitis, if you want my opinion.'

I turned on her. 'Lauren, we don't want your opinion ever again. In fact, I wish you'd just go and jump in the lake actually.'

The lake. Glancing away from Ruby for a second, I noticed the water, like black crinkled silk. The lighted flares shot ribbons of crimson across the surface. On the far side you could just make out the huddle of trees. It was then I noticed that someone was walking towards them. A white figure, moving quite slowly, as if struggling with some heavy burden.

'All right,' Ruby cried, grinding to a halt, 'I've done my bit, I've played your stupid game. I hope you're satisfied.'

'Satisfied?' Byron studied his nails. 'Only fools and cretins are *satisfied*.'

'You've had your song, now where's my Rosie?' Ruby shouted.

Byron glanced up, feigning astonishment. 'Your Rosie? Why yes, she went off with that odd-headed girl, I do believe.'

'Odd-headed? What d'you mean, odd-headed? You've let her go off with some maniac?' Ruby was beside herself.

I drew in my breath sharply. Claire Clairmont. That was *her*, on the other side of the lake.

'Not quite mad,' Byron said easily. 'Mad with *amour* for me once, though who could blame her?' Appealing directly to Nathan, he added, 'When a girl comes prancing to one's bed at all hours, what is a man to do?

242

I had to take the child of course . . .' He gazed wistfully across the lake. 'Little Allegra. A sweet thing. I placed her in a convent for her education. Was it my fault she died of the fever? Children die. They die all the time.'

'Died? Who died? Who's Allegra?' Ruby screamed.

I tried to explain. 'Allegra was Byron's child with Claire Clairmont. Ruby, look, don't panic, but I think that's her. Can you see that figure in white on the other side of the lake?'

'Ah!' Ruby's hand flew to her mouth. 'It's that child molester. I told you she was on the bus. I told you.'

It took Nathan and me to hold her back.

'Ruby, it's not what you think. These people aren't human.'

'Tell me something I don't know!'

'They aren't real, I mean. They're not flesh and blood.'

'You can say that again. They're heartless bastards. They're liars and child stealers and perverts!'

Nathan caught hold of her elbow. 'No, they're ghosts, Rube. And you can't just go picking fights with them. If you rush on Claire, she might just vanish and take Rosie with her.'

Rosie struggled from Nathan's clutches like a mad woman herself. 'Let me go! She's *my* baby. I want my baby. Let me go to my baby!'

'Your baby?' Lauren wrenched her attention away from Byron at last. 'But Rosie's your sister.'

Ruby pushed back the hair from her face. She looked exhausted suddenly. The turquoise make-up formed greasy smudges in the crease of her eye; the glitter dust on her cheekbones dribbled clownishly.

'Haven't you twigged yet?' she said wearily. 'Rosie's not my sister, she's mine. She's my daughter.'

'Your daughter?' Lauren sounded shocked. 'But you're so . . . so young . . . I mean . . .'

Ruby laughed bitterly. 'Get real, Lor, please. It happens, you know. I'm Rosie's mum and it'll be all my fault if something's happened to her . . .'

As I watched Ruby stumble away from the ghostly gathering into the darkness I felt like I was the dumb one, not her. Ruby might be totally ignorant about the spirit world, but when it came to the real world, she was light years ahead of Lauren and me. Ruby knew what it was to be a mother. She knew what it was to love someone more – a hundred million times more – than you loved yourself. She was a thousand years older and wiser than us suddenly.

'Let her go,' I said quietly to Nathan as he made to go after her. 'She's not stupid. She'll know what to do. She's Rosie's mother, after all.'

What right had any of us to keep a mother from her child? Who could say? Her love might be strong enough to defeat even the vengeful Claire. Maybe only love could do it. I really didn't know any more.

Chapter Twenty-one

For me, I sometimes think that life is death,
Rather than life a mere affair of breath.

Had Byron noticed that his nightingale had flown the nest? If so, he didn't seem exactly gutted about it. All his attention now was fixed on Nathan.

'Tell me, young fellow,' he drawled. 'What is this box contraption which you seem so attached to? Has it some scientific application?'

Nathan fished in his bag and brought out a pack of photographs. 'I just had these developed. Why don't you take a look?'

I peered over Nathan's shoulder. I expected to see the kind of thing he photographed for *The Buzz*: rock concerts and opening nights and minor celebs. But these pictures were of all kinds of stuff: an oak tree, its wintry branches like writhing black snakes; some kids on skateboards; an old man's face.

'The box does this?' Byron seemed impressed.

'No, I do, with the box. It's a camera. The camera records an image on film, and these are photographs.'

Nathan's voice had a strange edginess to it, like he couldn't believe he was actually talking to a dead person. I understood how he felt. Conversation with a ghost is a bit like speaking in a foreign language. You don't even know if your words make sense. You take the plunge and hope for the best.

Beside me I heard Lauren sigh. 'Great, a photography lesson. Where is it getting us exactly?'

Where was it getting *her*, she meant, of course.

Byron pondered. 'If you were to, say, point this box at me, you would capture my image in an instant?'

'You've got it.' Nathan spoke in a strangled tone, as if his throat was tight.

'You could capture me dressed like so, in my *magnifique* costume?'

'Sure. No problem.'

Byron lifted an eyebrow. 'Truly, this is an age of miracles. Can this be an end to that excessively dreary business of sitting for one's portrait?'

Nathan pointed out that some people still had their portraits painted. 'People like the royal family, and celebrities and that. But you know what they say: the camera never lies.'

'The camera never lies,' Byron mused. 'I like that. I should like my public to see me as I truly am. I assure you, I waste interminable hours lolling in some studio, my posterior growing numb while some clumsy dauber strives to capture my likeness.'

'But your lordship' – Lauren seized her chance to lather on a little more flattery – 'you look fabulous in your portraits; like a film star.'

'You think so? Most of my portraits are so dire, I assure you I burn the things. I have no choice. If my public should see them, I would be lost. There was a sculptor once who would insist upon my grinning like a cretin. Who would buy the books of such a fellow? I ask you.'

Nathan agreed he could see the problem. 'What you need—' He broke off to clear his throat, and I realized how tense he was suddenly, gripping the camera. 'What you, er, need, is some good publicity shots. Truthful, yet flattering. Catch you in your best light . . .'

Byron preened himself. 'This is true. Well, firelight does wonders for the complexion, does it not?'

'Perfect,' Nathan muttered. 'Bloody perfect.'

'What are you doing?' I whispered, as he fumbled in his bag, swapping his Nikon for a camera about the size of a cigarette carton.

He winked. 'Digital. Trust me, OK?'

'Wait!' Byron held up his hand as Nathan pointed the new camera at him. 'I shall signal when I am ready. And pray do not ask me to smile. I never grin unless it be to grit my teeth in pain.'

'Don't worry,' Nathan assured him. 'Just, you know, relax . . . be yourself.'

Being himself was one thing Byron was good at. Pulling himself up to his full height, he adopted the famous scowl and gazed haughtily into the camera lens.

Lauren and I exchanged glances. This was all a bit galling. Byron seemed to have totally forgotten about the pair of us, never mind poor Ruby, vanished into the darkness after a phantom baby-snatcher.

'I hope Ruby's all right,' Lauren whispered.

For a second I was astonished. Lauren, voicing concern for someone other than herself? Could this be right? Then, glancing at her, I noticed that the feverish

247

love-struck look had finally gone. Lauren had come down to earth at last. She'd realized that there was only one person Byron had ever had the hots for. *Himself.*

A silk scarf fluttered limply from his fingers. 'Well? Am I to stand here all night like a perfect fool?'

The session began. I held my breath in awe. Had there ever been a fashion shoot quite like this one before? Here was Nathan leaping about like a monkey and yelling that stuff photographers are supposed to yell at their models, like, 'This way . . . hold it there . . . head up a bit . . . yeah, great, lovely . . . shoulders back a bit . . . a bit more to the left . . . what about with the turban off? . . . great, fantastic . . .' and so on.

Meanwhile, Byron pouted and preened and strutted about like he'd been posing for the camera his entire life. He even made suggestions of his own, drawing the sword from the scabbard and wielding it in the air in a heroic fashion, as if about to behead an infidel.

'Lovely . . . perfect . . . you're a natural, you are!' Nathan flattered him as he clicked. 'Any minute now, and you'll see yourself as you really are.'

'I hope Nathan knows what he's doing,' Lauren whispered doubtfully.

So did I. There was something funny about the modelling session in a grotesque sort of way. Perhaps one day I might even laugh to think of it. Not now, though, with the monks huddled together at the edge of the lake. In their black robes they were hard to distinguish from the trees. Were they praying, or uttering curses? The sombre background droning nearly drove me mad. No wonder Boatswain and Smut were slinking, whimpering, about their master's legs.

'There we go. Didn't hurt did it . . . ? Now, just hold on a minute while I find your image on the screen.' Nathan declared the photo session over.

A minute. It seemed the longest minute ever as Nathan stood there clicking buttons. I hardly knew what I expected to see. I just remembered what had happened when he snapped Byron in the street with Ruby. All that showed up was a dark smudge, like an inky thumbprint. Would the digital camera make any difference? What would Byron say when he saw himself as a swirl of mist or, at best, a faint shadowy outline?

'Well, what do you know?' Nathan murmured under his breath, as he gazed at the squared image on screen. He crouched, plugging the camera into a box about the size of a powder compact. At once, the pictures began printing out, a stream of images into the darkness.

Byron was impatient. 'Well? Do not torture me, boy, I beg you. How do I look?'

Lauren and I peered over Nathan's shoulders, resisting an impulse to snatch the prints from his hands.

'Come on. Show us. How did they turn out?' Lauren pushed the cloud of hair back from her face to see better, then, clapping a hand to her mouth: 'Oh . . . he's . . . oh, Nathan Daly, what have you done?'

Nathan just shook his head in disbelief.

'What? What is it?' Snatching the top print from his open palm, I held it up in the firelight. 'Oh God.'

This was no swirling mist, or half-formed face. The costume was all there – the silk turban, the dashing sword,

249

the cape were striking enough for any colour supplement fashion page. The difference was, Byron wasn't inside it. At least, not the Byron we knew. The gorgeous sulk was now a toothy grimace, those eyebrows I'd so admired, a jutting shelf of bone. The disdainful gaze, which caused women to swoon and snip off their locks, was no more. Instead, the yawning hollows of Byron's eye-sockets gazed accusingly out of the picture at me.

'*I lived, I loved, I quaff'd like thee . . .*' For some reason I found myself repeating the words out loud.

It struck me suddenly that this was what beauty and talent and fame came down to in the end. An empty skull, like any old skull belonging to any ordinary, ugly and totally clueless type person. Well, what had I expected? Gold-plated jawbones? Some mark of genius to distinguish the greatest poet ever from the likes of Mrs Croop downstairs?

'Want to see the rest?' Nathan pressed more pictures into my hand.

I gasped. 'He's only got one foot. Oh, how did that happen?'

The rest of the pictures were all of a skeleton, in which the lame right foot was missing altogether. Worse even than that, the noble skull was grinning as skulls do. It was as if Byron's skeleton had defied him after all, and said 'Cheese' for the camera.

'Oh, this is insufferable!' Byron exclaimed. 'Enough of your torture! Come, let me see. Has it caught my likeness well?'

'No!' Lauren caught hold of Nathan's wrist. 'Don't! You can't show him.'

Byron clicked his tongue, amused. 'What is this whispering? Does it flatter me so much, you fear it will make me vain?'

'Judge for yourself.' Nathan took hold of the skull close-up and held it right before Byron's eyes.

We held our breath. Would he go berserk and attack us with the sword? Would he set Boatswain or the bear onto us?

We waited for Byron to speak. I almost hoped he would. Some withering witticism; something we'd never forget. Instead there was only silence. The kind of silence you imagine existed before the world began.

Something awful was happening to Byron now: it was horrible to watch. So horrible I had to peer through my fingers, as the silks and velvets rotted into dust. As the chestnut curls fluttered to the ground like dead leaves, I imagined his expression. Was it horrified? Accusing? Would he blame us all for vanquishing him like this?

Yet, when I dared to look, there *was* no expression on Byron's face. How could there be when there was *no face*? It had fractured into a thousand pieces, flesh peeling back from yellowing bones. The sound of the sword clattering to the ground made my heart thud.

Lauren hid her own face in her hands. 'It's terrible. I can't bear it. His beautiful face, his beautiful face is ruined.'

Nathan said softly, 'Like I said. The camera never lies.'

I must admit it was kind of a weird feeling. I mean, on the two previous occasions when Lauren and I had finally managed to send our ghostly visitors back to their graves, we'd breathed a sigh of relief. Now our sighs were more the wistful kind. The poet might have been a poseur, he might have been a bit of a love-rat, but well . . . he was so gorgeous you could almost forgive him for that. Now that he was gone, taking the monks, the dogs, the servants with him, there was only the chilly moonlit night. And us.

I looked around and saw that the grounds were back to the way we'd first seen them. Trim lawns and flowerbeds, the surface of the lake unclogged by reeds. Instead of the lighted flares, the blinding dazzle of security lights spooling out of the darkness.

Then, from the other side of the lake, we heard a shout, a baby crying and crying as if it would never stop. Rosie!

This time we didn't wait. We all ran, skirting the edge of the lake where the path was lit, Nathan streaking ahead of us, shouting over his shoulder, 'She's over here!'

She, he said. But who was *she*? I froze for a moment beneath a cedar tree, almost expecting Claire Clairmont to come sidling out of the darkness. When I saw Ruby staggering along the path towards us cuddling Rosie to her, my eyes filled with tears.

'She's all right. Rosie's all right. She's safe. Shhhh . . .' Ruby was sobbing and laughing at the same time. She was jigging Rosie about enough to make the baby's brains rattle around in her head. 'Ruby's here, pet, Mummy's here now.' She went on planting smacking kisses on Rosie's curly head. It was like now that she'd found her, she couldn't get enough of her baby; like she'd eat her all up if she could.

'What happened, Rube? Is she gone?' Nathan put his

arm around her, tickling Rosie's cheek at the same time.

'Yeah,' Ruby gulped, 'she's gone.'

She couldn't tell us much more than that. Not at first. And we didn't ask. It was enough that Ruby had her baby back in the land of the living, little hands clutching fistfuls of hair, whinging the old refrain, 'Me want. Me want . . .'

'Her pushchair.' Ruby suddenly seemed to snap back to reality. 'Oh hell, it's back at the abbey with all her stuff.'

'Well, we're not going back there now,' Nathan said. 'Don't worry. We'll club together and buy her a new one. The sooner we get out of this place the better.' He offered to carry the baby but Ruby shook her head.

'No offence, Nate, but she stays with me. She's not that heavy, are you, Rosie Posy? I'll manage.'

The drive lay ahead of us, a dark ribbon of tarmac threading its way through the wooded parkland. I held onto Nathan's hand as we followed it, stumbling over the pedestrian humps, anxious to reach the gates.

It seemed to take for ever getting down that drive. At times I imagined I could hear the rattle of carriage wheels behind us. Maybe the ghostly relic of Byron's funeral carriage was on its final journal to that little church I'd read about? Maybe now Byron would finally rest in the family vault with his mad, wicked ancestors? Who cared? One thing I knew, I wasn't looking behind us, no way.

Not until we reached the gates and Nathan had called us a taxi; not until we were finally on our way to the station did I dare to look back. But there was only the empty road behind us.

253

'Some special event going on back there at the abbey, is there?' the taxi driver wanted to know.

There was a pause before Nathan answered, 'Nah, nothing special that we know of, mate.'

The driver scratched his head, surprised. 'Thought there might be one of them exhibitions — historic vehicles, that kind of thing. Just had one of them horse and carriages holding up the traffic on my way to pick you lot up. Blessed nuisance, they are, if you ask me. Dangerous at this time of night without proper head-lights and that. Jogging along like it had all the time in the flipping world.'

The last train back to London would be along in forty minutes, the station master told us. Now there was nothing to do but hole up in the fuggy waiting room, drinking weak foamy coffees from polystyrene cups, and listen to Ruby's story.

'I s'pose you all want to know why I lied and that — about Rosie being my sister, I mean.' Ruby seemed unable to look us in the eye. She sat awkwardly on the orange plastic chair, coffee in one hand, her free arm tight around Rosie, who was fast asleep on her lap.

We all shifted uncomfortably. 'Only if you feel like telling us, Rube,' Nathan said kindly.

Ruby bit her lower lip. 'I do. Really. It was wrong. A mistake, I mean, pretending I wasn't even her mum. I was going to tell you some time, I was going to tell everyone, when I, like, got myself sorted out. My career and that. I thought being a young mum would ruin my chances in show biz. I thought no manager or promoter would ever sign me up if I had a baby to lug about. Doesn't matter how much talent you got, how good looking you are, once you're a mum, you're a mum . . . You're not, like, a real person in your own right any more. You've got this other person who relies on you for every little thing, who's more important than you are. And it's not just for a few weeks, it's the rest of your life.' She glanced up at us, like she was ashamed. 'Oh, I'm not explaining this well.'

'No, I understand.' I tried to help her. 'I'd die if it happened to me. It must be a real bind having a kid at sixteen.'

'Fifteen,' Ruby corrected me. 'I was just fifteen. I got a bit pissed at a party one night and that was that. Never saw the bloke again. I was going to leave home right away, but that would have meant going in one of them hostel places. That would've been, like, everything, all my dreams, up the spout. So I told my mum I'd work, like, really hard, take several jobs if I had to, while they put me on the council waiting list for a flat.' She gazed down at Rosie's head. 'Well, I know you lot think my mum's terrible, but you couldn't blame her getting fed up. I mean, she's had her share, with all us kids. She wanted a bit of life, and there she was stuck with a grandchild.'

Lauren and I looked at each other. Now it was all beginning to make sense. No wonder Ruby's mum had kicked up such a fuss about her 'swanning off to Newstead' on her own.

Ruby continued, 'I was always dumping her on people, off-loading her. It seemed easier to tell people she was my sister. I even told myself that once or twice. It wasn't until I thought' – she hesitated, her voice trembling – 'I thought I'd lost her, that I realized how much I loved her.'

Now it was my turn to feel ashamed. I looked down at the polystyrene cup crushed in my hand. 'I should have warned you,' I said. 'I heard the baby crying that night after dinner. I—' I was going to tell her the story of how I tried to grab Rosie from Claire's arms, but Ruby just waved a hand to silence me.

'No, you did try to warn me. I wouldn't listen, would I? I just wanted to believe Ron was going to change my life, hah! You never told me what happened to Ron, did you? No, don't tell me, I don't want to know. I just hope I never see him again.'

'Don't worry,' Nathan said. 'You won't.'

Lauren leaned forward. 'Ruby, what happened? With Claire, I mean?'

Ruby sighed. 'It wasn't like you'd think. I found her just sitting on this log, crying. She looked so lost and sad, I even felt sorry for her. Then she said she was really really tired. She said she was glad she didn't have to walk about so much any more, and that she'd go and lie down somewhere. And then she just, like, handed Rosie over to me.'

Ruby blew her nose on a napkin. 'She wasn't a pervert, was she, or a baby-snatcher or anything? She just disappeared. I mean, she was there one minute, then she wasn't.' She looked at us fearfully. 'Real people don't do that kind of stuff, do they?'

'No,' I said. 'Real people don't.'

Ruby buried her face in the baby's hair. 'Abbie, you

256

don't think this'll have, like, a really bad effect on Rosie? Psychologically, I mean. It's just that I wonder, you know, what happened, what was going on all that time, when I thought she was safe in the nursery?'

I looked at Rosie, now sleeping contentedly on her mother's shoulder. 'I shouldn't worry,' I said. 'Maybe babies see things, experience things all the time that we don't know about. Like animals do. She's back with you now. That's all that matters.'

'Yeah.' Ruby smiled through her tears. 'That's all that matters.'

Epilogue

What is the end of fame? 'Tis but to fill
A certain portion of uncertain paper:
Some liken it to climbing up a hill,
Whose summit, like all hills, is lost in vapour;
For this men write, speak, preach, and heroes kill,
And bards burn what they call their 'midnight taper';
To have, when the original is dust,
A name, a wretched picture, and worse bust.

Had our taxi driver really seen Byron's funeral carriage, making its final journey to the family vault that night? I'd like to think so. I'd like to think Byron's bones are resting easy at last, even though he swore they wouldn't. I'd like to think we'd got shot of him frankly. For good. For eternity. Totally.

Unlike Lauren. Poor Lauren. I suppose she had the Byron bug worse than any of us, and now she's having difficulty banishing him from her mind.

For instance, our adventures at the abbey took place a whole month ago, but when I ask her, 'Lauren, I want your honest opinion. Do you think Nathan Daly's good-looking?' she just looks up from the poem she's writing and raises one eyebrow. Then she says, 'Please don't take this personally, Abbie, but compared to Byron, all men look like monkeys to me. Or toads.'

'Toads?'

'You did ask for my honest opinion. Now, if you don't mind, I must get on with my poem.'

This is a new thing with Lauren. She's given up on her heal-the-world plans, and is now the youngest member of the Northgate Poetry Society.

OK, I have to admit that the Luscious Lord is a hard act to follow looks-wise. Nathan may not have Byron's eloquent eyebrows or pouty lips, but he makes me laugh so much it hardly matters. The only time we stop yackering together is when we're kissing and stuff. Also he's got this really kind heart. What kind of bloke would offer to come with me to take Rosie out for the day, for instance, just to give Ruby a break?

Ruby's moved out of her mum's place and is living in this flat over Pizza Pronto. It's a bit of a dump, frankly, but it's amazing what a splash of white paint can do. I look after Rosie sometimes when Ruby goes to auditions. There's no keeping Ruby down for long. She's still convinced she'll be famous before she's twenty. And know what? I think she will be.

So what about me? Well, the other day I introduced Nathan to phrenology, and he thought it was, like, really cool, and then he had this great idea that maybe I could do a column in *The Buzz*. We've even thought of a name for it – 'Head Case'. He's talking to his editor about it this week. Meantime I'm going around with Nathan a lot on his assignments, and it's given me this idea I might become a journalist one day.

Suddenly there's so much I could do. Suddenly

everything is going right for a change. It's like the gods have taken pity on me at last. Like they're up there saying: 'Hey, that Abigail Carter's not so bad. Let's give the girl a break!'

At least, I hope so.

CAVAN COUNTY
LIBRARY

The Henry Game

by Susan Davis

'You're not scared are you, Abbie?'
'Not exactly scared. Why should I be? It was my idea.
I mean, if he suddenly materialised right there on the
table, then I'd be scared. As long as he stays in the glass,
we're all right.'

It only started out as a game: three teen girls, one
homemade ouija board and an unusual way of
spending a hot summer afternoon. But when Marina,
Abbie and Lauren discover they've summoned up the
spirit of a long-dead randy royal, the 'Henry Game'
suddenly turns into something more sinister. Are the
girls in danger of losing their heads?

'Simply a great read . . . Susan Davis is observant,
witty, and spooky too.' *Fay Weldon*

0 552 54793 X

CORGI BOOKS

Delilah and the Dark Stuff
by Susan Davis

'I don't do dark stuff. Dark stuff comes back on you three times over.'

After bad experiences with spooks Abbie and Lauren have sworn off the dark arts. Then self-proclaimed teen-witch, Delilah declares she can use her craft to clear up Lauren's eczema and spice up Abbie's love life . . . It seems like harmless fun. But there's a sinister figure stalking the girls and when Delilah starts to dabble in the dark stuff the girls find themselves in very deep water . . .

0 552 54794 8

CORGI BOOKS

The Sisterhood of the Travelling Pants

by Ann Brashares

Four best friends, one pair of jeans and a few important rules:

- You must never wash the Pants

- You must never double-cuff the Pants. It's tacky. There will never be a time when this will not be tacky

- You must never say the word 'phat' while wearing the Pants. You must also never think 'I am fat' while wearing the Pants

- You must not pick your nose while wearing the Pants. You may, however, scratch casually at your nostril while really kind of picking

- You must write to your Sisters throughout the summer, no matter how much fun you are having without them

Quirky, original and heart-warming, *The Sisterhood of the Travelling Pants* is an irresistible celebration of female friendship and self-discovery.

0 552 54827 8

CORGI BOOKS

Hope Was Here
by Joan Bauer

Life's never been a bowl of cherries for Hope, but at least with her Aunt Addie around, the food's been good. Addie and Hope have worked in diners from New York City to Atlanta. Now they're getting ready to transform the tastebuds of Mulhoney, Wisconsin. Butter pecan pie is sure to be a hit but someone in Mulhoney is cooking up something a lot less wholesome . . .

Can Hope find the antidote to the poison at the heart of their small town? It's a tall order, but then again that's her specialty!

A Newbery Honor book 2001

0 552 54972 X

CORGI BOOKS